THE UNQUIET HEART

GORDON FERRIS

CORVUS

First published in Great Britain in 2008 by Crème de la Crime

This paperback edition first published in the UK in 2012
by Corvus, an imprint of Atlantic Books Ltd.

1 3 5 7 9 10 8 6 4 2

A CIP catalogue record for this book is available from
the British Library.

Paperback ISBN: 978-0-85789-555-4
E-book ISBN: 978-0-85789-495-3

Printed in Great Britain by Clays Ltd, St Ives plc

Corvus
An imprint of Atlantic Books Ltd
Ormond House
26–27 Boswell Street
London WC1N 3JZ

www.corvus-books.co.uk

For Bill Ferris [1925-92]
RAF and Parachute Regiment, Palestine 1946

Thanks to:

To Tina Betts, my agent at Andrew Mann for the hard questions and helpful nudges. Sarah Ferris for her wise and impartial contention that this one's even better than *Truth Dare Kill*. And Nic, Emma, Becci and Rina at Team Corvus for this second coming.

But for the unquiet heart and brain
A use in measured language lies;

In Memoriam, V: Stanza 2.
Alfred Lord Tennyson

Author's note:

I have taken the liberty of weaving into my fiction some real events involving real people in 1946. For example, while Heinrich Mulder is a composite, Menachem Begin is real. The B1A unit in MI5 really existed, and most certainly, the events in Palestine happened. My intention was not to take sides in this complex and contentious run-up to the birth of a nation, but to suggest that truth depends on your vantage point in history.

ONE

A pub fight doesn't start in a pub. It begins that afternoon when you're laid off at the yards. It starts a month back when you look in the mirror and see your old man gazing back at you, and this revelation of mortality starts eating at your balls. It begins a year ago when you come home from the war flashing your medals – and find the wife has left you for one of those fellas with feet just flat enough to keep him out of khaki but swift enough to be a bookie's runner. Something sours the day or the year or your life and you bring it into the pub like a rat in your belly. All it takes is a clumsy shoulder, a spilled drink, a guy with a small brain and a big mouth, and the first punch gets thrown.

You would think it was the big blokes you had to be careful of, but big guys usually have nothing to prove. It's the pipsqueak you need to sidestep, the little man who feels shat on all his life for having to look up at folk all the time. There seems to be an inverse law operating: the smaller the man the bigger the chip.

Normally – unless I'm the cause of it, or it's to help a mate – I quietly pick up my pint and move to the lounge bar till they get it out their system. If it's really bad, and there are tables and bottles flying, I find another pub. I should have stuck to my rule this evening.

I'd had time to kill, so I walked down Albany Road, crossed the Old Kent Road and headed into Bermondsey. It had taken a pasting. Incendiaries had gutted whole streets and you could take short cuts through rows of houses following the paths taken by Jerry's visits. I took back streets and footpaths, twisting and turning until I connected with Jamaica Road. Then into the warren, past gaps like old women's gums among the warehouses and tenements. I emerged by the Thames and leaned on the wall to watch the darkness settle on the water and the mists swirl and flow like a ghost stream above it. I dropped my second cigarette into the current and headed east, along the spine of Rotherhithe, following the curve of the river.

The Angel sat by itself, poised over the water. It was the latest incarnation of a hostelry that had stood on the site since Captain Kidd sailed upriver in chains on his way to a good hanging. The bombs that fell the night the East End was aflame had taken out a row of houses opposite and half the buildings alongside. A church had been flattened just a hundred yards away. But the Angel was untouched, proving to the wittier locals the power of prayer.

The wind whipped up the Thames like a banshee. I clamped my hat harder to my head and pulled my mac tighter against the flurries of rain. Flaming June indeed. There was hardly a street light for miles, but the occasional gap in the clouds let the full moon pour on the rippled surface of the water. My shadow stretched out behind me.

The noise from the pub eddied and whirled on the stiff breeze. I crossed the road and stood in front of it, wondering why I'd agreed to this meeting. I looked behind me and then back at the pub. The mouldering wood suggested they were the original panels, and no painter had been allowed near in three hundred years. A tired sign creaked on its chains: a faded angel gazing down at me, blind and uncaring. Behind dirty windows silhouettes of drinkers nodded and laughed like a magic lantern show. I pushed the door open and walked back in time. The original customers were still on a bender: blackguards to a man, with strong piratical tendencies.

The place was sweating and jostling and roaring. It was half nine, twenty minutes before last orders, and men were buying multiple rounds as though the end of the world had been announced. Which of course it would be, in twenty minutes. The thought of cutting off the supply of Dutch courage and alcoholic bonhomie was beyond bearing. Make that a double, and have one yourself!

I looked round for my man: a tall bloke, I'd been told, wearing a flat cap and carrying a newspaper. The one-roomed bar was full of flat caps perched over shouting mouths in flush-faced groups. A few men drank alone, supping at their ales to wipe out the past and get a rosier view of tomorrow. One man caught my eye. He was better shaved than the rest, and his eyes less bleary. A paper was rolled tight under his hand like a sergeant major's baton. He'd seen me as I walked in. His eyes swivelled left and right like he was crossing the road. He nodded, got up and came towards me. He was my height, white-faced, serious-eyed, a penitent. I hoped he'd got something to confess.

"McRae?" he asked, in a voice pitched to be heard above the roar. In that one word I heard the cadences of Ireland.

I nodded. He waved a part-drunk beer at me. I nodded again. He indicated I should grab his seat while he got a round in. He

3

gave me his paper and went to the bar. I squeezed behind the table and sat down with my back to the wall, eyes stinging with fag smoke and the rank stink of old pubs and sweaty men. It was a smell common to bars from Sutherland to Southend, and hauled me back to the Working Men's club in Kilpatrick, and the time my father took me in to show me off to his pals. Small men with bright eyes and scrubbed faces, but nothing could erase the black pits of coal dust around their noses.

I unrolled the paper and smoothed out the front. The picture shook me, though I'd seen it a dozen times in the last ten days now. It didn't do her justice, but it was enough. I rubbed my eyes and looked up, just in time to see the action.

It happened fast. They must have planned it well. I saw my man take a push from a thickset man with curly hair. My man turned and joshed him and turned back to the bar. The big guy wasn't to be ignored. Another push and the drinks were all over the bar. A push became a punch and my man went down. Two other heavies appeared and began to shove and shout at the bystanders. It didn't take much to start a fight. This was the wrong end of the Old Kent Road and people had old-fashioned ideas of honour and face. The last of the duellists.

My rules of self-preservation went out the window. Though it was a stranger in trouble he had information I wanted badly. Or so I'd been promised by Pauli Gambatti who'd set up the meeting. With blokes like Gambatti it's hard to know whether they're doing you a favour or stitching you up. It shows how desperate I was. I would try anything, go anywhere to find out what happened to Eve Copeland, whose accusing eyes stared out at me from the newspaper.

I sprang to my feet, fists clenched, ready to get stuck in, to get my man off the floor. A kicking is always a bad event. I made two steps before my legs were clipped from under me and I went down like Charlie Chaplin. I made to rise and found a knee on my back and a hand like a shovel on my neck. A voice leaned over, a thick, European brogue in my ear:

"Forget her. It is not your fight. None of it is your fight. You hear me?"

I nodded as well as a man might with his face in the sawdust. The stench of the beer-soaked floorboards filled my nostrils. All I could see was clattering feet like a rugby ruck. I prayed my head wouldn't become the ball. The shouting went on, then it stilled, and the knee came off. The hubbub picked up again, and I turned over as fast as I could. I saw a pair of legs disappearing through the crowd: black boots with heavy tacks on their soles. All the better to kick you with. The man who'd knelt on me turned briefly and I had a good look. Cadaverous cheeks as though he was sucking them in for a bet, and blue eyes that laughed at me under his cap. Then he was gone.

I got to my feet feeling stupid. So much for my SOE training. I brushed off the sawdust and the fag ends and looked for my man. A crowd stood round where he'd gone down. I pushed my way through. He wouldn't be telling me anything now. He was face down in his own red pool, his head turned to one side. His eye stared at something we couldn't see, and his breath came in little pants. A broken bottle lay beside his throat. Shards of glass glinted red, lodged in his neck. He was beyond first aid, or indeed second or third. Bugger. His already pale face was blanched. Lank hair spread round his head, mopping up his own blood. One hand twitched, trying to plug the holes in his neck. The other reached out and hung itself over the brass foot-rail like a drowning man. Suddenly the tension went out of his body. With a glint and a clunk, a knife dropped from the dead fingers.

As an ex-copper I knew my civic duty was to stay and answer questions and help them all I could with their inquiries, even accompany them to the nick and spend all night making a statement. So I joined the fast and shifty queue that was moving out the back door. The landlord held the door. He wasn't wishing us good night. He was thinking of his licence and the mess on the floor and endless questions coming his way. I came out in a side street and scampered into the dark with all the other cockroaches. This far from civilisation, it would take a while for the bell of a squad car to reach us, but no sense in loitering.

I had no doubt my man had just been murdered. It was a set piece. But who set it? Gambatti? A complicated way of doing business. Someone who found out Gambatti had arranged the meet? But why did they wait till I showed? To warn me off? To make me a witness? There are easier ways of getting through to me, though I supposed I should be grateful for the warning. But I couldn't afford to heed it.

My heart lurched again. If they could kill a man to stop him talking, what might have happened to Eve? What was so important? I walked the long dark miles home to Camberwell, mulling over the upheaval in my life that started just eight weeks ago when she walked into it. I should have stuck with my first feelings about her and thrown her out...

TWO

Eight weeks. If you were a student of morals and manners you could earn yourself a PhD by sitting behind my desk for eight weeks. They all pass through my office: the crazies with a grudge who want me to spy on their neighbour; the tortured and vengeful who want the goods on their two-timing lovers; the desperate who think you can find the son missing since D-Day; or the wife who walked out years ago and won't ever come back, and you can see why.

They dump their sins and suffering on my desk with diffidence or bluster, tears or temper, certainty or fear. Most times they know the answer; they just need someone else to prove it or say it out loud. It seems to help them if they pay for it, though not all of them do. They want solutions and absolution from an ex-copper trying to make a living as a private detective in a rundown flat in a bombed-out corner of South London. I don't tell them I'm also a former Special Operations agent and a one-time inmate of a concentration camp; every Londoner has a war story. Every pub echoes to their tales. They don't need to hear mine.

I try not to turn anyone away. But I don't always take on a case. It's hard to be prescriptive. Hunger stretches a man's ethics. I've tried drawing up a list of stuff I will do and stuff I won't. I made a deal with myself when I started this business that I wouldn't do anything illegal or immoral. But it's not as if I wrote it in stone. Like when I had to do a bit of breaking and entering to catch a bigamist: I found myself torn between the legalities of jemmying a window, and the moralities of keeping two women ignorant but happy. Ends and means. It's a daily wrestle with a rickety conscience.

I'm not alone. In this first full year of peace we still have rationing, and rationing brings out the spiv, and the spiv has more customers than he can handle. Who *doesn't* need an extra slice of meat for the kids? Who *isn't* fed up with their car on blocks, when a gallon of black market petrol takes the family to Brighton to put some sea air in their smog-black lungs? The law makes us all criminals. The latest regulations from the pinstripes at the Home Office test our loyalty, and after six years we've had enough. It's about personal survival. We suspended the ten commandments in '39 and it's hard to slip on the strait-jacket again; especially if you felt deserted by God himself.

Occasionally there are diversions. Like the woman I was waiting for. Eve Copeland wasn't the first reporter to take up my time, but I was hoping she had something fresh to offer. Business was sluggish right now, after the flurry of interest a couple of months ago when my face was in all the dailies. Few of the inquiries had turned into jobs. Several just wanted to pick over the entrails. It was getting that I could spot a leech at twenty paces. At least this lady had called the day before to book an appointment. I like that. It makes a change from the people who think that because I leave my office door open and a kettle on top of the filing cabinet, they can use it as a caff.

The little clock on the mantelpiece said ten past nine. She was late. It meant I could tidy my desk and put on my no-nonsense air of busy preoccupation – two seconds. I lit another cigarette to stop my fingers from drumming on the table and I checked the time again; I had one big job prospect – warehouse pilfering – and had to get over to Wapping by noon. Eve Copeland needed to get a move on or she'd miss her chance.

She arrived at my door breathless from the three flights of stairs. She may have sounded businesslike down the wire but the phone is a dangerous invention; you build a picture of a person from a voice, and when you meet them in the flesh it's usually a disappointment. It was the reverse with Miss Copeland. Her voice had said pushy Londoner; her face said I'm the most interesting thing that's come into your life since Johnnie Walker Red Label – quite an achievement, given my relationship with Johnnie.

I should be used to suspending judgement on people, especially pretty women with a business proposition. But I'm a sucker for blatant femininity. Something I'm working on. She strode towards me in a dark green gabardine belted to empha-sise a slim waist. A black beret topped her out. She'd just stepped out of one of those sultry French pictures they some-times show at the Odeon Camberwell Green – watch out for the men in the one-and-nines with raincoats across their laps. I could picture her under a street lamp in Boul' St Michel, a ciga-rette hanging from her painted mouth and asking for a light.

I got to my feet as she cut up my lino and plonked herself down in my client chair. It creaked with the impact. Not that she was overweight; just a wee bit exuberant for the quality of the furnishings.

"I can help your career," she burst out.

I blinked. "You think this is a career?" I sat down slowly and waved my hand round the tired attic. Brown lino, brown walls, yellow-stained ceiling that sloped on two sides. A desk, a phone, a filing cabinet and a door to my bedroom. And me.

She took in the room and me with a long slow look. "What is it, then? A hobby?"

The diction was street-London, but there was a trace of something else in her voice; like she was hiding a posh accent to fit in. I guessed that her particular gang in Fleet Street didn't wear blue stockings.

"Congratulations, Miss Copeland. It normally takes people at least a couple of days to start questioning my prospects." I made a show of checking my watch. "It took you ten seconds. Do you mind if we start somewhere simpler? Like who you are and why you're here?"

She cocked her head and inspected me for a while. I returned the stare, noting the big features, any one of which would look out of place on an ordinary face but all together on her strong canvas of bones and angles added up to something a little short of beautiful and a little beyond fascination. Strands of chestnut hair spilled from the jaunty beret, a tarpaulin over a briar patch.

"Where are *you* from?" she asked me.

"Isn't my accent a bit of a giveaway?"

She raised her thick eyebrows. "Which *part*?"

"Glasgow. Sort of. Do you always answer questions with a question?"

"Do you always look a gift horse in the mouth?"

I waited. And won – this round.

"I told you on the phone I'm a reporter. I work for the *Trumpet*."

"I don't read the *Trumpet*."

"Why?"

"Too many cartoons."

She coloured. "The words aren't bad, you know!"

"I find better ones in *The Times* crossword. What *can* I do for you?"

I prayed she had a new line. I'd been tripping over journalists since the Caldwell case blew up, each of them trying to get his angle on the story. Not that I could deflect them from what they'd planned to write before they spoke to me. I'd learned in Glasgow in my police days that you could make exactly the same statement to six newshounds, and six different fairytales would appear the next day. A waste of time, but I was prepared to waste a little more of my time just to hold the attention of Eve Copeland, ace reporter, with nice legs.

"I'm looking for a new angle on the Caldwell murders."

I let my forehead fall on to my desk. Then I raised it with a pained look on my face. She was trying not to smile.

"That was January, three months ago. I've seen a hundred theories from you people, none of them based on the facts. There are no new angles. Major Anthony Caldwell was mad as a hatter and took up killing young women because he liked it. End of story."

It wasn't, of course; it was the beginning. But it was all that anyone was going to get out of me. She ignored my theatrics. As I raised my head she had her eyes fixed on the scar across my skull that even my red mop can't hide. She pulled a shorthand notepad from her raincoat pocket and flicked it open. She poised a pencil over the page.

"Do you believe that?"

"I'm not a psychiatrist."

"But you've known a few," she said with a lift of a heavy eyebrow.

"I spent a few months in a loony bin if that's what you mean. All better now." I tapped the trailing end of the scar that terminates just above my left brow, and smiled to signify the end of that little probe.

"That's how we ran the story. Not one of mine." She made it clear how little she thought of her fellow hacks. "I've been reviewing the facts and some things don't add up. I thought there might be a more interesting truth behind it."

"Five murders wasn't interesting enough?"

She stared defiantly at me. The eyes were black olives swimming in milk, and the skin round them was a soft brown with a little fat ridge beneath the lower lids; harem eyes behind the yashmak. "Not in themselves, no. They're just numbers, unless you know something about the murderer's mind, or the victims'. My readers want the inside story, the human story."

"Tell them to read Tit Bits."

"I see we start from rather different views of a newspaper, Mr McRae."

I shrugged. "What didn't add up?"

"Don't tell me you're interested?" She balanced her pad on her lap and raised both hands to her beret. She dug out a pin that had Exhibit A in a murder trial written all over it, wrenched off the cap and shook her hair out. The briar patch exploded. This woman was unscrupulous. She went on, careless of the effect on me.

"It was the sister. Not the Caldwell woman, the upper class one..." She flicked through her pad. "Kate, Kate Graveney."

"What about her?"

"She was… unexpected. I'm good at my job, Mr McRae. Thorough. I do the leg work. My colleagues prefer to sit in the pub and make it up. I go look for myself. And I ask questions. I asked some of the girls in Soho, the working girls. It helps being a woman – at times. They told me that the classy Kate operated a little side business, she was a competitor of theirs offering a service that none of them could – or chose to – provide."

I kept my gaze level and waited. I wondered if she'd met any of the girls from Mama Mary's house. I'd have a word with Mary later.

"You don't seem shocked," she said.

"Nothing much shocks me any more, Miss Copeland. Especially if it's made up."

"So it's not true."

"Even if it were, I imagine if you were to print it you'd be sued till the *Trumpet*'s last blow."

She had the grace to look rueful. "I know, I know. But there's another thing. The word on the street – and I do mean the street – is that Kate also knew about the murders. Maybe even helped. You know what those rich society girls are like."

"'Fraid not. I don't throw enough cocktail parties up here. Maybe I should. What do you think?"

"I think you're covering for this woman, but I don't know why. Love? Sex? A gentleman protecting a lady's reputation?"

"Will that be all, Miss Copeland?" I got to my feet.

"Call me Eve. Can I call you Danny?"

"Call me what you like, Eve. But I have work to do. If you don't mind."

"Wait, wait. Do you have any idea how hard it is to get taken seriously as a woman in this business?" She shoved her hair back from her face. Her big eyes suddenly lost their certainty. I sat down.

"No, I don't. I guess it's tough. Now all the men are back."

She nodded. "All with their old jobs guaranteed. I don't mind. It's fair enough. But things changed when they were away."

For the first time since she got here she was being sincere.

"It gave me a chance. I took it. I did anything and everything. I even got blown up in an air raid." She reached down and pulled up her skirt. She pointed to a white scar running from her knee and disappearing up her thigh.

"I had my own daily column, for God's sake. Then all the men came home and, bang, I'm back down the ladder. Not all the way. I still do a weekly. But I need to be ten times better than they are to get back to daily. Do you see?"

She was leaning over my desk, longing written across her exotic face. It made her suddenly vulnerable. Then I noticed: the East End accent had gone. Nothing replaced it. I mean she spoke without an accent of any sort.

I nodded. "We all need some breaks, Eve. But the Caldwell case is closed as far as I'm concerned. It's too personal. All tied up in my memory problems and headaches. I don't want to bring them back. Do *you* see?"

Her face took on new purpose. She pulled back. "OK, Danny, let's leave the past. I can't run to a lot of expenses, but what if I could pay you to let me inside?"

"Inside?"

"Your world. Villains and crooks. Fast women and mean men. The underworld. A Cook's tour of the wrong side of the tracks. I want you to introduce me to thieves and murderers. There are clubs I can't get into on my own, unless I change my profession." She bared a set of even, white fangs. I could imagine them sunk into a story and not letting go.

I stared at her. "You're having me on, aren't you?"

Her soulful eyes glittered with wicked interest. "Take me out on a case."

"Seedy hotels, following Mr and Mrs Smith?"

"You do more than that."

I shook my head. "Was this the career opportunity you had in mind for me?"

"I pay you for information. I write it up and we both do well out of it."

"You make me sound like a copper's nark."

"A man of principle, dispensing justice where the courts fear to tread," she inscribed in mid-air.

I laughed out loud at the image. But then I thought about where next month's rent was coming from. And I thought about being paid for spending more time in her lively company. Who could pass up an offer like that? I should have; I was barely over the last woman in my life, real or imagined. I needed repair time.

"Eve, it's a deal. If anything comes up, I'll give you a call, OK? My rate is twenty pounds a week. Can your paper cover that?"

"Fifteen."

"Eighteen plus expenses."

She nodded and grinned and stretched out a hand. We shook. Like a regular business deal. She crammed her thatch under her beret again and skewered it to her head. I saw her to the door and watched her spiral down the stairs. I would have whistled as I walked back to my desk but it would have echoed after her, and she would have read too much into it.

I thought about the warehouse prospect and wondered if I should have mentioned it. I decided to see how my meeting went this afternoon. Then I might call and let her in on it. And, if I was honest, it wasn't just about the money.

THREE

Tommy Chandler was short but wide. His barrel chest was constrained from exploding by taut red braces. He ran a warehouse in docklands that had largely escaped the bombs. Having one of the few intact depots should have been making Tommy a lot of money. In theory he was – but before he could bank any of it, it was disappearing. Tommy had rats in his warehouse, man-sized, and they were eating his goods. Tommy had called me a couple of days ago at his wits' end. I'd agreed to go down and take a look.

It took three buses to get from my office near the Elephant across Tower Bridge and down Wapping High Street. I went upstairs not just to have a fag but to get a view crossing the bridge. It does your heart good to see the cranes bobbing all along the river. I know the docks got a hammering, but give or take some missing teeth in the river frontage, plenty of warehouses were back in business – one of them my prospective client's. I got off in the Commercial Road and walked down the cobbles to Wapping High Street, glimpsing the river through bombsites as I went. Tommy's yard was bustling: a horse and cart were backing up to the warehouse doors while a van roared and squeezed me against the big wood gates on its way out. I had no doubt Tommy was the one shouting out orders. He took me inside.

"Why can't the police stop it?"

Tommy snorted. His beefy hands pushed at his shirt sleeves in frustration. A permanent cigarette hung from his mouth and left a yellow trail up his short moustache.

"Fuckin' coppers!" he wheezed. Tommy was a self-made man; he'd left behind none of the vocabulary of the docker.

"They come 'ere, and they ponce about and they fuckin' throw their 'ands up in the air and say they can't do nothin'. What are we paying these ponces for, that's what I want to bleedin' know?"

Tommy was pacing up and down a tiny glass office tucked into a corner of the great wood and brick building. He looked as if he was warming up for a bare-knuckle fight. Though if his chest was as bad as it sounded he wouldn't make the first bell.

"What security measures have you taken, Mr Chandler?"

"It's Tommy. Come on. I'll show you." He stormed out of his little office like a bull at a rodeo and we did a grand tour. He took me up ten flights of stairs to the top level. Despite his girth and his sixty-a-day habit he seemed to be breathing easier than me. Which would disappoint old Les at my gym. I was trying to get back to my levels of fitness in my army days by going to Les's a couple of times a week. He was a welter-weight contender before the war and now coached young kids from a big room above some shops in the Old Kent Road. Twenty minutes with a skipping rope and five rounds in the ring was still leaving me weak as a kitten. But it was a start. Maybe I needed to increase my fags to Tommy's level.

We walked over to one of the floor-to-ceiling gaps and looked down on to the great worm of the river. It was a long way to the deck of the waiting ship that sat with belly open to the plundering arms of the cranes.

Cargo boats were now returning in growing numbers from around Britain and from America and the Far East. Each of the warehouses tended to specialise. Across the river at Butler's Wharf and Jacob's Island, sailing clippers had been landing tea and spices from the East India Company for the last hundred and fifty years. Now, squat iron hulks rode the oily swell and burped grey smoke from their funnels. On either side of Tommy stood a coal warehouse and a scrap metal trader. Tommy took in silks from abroad and sent out cottons and lace from the north to every corner of the British Empire, what was left of it.

I watched his great cranes swing and groan, and fumble deep into the metal holds like giant fishing rods. The bales were pulled in through double doors that studded the warehouse walls from river level to where we stood, five storeys up. Groups of flat-capped men shouted and cursed below us, signing directions at the crane drivers like tic-tac men. They manhandled each haul through the doors into big barrows, then pushed them off into the building's entrails and stored them in dark corners. It reminded me a bit of the coal mine my dad worked in, but at least these men could suck in fresh air.

I could have watched this ant heap for hours, but I was running to keep pace with Tommy. Wheezing all the way, he led me down to ground level. We scampered across the yard and emerged on Wapping High Street through huge wooden gates. For a minute or two we watched horse-drawn carts and groaning lorries bounce along the cobbles, carrying loads around London and on up country on goods trains.

"Them horses are on the way out, you know. Bleedin' shame. Look at them beasties. Lovely. My dad had four. Great bleedin' Clydesdales. Big as fucking warehouses themselves."

We turned our backs on the road and traced the route in and out, starting with the gates. They rose in solid slabs of wood twenty feet in the air and about the same in width. Tommy showed me the courtyard side of the gates where spars of metal criss-crossed and reinforced the backs. He'd had huge new padlocks fitted. The keys were kept in a safe and only Tommy had the combination. Not even his three senior foremen had access. He pointed them out to me: Sid, a runty bloke with a set of dentures nicked from a horse; Stevie, a taller version of Tommy himself; and Albert, who'd left one of his arms behind at Dunkirk and used his hook to menace the dockers.

"An' I've got a team of night watchmen that patrols the whole bleedin' place every night of the week. And dogs loose in the yard. Alsatians that would rip your balls off and ask questions after."

"And still…?"

"An' still stuff gets nicked! It fuckin' vanishes like piss on a fire, it does. Nobody sees nothin'. Nobody hears nothin'. It's a fuckin' miracle. Houdini couldn't do no better."

I began to have my own thoughts, but wanted to hear his. "So what do you reckon?"

"If'n I knew that, sonny Jim, I wouldn't be bleedin' asking your expert bleedin' advice, would I?"

"You've had longer to think about this than me, Tommy. I've got some ideas but I'd like your insights."

He studied me with his raging eyes, and lit another fag and jammed it in the corner of his mouth. Then he fingered his braces, stained from his fat thumbs. He pulled the elastic out and let them slap against his chest. Maybe the pain calmed him down.

"Fair 'nough. Here's how I sees it. It's an inside job and my own men are robbing me blind. Must have spare keys. Maybe the locksmith's in on the act. They just walk out the bleedin' front door. Nex' thing they're floggin' it down the lane, as bold as you like. As though their old ma had found a bit of cloth in her attic an' didn't have no use for it."

His face was going purple at the thought of it. I stopped him before he blew up like a Zeppelin.

"Tommy, I think you're right. There must be inside help. Tell me, is there any pattern to this? Do they come on particular nights or weekends or what?"

"They come when I gets a new load in, a good load, silk, or somethin' they can flog for the most bleedin' money, that's when!" He lit another fag from the end of the current one.

"OK. When's the next *good* load due?"

"Four days from now. Thursday morning the *Clever Girl* comes in from Holland. She's out of Constantinople through the Med. She drops half the load in the Hague and the other half here. Nice stuff. The best. The bastards will be queuing up to nick it!" He thumped the wooden gate so that it shuddered.

"Not this time, Tommy. Maybe not this time. If I can have a crack at it. Me and a few mates of mine will spend the night here."

"I've tried that myself. Nothing. Not even a bleedin' mouse."

"Of course not. You're not hard to spot, Tommy. They just wait for you to give up and then it's back to business."

He was nodding furiously and smoke was coming out of his mouth like the Royal Scot. "I knows, I knows. What you gonna do, then?"

"I don't want you to tell anyone, not even your foreman. Not even your wife!"

"So what's the plan?"

"Some of my mates were Special Services..."

Back at the office I phoned the landlord of the George and left a message for Midge, one of my part-time, as-and-when, don't-tell-the-taxman employees who worked for beer money and had no problem spending it. They'd been stretched in the Forces and found it hard to settle down to a proper job. Like me. Midge would get word out to the others. I needed three, though I would have preferred twenty.

I thought for a long time about making the second call. The plan I had in mind was dangerous. No, not dangerous; risky. I know Midge and co. would be up for it, but why should I complicate matters by bringing a bint in on the act? A reporter at that? They would curse me black and blue. I decided to start with some small fry and see how she reacted. I picked up the phone and asked the operator to connect me to the news desk of the *Daily Trumpet*.

"You'll have to speak up, Danny!"

She sounded like she was at a Rangers match. "I want you to meet a friend of mine. Mama Mary."

"A nun?"

"Not Mother, *Mama* Mary. A very different line of business." And how.

"Where?"

"Soho."

"So she runs a whorehouse?"

"She calls it her pleasure palace."

"You're selling me into slavery?"

"Mama Mary has her fingers on the pulse. If it's illegal, she knows of it."

"The *Trumpet*'s favourite kind of woman."

We agreed a time and a date, and I hung up, but my smile lasted a while longer.

FOUR

As I roused myself from sleep, I remembered I was seeing Eve today for the first of our jaunts. The notion raised mixed emotions: she was easy on the eye but hard on the brain; the sort of feisty girl that attracts men like moths to a candle, often with the same tragic ending. A woman who can provoke thoughts of murder or suicide. Sometimes both. As I lay there gathering my wits I ran a quick mental check to make sure she wasn't part of an interesting dream. Nope. I'd phoned her office twice since our first meeting – once more than I needed to – to confirm arrangements. She was real enough, unless she'd hired a secretary from the spirit world.

I was beginning to believe I was cured. I'd stopped imagining women now. No more ghosts to haunt my waking hours. Doc Thompson had given me the all clear provided I attended a monthly clinic with one of his pals in Harley Street. It saved a long train ride to Wiltshire, but it cost two guineas a go. An arrangement which seemed all wrong: it was paid for by the Army Department, but I still felt like the Doc and his ilk should be paying me for providing grist to their psychiatric mill. I was seeing Professor Haggarty at nine this morning and Eve this afternoon. I would have cancelled the mad Prof, but he was an enthusiastic Irishman who had trouble hearing the word no.

I'm in a rut with my morning rituals. I sat on the edge of the bed and lit a fag and waited for the kick to get me going. It came in a brief buzz of nausea, followed by the first cough, then the head cleared. I picked up my latest Penguin from the floor by my bed and placed it carefully on the end of a growing shelf of orange and green covers. In our house we'd never owned books; we just borrowed from the big Victorian library. But now, at a tanner a go, I can't get enough of the smart wee paperbacks.

I tossed my pyjamas on the bed and wandered to the sink to light the gas flame under the immerser. While the water was warming I switched on the wireless and watched the light gather behind the dial and the sound of the Home Service break through. I like to listen to the seven o'clock news before switching to music.

I cleared the draining dishes and pot from my supper last night: mash, greens and two of the tiniest lamb chops I'd ever seen. Even the sheep were on rations. I propped my little mirror against the draining board, put a new blade in the razor, and turned on the tap of the immerser. Then I rinsed my face with warm water, worked up some lather in my shave bowl and scraped my cheeks till they glowed. I lit the gas ring, filled the kettle and put it on. By the time I'd scrubbed myself with the flannel and dried the pool on the floor, the first cuppa was imminent.

Warmth seeped in through the skylight window from the late spring sun. Birds were belting out mating calls. May is a great time to be in London, even a London tattered from five years of pounding by Hermann. It was also a nice switch from this time last year. In '45 I was hauled out of a Dakota at RAF Brize Norton on a stretcher and whisked off to have my head fixed. A year ago they were taking bone splinters out of my brain and screwing in a piece of aluminium. They joked about it coming from a cannibalised Spitfire, said I'd have my own built-in war memorial. As long as it wasn't from a Messerschmitt.

I went back to the mirror and massaged a dab of Brylcreem into my hair, kneading the ridge under the skin. I combed the red tangle to careful order so that the scar was hidden, apart from the end that ran down into my left eyebrow. Maybe I should try a kiss-curl.

The newscaster was talking about the meeting of the new United Nations, and what a great step it was towards world peace. I hoped so. We said the same in 1918. Then he switched to reports about the latest overcrowded boat sailing towards Palestine, with a thousand ragged Jews wailing their way to their promised land. I couldn't see why we were standing in their way, after what they'd been through. More stuff about new ration schemes; never enough of anything. Was this what we'd fought for? And was this why we voted old Winston out?

I switched over to the Light Programme, and as I dressed, I joined in the chorus with the Andrews Sisters: *"He's the boogie woogie bugle boy of company B..."* and crooned with Frankie, *"I'll never smile again, till I smile with you..."*

Then the toast was burning and I was cursing and scraping it into the sink. I coated both slices in thick marge and black-currant jam but the taste of carbon still came through. Tea helped, and the second fag of the day had me whistling again. The milk was getting a bit whiffy but good enough for the stray moggy that had adopted me. I filled a saucer and left it on the landing. She must have been waiting; she pounced like I'd tossed her a fresh salmon. I left her lapping and guzzling, and plunged down the steps two at a time. For now I was late.

But it was my lucky morning; the big double-decker was grinding away from my stop as I belted across the road and leaped on the platform. A smooth change at Piccadilly Circus, a number 12 up Marylebone High Street and I was walking through Prof Haggarty's door just as the clock on his receptionist's mantelpiece struck the hour.

"How's that for timing?" I called to Miss V. Allardice sitting stiffly behind her newly polished desk with its wooden wedge displaying her initial and surname. She pursed her lips, and kept typing, pretending not to have noticed me. Levity was frowned on within these serious walls. I suppose she was needed as a counterpoint to Haggarty.

She hit the return, the carriage slid across with an efficient ping and she deigned to look up. She unzipped her lips. "Good morning, sir. It's Mister McRae, isn't it? The Professor will call you when he is ready. Please take a seat."

She expected to be obeyed. She was just the sort you'd need on Judgement Day to keep order. No coffin lids opened until we say so, thank you very much. Everyone lined up in strict order of sinning, worse ones to the rear. I'd barely parked my bum on the hard seat when Haggarty's voice boomed down the hall.

"Is that McRae? Show him in, Viv!"

Miss Vivienne Allardice flushed at the treacherous revelation of her first name but she kept a steady grip on her sangfroid and her keyboard.

"Professor Haggarty will see you now, Mr McRae. Straight through that door…"

"Thanks, Viv."

She glared, and the glare turned to horror as I dropped my coat and hat on the chair. She leapt out to hang them up and reinstate order before I got through the door. Haggarty was standing in the corridor like a pub landlord welcoming his first customer after some remodelling by the Luftwaffe.

"How have you been, man? Come in, come in. Take a pew. Isn't this a glorious day? Better than you and I are used to in our wet native lands, eh?" His great paw dragged me in to his lair. After one session with the Prof, I knew I didn't have to respond to any of his early questions. I sat down in the big armchair set aside for his victims.

"So, how've you been?" he asked again, this time requiring a reply. He settled his great bulk in a double of my chair and flung my file on the table between us. It was a thick file. I'd given them plenty to write about.

"I've been fine, Professor. I get the odd bad head but it passes."

"Are you still using Scotch to clear it?"

"It works."

"Aye, so it does. For you. As long as it doesn't get to be a habit. How much do you drink?"

"A glass or two a day."

"Liar. But never mind, eh? I enjoy a tipple myself. What about smoking?"

I shrugged. Everybody smoked. "A packet a day, sometimes more."

"That, you should stop. Or at least use the ones with filters. But you're not here to chat about your lungs." He began to sift through his thick pile and pulled out a piece of black film. "The hospital sent me the X-ray we had taken the last time. Shall we take a look?"

He was on his feet and holding a foot-square panel of dark film up to the light streaming through the window. I walked over and stared at the outline of my skull. I didn't know what I was looking for. Something that told me what sort of man I was. Something less like poor Yorick. How could that be me? This is how I'll look ten years after they bury me, after the worms have had their fill. Is that all there is to us?

Haggarty's big finger traced the outline of the white wedge that sat across much of the skull like a smudge on the plate. "They made a good job, so they did. Nice. Neat. No sign of movement." Then he turned to me and looked down at me from his great height. "But it doesn't tell me what's going on *under* there." He stabbed the film, then prodded my skull in the same place.

"Nothing you should worry about, Prof, I'm sure."

"That's for me to find out. Let's have a chat. Are you keeping the journal?"

I pulled out a little notepad from my inside jacket pocket and waved it at him.

"Good man."

We took our seats again and got down to it. He made me talk through the last month and the number of headaches. According to my records they seemed to be getting fewer.

"And what about the dreams?"

"They're not like before. I mean I don't have one of my fits and wake up and find cryptic notes." I pointed at the pad. Thank God. It had been like living with someone else in my body, sometimes being taken over and waking from a fugue to find this parasite had left me a message. Usually a nasty one. From the time in the camp.

"I still get nightmares, but somehow I know that's what they are. Which makes it bearable. Does that make sense, Prof?"

29

"Perfectly. These nightmares – are they about Dachau?" He said it the way everybody does since they showed the pictures; as though voicing those two guttural syllables would reopen its gates and let evil loose. Or maybe that's just how I hear it. It still makes me flinch.

"It's not that clear. Let me check." I opened my pad and ran through some of the jottings. "There's one that keeps popping up. It's hard to describe. I'm in a big space without colour or definition. Alone. And I'm being crowded by big boulders. They keep closing in on me. It's not violent or scary, just oppressive somehow. An air of gloom and foreboding. Pretty obvious, I guess."

"Really? And what might these boulders be?"

Haggarty had that look in his eye, the one that says I'm interested in what you're saying but not necessarily because you're talking sense.

"I'm trying to get on with my life. But things keep getting in my road. Obstacles…" I trailed away.

He was nodding. "Sure, sure that could be right. But it might also be that you're trying to hide something from yourself. And you won't let it go."

"Hide? What would I hide from myself?"

"Feelings? Recognition of yourself? You went through a rough time. For a while there you lost yourself. A year of your life erased, and you couldn't connect the time before with the time after."

I nodded. "I could remember who I was, but not recognise who I'd become?"

"Possibly."

"You blokes never come off the fence," I laughed. "But if you're right, what do I do about it?"

"Nothing. You're sane – as sane as me." He ignored my raised eyebrow. "You've got a job – a strange one, mind – but you can fend for yourself. The fact you've got holes in your memory isn't unusual. How many of us can recall every bit of our time for the last week, far less a year? From what you've told me, you've got plenty enough recollection. And a lot of stuff that's better forgotten."

"So I just put up with the dreams?"

"Sure, we all dream." He said nothing for a moment, then leaned forward over the table. "Tell me a thing. What language did they speak… in the camp?"

"I hadn't thought about it. All languages. There were Poles, Roma, French, Germans of course… lots of German Jews."

"What language did *you* speak?"

"I suppose French. I took French at school for my leaving certificate."

He looked down at my file and casually asked, "*Sprechen sie Deutsch?*"

"*Ja, ein bisschen. Ich habe… Meine Gott!*" I put my hand up to my mouth.

"Coming back, is it? Don't be so surprised. Even though you had a hard time of it, you would have picked up the language around you. Like a kid does. I expect you have a good basic grasp."

I wasn't listening to him. I was lying in my cramped bunk whispering to the other men around me. We were discussing the news filtering through about the progress of the allies. The guards were getting edgy. The word was they were within fifty miles. It seemed impossible. Seemed wrong to hope. I tugged at the filthy bandage around my head to ease the pressure. I was asking them what they thought the guards would do. Would they kill us all to get rid of the evidence? Should we try to break out?

I strained to hear my words and for a moment, my head filled with new sounds and structures. We were talking in German. It might not have been High German, given the polyglot culture of the camp, but it was recognisable.

"I had no idea, Prof. All I've been doing is trying to recall incidents. The language side of it never occurred to me. You don't get far trying to order a pint in German in Camberwell Green. Some of those old boys still have their Home Guard rifles under their beds."

"I don't suppose I'd recommend it as a new educational approach. But another language is always handy. I suggest you try to find a way to consolidate it. Make sure you don't lose it. It was hard enough earned."

At the end of our session he walked me to the door. "You're doing fine, Danny. Just fine. See you in a few weeks."

I collected my hat and coat from the cool Miss Allardice.

"*Danke viel mal, fraulein. Guten tag, auf wiedersehen*, Viv."

It was unkind, but worth it to see her perfectly smooth jaw drop and her eyes take on a look of panic as though Goering himself had just touched her up. I threw my coat over my shoulder, jammed my hat on and walked to the bus stop, whistling again, this time "Lili Marlene"; the German version of course. I checked my watch. Eleven-thirty. I was meeting Eve Copeland at one o'clock in pub near her newspaper office in Fleet Street. I'd get the bus down to Trafalgar Square and walk along the Strand.

FIVE

Walking down Fleet Street is like going back in time. The straggling lines of buildings are black with soot but still have that air of lofty grandeur I associate with top hats and carriages. There were plenty of bowler hats about, and wigs – lawyers from the Inns of Court – but the air was thick with traffic smoke, and the stink was enhanced by the odd steaming pile of horse manure. Hard to imagine the old river somewhere under the road, burbling down to the Thames.

The best view, through the arch of the railway line that sliced across the street, was the dome of St Paul's. No one knows how it survived; it's not as if Jerry was trying benevolently to miss our cathedrals. Look what they did to Coventry.

The Wren was dark and low-ceilinged; their original customers must have been a lot shorter. I settled in with my papers and beer. I read the *Trumpet* from cover to cover, got stuck on *The Times* crossword, and finished a pint and two Players before Eve materialised next to my table.

"You're reading the wrong rag, you know." She flicked my *Times*. She was flushed but not a bit embarrassed at being half an hour late.

I sprang to my feet. My memory hadn't betrayed me; teasing eyes and turbulent hair. Something flipped inside me, a forgotten thrill. I'd be quoting Burns to her next.

She slung her coat over the spare seat and sat down opposite me. She looked round to get her bearings. I'd chosen a corner spot and we were sufficiently far from the next table not to be overheard. Not that the two old boys had any interest in anything other than their next domino. It was war; they clutched their tiles to their chests like they held details of Hitler's last secret weapon in their hands, silent except for the occasional crash of a tile on the wood table or muttered oath before "chapping". Eve caught me eyeing them and smiled at me. A good smile. A conspiratorial smile.

I pulled the *Trumpet* out from under my coat and flourished it. "I've already done my homework. Yesterday and today."

"Good. That's how to butter up your clients. What did you think?" She put on her inquisitorial look.

"The truth, or do you want me to make you happy?"

She laughed. "The truth makes me happy."

"There are some very, very good… cartoons."

"Bastard."

"And… some of the writing is pretty good too. I'm not just saying this. Your column is about the best in the paper. It's well written, and makes its point."

"Hmmm. I *think* you're being sincere." Her head lifted and her sallow eyelids narrowed like a haughty face on a Pharaoh's tomb. "But I don't know you well enough, Daniel McRae."

"Trust me, I don't know why you're worried about losing your job. I don't see any competition. Not in here."

"Remind me to introduce you to my editor. I need to be ten times better than the next man. That's how it is. I need new material, new angles, new stories. All I do is report what I hear sitting in the Old Bailey." She pointed up towards the Aldwych. "And then some follow-up with the victim's family. The *personal* angle. Any fool can do that. I want to report stories *before* they get to court." She had that gleam in her eye again, the one I saw in my office when she got enthused at the idea of patrolling the dark side of town with me.

"Right, then. Have you got your walking shoes?"

She looked down at her leg and lifted her foot.

"Will these do?"

I admired her slim brown leg for a moment longer than I needed. "They'll do nicely," I grinned.

"I meant the shoes," she said dryly. "Where are you taking me?"

"Tea with Mary."

We cut through the green stench and slippy cobbles of the market at Covent Garden. Several stalls are still serving fruit and veg, but the real business finished long before sun-up, unloading the fresh produce from the lorries and carts. The bars down Longacre are full of the porters who breakfasted on full fries and stout, and stayed on for the fun of it.

We resist their siren calls and cross Charing Cross Road into Soho. Along Rupert Street, trying to look businesslike rather than furtive. But a red-light district on a sunny afternoon isn't an easy place to blend into. The denizens of the night are creeping about in mufti pretending to be normal citizens doing normal things like shopping, getting a haircut and chatting with their mates on street corners. It feels like a stage-set before the evening performance. We get the odd offer: two for the price of one, guv? You and your girl looking for a threesome, luv? But there's no conviction in the solicitations, just practising their lines for when the curtain goes up.

"And this Mama Mary, you know her purely through business?"

I pretended not to hear the irony in her voice. "I helped her with a little thieving problem. Then she helped me over the Caldwell case." That was as far as I would go. I just hoped that Mama Mary would heed my phone call plea to stick with that line. It was no business of Eve Copeland what I got up to in my private life, but I didn't want her thinking badly of me.

We stopped outside the green door. "Now remember our bargain, Eve. Whatever is said in here is off the record. No mention of Mary or her girls in anything you print. Or all bets are off..."

"Relax, Danny, I'm like a priest."

"You are nothing like a priest. Shall we?" I knocked and waited. Mama Mary must have been watching for us. The door eased open, a bird-like head darted out, looked each way, and a tiny but strong hand dragged us both inside. We crowded into the hall with its tasteful fake Rubens, a big fleshy girl with dimples in her rear.

"Scared what the neighbours might say, Mary?"

"Scared of big fat rozzer. Always sticking nose in."

My blood cooled. "Not Wilson? Don't say he's back on the beat?"

"No, no. Silly man. You stopped him plenty good. Shoulda stopped him dead. Tea for you too, missy?" she asked Eve as she brought us into her private room.

Eve was too busy gawping at the sea of crimson to respond.

"Sorry? Tea would be lovely. This place of yours, Mama Mary, it's very... very..."

"Red," I whispered.

"… charming," she finished.

We slithered among the silk and satin cushions, and Mary smiled at us as she poured the tea.

"Danny say you write in paper. Not 'bout us!"

"No, no. Mary. I promise you. I just need some help. Some advice."

"I got advice. Stop. Don't you go looking for trouble. Enough come to you."

"It's my job, Mary. All I want is to get a little closer to the action. Danny tells me you know everything that's going on in …"

"… in bad part of town? That what you mean? Sure, lady. I got best ears in business." She giggled, which might have looked charming in someone half her age. Though with her tiny physique, her black wig and her thick painted face, I couldn't begin to put a year on Mary.

"Mary, one thing before we get started. I know how much you like silk…" I glanced round the room. "The redder the better, eh? Do you mind telling me where you get it?"

She screwed up her face so that her eyes became cunning slits.

"Why you interested, Danny? I paid all this." She swept her hand round the room festooned with shiny hangings.

"I'm sure you paid for it, Mary. But maybe not full price. I'm not going to report you and this is off the record for Eve here. A customer of mine keeps losing some silk. I want to know where it turns up. I have my suspicions."

Mary sat thinking for a second or two. "OK, Danny, I trust you. But if I get in trouble 'cos you, then I send boys to cut off balls, OK?"

I coughed and dodged Eve's stifled laugh. "Fair enough, Mary. What do you know?"

"Place in Whitechapel. On top of shop. Always got plenty stuff. Got stall in Petticoat Lane, but that rubbish. Good stuff, you need to know right man." She tapped her head indicating she was in the know.

"Do you have a name, Mary? Just between these four walls. Promise."

"I tell." She shrugged. "No do you good. Big top guy too big to touch. Gamba, they call him."

"Gamba? Gambatti? Pauli Gambatti?"

I whistled but it was no surprise. Gambatti had his finger in every dirty pie from Stepney in the east to Gray's Inn in the west, and from the Thames up through Whitechapel and Bethnal Green to Hackney in the north. The western edge of his territory collided – in frequent bloody disputes – with Jonny Crane, boss of Soho and Holborn. His patch covered the warehouse area of Wapping. Out of the corner of my eye I caught Eve's face. Her eyes were alight and her teeth were bared.

"Know him?" I asked her.

"I know *of* him. A name that comes up a lot in conversation. But I've never been able to use it in a story. He's got expensive lawyers."

I left it at that. We drank more tea, and Mary told us of dark rooms where poker was played, drinking dens that were open all hours, dog races where both dogs and punters were drugged, and pubs where you could arrange for a business rival or straying spouse to be fixed – permanently, if required – for less than fifty quid. Eve wrote and wrote and when we emerged Soho was dipped in a golden glow from the last of the sun, and Mama Mary had broken off twice to welcome her first guests of the day to the pleasure palace: men dropping by on their way home from work.

"I need a drink," Eve said as we stumbled into the light.

"As long as it's not tea."

"Never. I will never drink another cup of tea."

"I know a place." I checked my watch. "And they're open in ten minutes."

I steered her through Soho, noting the subtle changes that were taking place. Lights coming on in dark doorways, bouncers rolling their shoulders, heavily made-up girls beginning their patrols. The streets were filling with men with hats pulled down despite the early summer warmth. As we walked, we touched occasionally; I even held her arm from time to time to see her across a road or past a pushy procurer. She didn't seem to mind.

We joined a small queue outside the Dog and Duck in Greek Street. Neither of us looked at each other, not wishing to advertise our need. At exactly six o'clock the bolts rattled; the door gaped open and a rush of stale air wafted over us. I got us drinks and led the way upstairs. We were the only customers in the small dark room. It smelled of two hundred years of beer and smoke.

"Cheers!" I raised my pint glass.

She smiled and clinked her vodka and lemonade. "Cheers, Danny. Thank you. I liked Mary."

"She's a tough little cookie, but honest. As honest as a madam can be, I suppose."

"She seems to like you."

"I told you, we helped each other."

"But I'm not sure if I got anything that will make my readers sit up and buy more papers." She took out her notebook – a black leather-bound pad that fitted into her raincoat pocket. She flicked through it, frowning. "Sorry, I don't mean to be ungrateful. It's just I need more…"

"… excitement? Look, if you're up to it, we could grab a bite and then try one of the clubs or illegal bars. I think I can get us in."

She shook her head, and I felt curiously let down at the prospect of saying goodnight.

"I *can* make something of it." She raised her hand and drew a headline in the air. *"Illicit gambling den! All-night bars of Soho!* But it's been done. And everybody knows it goes on. I need action. Bring me the head of a gangster," she challenged. *"Crime boss captured in shoot-out.* That's what makes the news."

"If only we had Prohibition." I sat back and examined her, trying to see the situation dispassionately, as if what I was about to suggest was simply business. I digested her quirky features – nose too long, eyes too big and mouth too full. Some women – not always the prettiest – set your blood racing. You want to do foolish things in front of them to keep their interest: cartwheels; picking fights with strangers; robbing a jewellery store. Eve had that quality. I wanted to impress her, to keep her near me.

Yet I knew nothing about this woman. I looked down at my beer and tried to picture her climbing a wall, running for cover, perhaps swimming for her life. I thought of the agents I'd worked with – women so brave and selfless it made you feel namby-pamby. Was she up to their mark? No one ever knows until they're tested. And by then it's too late.

But Eve Copeland seemed to have fire in her belly. Look

what she had achieved. And the way she'd sought me out. It said a lot about her determination. I lifted my gaze again into her questioning eyes. Unless I had failed to get the measure of her, I'd seen this sort of steel in only a few people in my life.

"Are you scared of water?" I asked.

"I'm a fish. You should see me at the Lido."

"I'd like to.' I smiled at the thought. "OK in boats?"

"Big ones or little ones?"

"Little to start with. Can you take a risk?"

"Life's a risk. What is it?"

"What I'm about to propose is dangerous. You could get hurt... badly. Depends what we run into. *Who* we run into."

"Are you going to tell me before I start screaming?"

"There's going to be a raid. On a warehouse."

She was sitting forward now, her dark eyes gleaming. "That's more like it." She looked round the empty bar and lowered her voice theatrically. "Tell me more."

"Bales of silk. Mary described the end result. We'll have a ringside seat at the start. The warehouse owner's being robbed blind. Tomorrow there's a fresh shipment in from Holland on the goods ship *Clever Girl*. I'm going to try to stop them."

"Count me in!"

"There's one thing. Mary mentioned a name. It shook you. Pauli Gambatti. I think he's behind this. If he is, he won't be happy. In fact he'll go berserk. And he'll know you were on the inside if you write the story. Still want in?"

She handled it well, barely blinked. But I could see her pupils dilate. She forced a smile.

"I'm in! Look, I'm starving. One more of these and I'll fall over. How about an early dinner? My treat. It's on the paper. You can tell me all about it."

She knew an Italian restaurant just off High Holborn. It was one more Italian than I'd ever been in, if you don't count Glasgow chippies. She told me it had been shut for much of the war after Churchill had ordered the internment of "enemy aliens". The aliens seemed pleased to see her. I just hoped they harboured no hard feelings as they stirred their pots. We took a corner table, and I had to ask the stupid question: "Do you come here with your boyfriend?"

She looked amused. "That's very personal."

"You're joining my gang. I need to know a bit about you." It was only half a lie.

"No boyfriend. Too busy. And even if I had the time, not enough good men to go around. *Single* men. Why aren't you married?"

Back to her defensive tricks again. "I've been busy too." I tapped my skull.

"Before the war."

"There were girls." I shrugged, and thought of the sparky shop lassies in Glasgow on a Saturday night, mad for dancing, mad for men. Get a fella, get pregnant, get married, get old. "And you?" I asked.

She looked distant for a moment, and I was about to change the subject. "There was a boy. I don't know what happened to him." She shook her head.

"Sorry. Any sisters? Brothers?"

"Someone you can invite to the funeral?" she parried.

"It's not going to be *that* risky."

"Shame." She relented. "No, no family. Only child. Mum and dad both gone." Her jaw tightened and for a second I glimpsed a different Eve Copeland. Then the barrier came back up. She picked up her fork and jabbed the back of my hand, hard

42

enough to leave a mark. "This really is a job interview, isn't it? Next it'll be hobbies and interests. Then why do I want this job and what my qualifications are, and..."

"OK! Enough! I give in." I laughed and rubbed my hand.

We broke off the swordplay and ordered some lasagne and a glass each of red wine. I took her lead on the food. The Tally caffs in Glasgow only served fish suppers and ice cream. The wine was better than the camel piss I'd tried in North Africa when I had a forty-eight-hour pass, but not much. I'm a Scotch drinker through and through. But the acid red seemed to mellow her.

"Danny, I'm very boring. I work hard at the paper. Any spare time I have, I read. I read till my eyes bleed. That's my life."

"That's not boring. What do you read?"

"Anything. Everything! There's so much." Her face glowed.

"Library?"

She shook her head. "I love being the first to open a book. It is a complete indulgence. But at sixpence a go..."

"Penguins!" Without thinking, I stretched out my hand and laid it over hers. She didn't seem to notice, just nodded sheepishly as though admitting to a cocaine habit. I left my hand over hers.

"You too?" she asked.

"I've had to put up a new shelf. Who do you read?"

"Hemingway, Linklater..."

"Mackenzie, Christie..." I raised her.

She riposted with, "Orwell, Priestley..."

We were showing off. But isn't that what you do when you find a fellow clan member? In the excitement, our fingers seemed to become laced.

"OK, OK. Here's the test." I squeezed her hand. "Steinbeck."

"Tortilla Flat, Of Mice and Men..."

"*Grapes of Wrath*! What did you think of *Grapes of Wrath*?"

"I wept," she said simply.

"Will you marry me?"

"And share my Penguins? Never!"

They tried clearing our table and sweeping up around us. Finally they put upturned chairs on the tables, so that we sat in a forest of thin columns. We took the hint at last and I walked her home through Bloomsbury to her digs in Russell Square. It felt companionable and right to hold hands all the way. Her fingers were long and slim and hot. We weren't sure what to do on the doorstep and ended up with a brush of lips on lips. It was enough to get a taste of lipstick and wine and cigarettes, and I wanted more. But she seemed to blink, as though coming out of a dream. She backed away and slipped inside. Yet something had begun. It was easy to involve her in my business. Easy to get involved with her, period. That's my excuse.

SIX

I woke early, but lay wondering at the turmoil in my mind. Nothing had happened last night. Had it? Why should it? She was my client. I was working for her. Running a detective agency didn't put me among the bankers and accountants, but it warranted professional standards. Didn't it? Besides, if I wanted to pick up a girl who liked books as much as me, I should hang around libraries. And yet... we hadn't been able to stop talking, comparing notes, trumping each other, flashing our best sides. We were kids showing off, excited by the promise of adventure. That's all. But I should have kissed her again. Properly.

I got up and dressed and stopped myself three times from lifting the phone and calling her newsdesk. It's a character defect with me, overreacting at the merest sniff of a chance with a lively girl. I shoved her out of my head. I pulled my chair up to my desk and switched into SOE planning mode. I had work to do. But as I began to lay out the operation, all I could see were the risks for her. Maybe I should have called her and put her off. I had the phone in my hand when the boys arrived. I put it back in its cradle.

They were punctual: army training. I'd met them in the pub

a couple of months ago, and over a few ales we became instant pals. As with Eve, you recognise your own type. I get them to do some stuff for me: recces of hotels and offices, tailing philanderers, that sort of thing. I can trust them. Four of us cloistered in my little office. Four men, two chairs. I took one, Midge the other. Midge Cummin, by common but unspoken assent, was my number two. An ex-sergeant in the Paras, one of the few who survived Arnhem. He was unemployed and living off the pittance of his demob pay supplemented by jobs like this, but his boots shone like he was Honour Guard at Sandhurst.

The other two sat on the floor with their backs against the wall. A pall of smoke already hung from the ceiling and at the rate we were puffing the cloud would envelop us all within the hour. I opened the window and watched the breeze stir and suck at the foul canopy. Maybe Prof Haggarty was right; I should give up the fags.

I went through my analysis of the layout at Tommy's warehouse and briefed them on the plan, such as it was. There would be a lot of improvisation. I asked Big Cyril what he thought about the timing. He was squatting against the wall tugging at his beard. He was Navy and looked exactly like the bloke on the back of a packet of Players. Cyril Styles was the quiet man who killed with his bare hands, or with a knife or anything that came to hand, in his former life as a platoon leader in Special Boat Squadron.

"It depends on the tide. I've checked the tables and we should get floated at 21.35. It's already dark by then. But you said we've no idea what time the raid will happen?"

"That's true," I said. "We could be wasting our time tonight, but you'll get paid for turning up. I agreed with Tommy Chandler that if nothing happens this time, you'll still get a couple of quid each. The bonus – twenty a man – gets paid when – if – we nail these bastards and stop the thieving."

"Sounds fair enough to me," chipped in Stan Berry. We all reckoned Stan's mom had slept with a Jack Russell. He was five foot nothing, wiry, and kept his hair short and spiky. He couldn't sit still on his scrawny arse for longer than two seconds. For the last twenty minutes he'd wriggled and twisted like he had fleas. But this was the guy who'd bailed out of his burning Lancaster over Cologne, spent six months in a German POW hospital before escaping on crutches through the lines to France, then Spain, and took the next seat on the next Lancaster to bomb the bastards again. For the crap food, he said.

I would put these three men up against a gang ten times their strength and still bet my house on them. If I had a house. But it was important never to get all four of us in the same pub. Unless they were watering the beer.

"Right. You all know your job. Midge takes one boat, Cyril takes the other. I'll be with Midge, Stan goes with Cyril. And remember – no killing! This isn't Jerry. Hear that, Cyril? No knives, no garrotting, and absolutely no guns."

"What if they've got 'em?" asked Cyril, disappointed.

"Or there are ten of them," chipped in Stan.

"You've got surprise and experience on your side."

"You sound like my old sergeant major just before he sent us out against a Panzer unit," said Cyril.

"What happened?" asked Stan.

"We lost," said Cyril dryly.

"Still, we've got these." Midge picked up one of the pickaxe handles he'd brought and thwacked it into his hand with a ringing smack.

"But try not to brain them, fellas, OK? We want to hand them over to the bobbies in one piece, everything in working order. If we can."

I stared each one in the eye till I got the look that said they understood.

"There's one other thing. We'll have a passenger tonight. A reporter who wants a scoop. I'll take personal responsibility. None of your names will show up."

"What the fuck, Danny? A passenger? This is no time for a fucking passenger," said Midge.

"I said it's my responsibility. OK?"

There were a few more grumbles but no serious objection. I wonder what they'd have said if I'd told them the reporter was a girl? One shock at a time.

At eight o'clock I was walking along the cobbles towards the Anchor Tap, a pub in Horselydown Lane, the frontier to a run of narrow streets and warehouses just down river from Tower Bridge. The streets were empty; the warehouses shut for the day, and all the workers – draymen and lightermen – safely home with their feet up listening to the wireless and reading their papers. Sensible blokes. But they'd left their spoor on the air like a tribe that had just folded its tents: acrid fumes of coal fires from guttering braziers, the sharp stink of urine and dung from the Clydesdales, and ripe malt and hops from the Anchor Brewhouse. It set my senses alight and made me wish I was meeting this girl for a quiet drink instead of a gang for a midnight ruckus.

I pushed though the swing doors, into the bar area and ducked into the little back room behind it. Four rough lads were throwing darts, another was sipping his pint and scanning the racing section, and a bargirl stood polishing her counter and dreaming of the first kiss from her beau when she got off work at ten.

No Eve. Late, as usual. I turned to walk through to check the other rooms when the fella with a paper coughed. I turned. He was waving at me to join him. Then I saw the dark eyes below the brim of the flat cap and the slenderness of the hands holding the paper. I nearly burst out laughing. I signalled to her to follow me and went on ahead. One of the darts players gave me a funny look as though he'd spotted a rendezvous between homos.

The Tap is a warren with a dozen boltholes downstairs and up. I took a seat in an empty room down the narrow corridor and waited. She appeared in the door clutching her paper and her pint. Smaller than your average bloke but no midget, she wore a scruffy pair of flannels, a jacket that must have come from a jumble sale of lads' cast-offs and a creased blue shirt and tie. I guessed she'd bound her breasts to keep them flat. The boots looked like genuine labourer's with hard toes and plenty of scuffs. Her face was scrubbed of make-up and showed off its strong lines. Her tangle of hair had been ruthlessly shoved under her cap. It bulged under the strain. In a weird way the look suited her, and I had a very odd fancy to grab this pretty lad and give him/her a sound kissing.

"You look like a docker. Quite a pretty one, mind."

"Was that a compliment?"

"For what we're up to, yes."

"What do I have to do?"

"Nothing. You are here purely as a spectator. If things get messy, stay clear. Whatever you do, keep out of the lads' way."

She nodded and looked suitably serious, yet there was a glint of mischief in those interesting eyes that made me wonder if she really understood what I'd got her into. I tried to put it across.

"If things go pear-shaped, you have to be prepared to dump the jacket and the boots, and swim for it. And this is no sweet-smelling lido; this is the Thames. More turds than fishes. Do you understand?"

"I don't intend to drink it."

I sat back. Either she was a bloody good actress or she didn't realise what a thoroughly stupid idea this was. And how likely it was to go horribly wrong.

We left the pub at nine. Once we'd gone beyond the pool of yellow light from the pub, darkness gathered round us like a silent crowd. These were warehouses, not residential streets; no need for the lamplighter to string his fire from hissing globes. The four- and five-storey brick buildings loured above us. Overhead, cranes and walkways linked the river-fronted warehouses with the rear ones. You could unload your ship and shift your load to storage through rat-runs in the sky. In the day it was full of shouts and crashing doors and creaking hand carts. Now, it was eerily quiet, and I didn't enjoy the claustro-phobic narrowness of the streets. Our boots rang out on the cobbles and echoed round the maze of alleyways.

We came to Shad Thames, the eastern boundary of this enclave. I held her back in the shadows and peered across the road into the gloomy arches of St Andrew's Wharf. I checked my watch; the luminous dial glowed green. Nine-fifteen exactly. I looked again across the road. A light blinked twice then stopped for a count of five. Twice again, and we crossed the road and penetrated the gloom. Hands guided us forward and I could smell the salt. As my eyes adjusted I could see the three shadows grinning at me.

"All set?" I asked, not whispering but keeping my voice low.

"Set, skipper." I recognised Midge's voice then his face as we emerged into a pool of moonlight. We stood on the wharf side looking down on the gathering waters of St Saviour's Dock. Below me, moored by rope to the wharf, were two boats, each with a two-stroke outboard motor. Big Cyril had done well. To our left the dock widened into the grey-glistening Thames in the Pool of London. Across the other side among the darkened crenulations stood Tommy Chandler's warehouse.

I turned to the men and indicated Eve. "This is the reporter I told you about."

"Does he have a name?" asked Stan, his inquisitive eyes running all over Eve.

I saw Eve's eyes widen as she realised I hadn't told them.

"Fellas? Just to set the record straight. It's not a *he*. This is Eve Copeland, ace reporter on the *Daily Trumpet*."

"Fuck's sake, Danny!" said Stan, more offended by Eve being taller than him than by her sex, I suspected. He was echoed by the others.

"Enough! I said I'd handle this. She's—"

Eve interrupted me. "I'm just along for the ride. I promise you, I won't get in the way. And if things work out the way Danny says, you'll all be front-page heroes."

The men grumbled but were softened by her attitude, or the promise of stardom. I called them back to business.

"How's the tide running, Cyril?" This was his specialty. I hoped he wasn't having flashbacks to the Dieppe raid. But as far as I could see he was enjoying it. Just like old times.

"We're at the last half hour of high tide, Danny. The current's running like a greyhound. It'd have us all down at Richmond in two shakes if we went out now. But I'm assuming

Jerry will have thought of that too. If they're coming out to play tonight."

"Jerry?"

"Habit. Sorry."

"Is the *Clever Girl* berthed?"

"She's alongside. You can see her prow if you walk five yards."

I did. I could see the sharp outline of her forward half across the water. Tommy told me she was a three-thousand tonner, one-funnel job. She took up three-quarters of the mooring in front of the warehouse.

"When's the best time – if you were planning to nick the goods?" I asked.

"In an hour the tide will hit high-water mark. That's when there's calm, when the water balances," said Cyril showing us with his hands.

"How long does it last?"

"Ten, fifteen minutes."

"When's the next high tide?"

"Three a m. That's the one I'm betting on," said Midge. "Dead time."

"You could be right. But we need to be prepared for either. We'll take turns watching. The rest of us settle down. This could be a long night."

Midge took lookout first, sitting out at the end of the walkway in the shadow of a thick pile, gazing across the swollen river. Eve and I sat with our backs to the wharf wall. The wood warmed up under us and as there was no breeze, the evening air felt mild. We shared a cigarette, cupping the glow, and kept our thoughts to ourselves. Mine dwelt on other nights waiting for action. The weapon drops in France, with the wood-burning Gazogene truck parked in the wood. The quiet breathing of the Maquis around me, ready to chase the crates of ammo and guns swooping down out of the night sky. Or before that, under a desert night flooded with stars, waiting for the roar of the guns to split the dawn. Back further, to a past that belonged to someone else; waiting for the daybreak of my first big police raid on a bunch of counterfeiters I'd been tracking for months. Wondering if I'd thought of everything. Wondering about the deployment of forces. Wondering about my own courage.

Was it fear that cramped my guts now? Or excitement? I felt the heat of Eve's body and despite her lack of make-up and perfume, could smell her skin above the coarser smell from her borrowed clothes. I thought about putting my arm round her, but instead found my head slowly tipping forward, and I was asleep.

"Danny! Skipper!" Someone was hissing at me.

I woke fast, not remembering where I was. Then it returned. Eve was already awake beside me, and might not have slept at all. We got stiffly to our feet. Midge was standing over us.

"There's movement by *Clever Girl*. It's quarter to three. Tide's up and river's flat." Midge told me. Stan stood beside him. I looked along the boardwalk. Cyril crouched behind one of the big wood piers, staring out across the black water. Our two boats sat quietly in the water of the dock about three feet below us.

"Let's go."

I whistled and saw Cyril turn and slip back into the shadows, then reappear a moment later by our side. Midge was already in one boat, Stan in the other. I got into Midge's and helped Eve down. Through her hands I could feel her shaking but her face was charged with excitement, not fear. Each of the men pulled out a dark balaclava and pulled it on. I took out another and gave it to Eve. Without hesitation she tugged it over her head till all I could see were two dark eyes gleaming out of the big white pools. She grinned and I saw her teeth. Suddenly we were five anonymous men up to no good.

I gave the signal and we started up the little outboard motors. It took a couple of tugs and a bit of priming but both spluttered into life. The noise seemed loud enough to raise Old Father Thames himself, but it would dissipate when we were out of the narrow dock and into the main river. There was always noise at night anyway. River folk didn't work nine to five.

Stan's boat led the way and we edged out to the mouth of the inlet. Then we stopped while I took a good hard look across the water. The Pool of London is three or four hundred yards wide at this point and deep enough to take the Queen Mary. A quarter moon dipped in and out of clouds, and it was hard to pick out any shapes against the black wharfs. But I could see the outline of *Clever Girl* clearly, and just down-stream from her, a smaller craft, long and flat. A barge. It hadn't been there earlier. For a second I caught sight of a man walking along the gunnels and then dropping out of sight. The wheelhouse was empty. I peered above him at the ware-house wall. All the doors were firmly shut except for one. Directly above the barge. A figure appeared in the doorway and looked down.

We stuck to the south bank for a hundred yards upstream until we were nearly under Tower Bridge. Then we cut straight across the river, slicing through great eddies and whorls of hesitant water. If we weren't about to go into battle it would have been a romantic trip. When we reached the north bank we cut the engines and found ourselves almost stationary as the tide made up its mind which way to run. We now had the bulk of *Clever Girl* between us and the robbers.

We took up oars, Midge in my boat and Stan in the other, and slid downstream. As we came round the hull of *Clever Girl* we kept our heads low. No one on the barge was looking our way and we eased ourselves between the two boats and hooked our ropes round the chain of *Clever Girl*. We were directly under the squat prow of the barge. I stood up, feeling my boat rock beneath me. I inched my head up above the bulwark and peered over.

The hold of the barge stood two feet proud from the deck. It took up most of the deck space. At the stern was the empty wheelhouse. The tarpaulin that covered the hold was rolled right back. One man stood on the gunnels beside the hold, next to the wall of the warehouse. Ten feet above him the door gaped open. A knotted rope dangled from the arm of the pulley that jutted out above the door. There was no one else in sight. I guessed there was at least one man inside the building, probably two, and they were off looting.

Sure enough I heard the sound of wheels, and suddenly one of Tommy Chandler's handcarts came into view. A big bale of silk sat in it. Two men were pushing it. I ducked down as they came to the edge. I waited until I heard the sound of exertions and then the thump as the bale hit the hold. We felt the impact through the hull. I waited again till I heard the sound of the cart retreating then risked another look. The doorway was empty; they'd gone to refill. The man on the barge was gazing into the hold. He turned and stared up at the open door, waiting for the next batch.

I pointed at Midge's boat and raised two fingers. Midge nodded, tapped Cyril and the pair of them stood up. I waved, and they slithered over the top, like eels. Their empty boat slopped and bumped against the barge. I peeked over the bulwark again. They were crawling round both sides of the hold. One, I couldn't tell which, got to the end of the side nearest me, and waited for the other to make his way round two sides. The nearest suddenly pulled off his balaclava, got to his feet and walked smartly towards the man.

"Got a light, mate?" said Midge.

The man whirled round. His expression was a treat: somewhere between terror and confusion. Exactly what Midge wanted. The man looked up at the door and back at Midge who was now within three yards of him. He didn't know whether to call a warning or reach for his matches. That's when the shadow behind him filled out and the club tapped him neatly behind the ear. He fell with a thump. Cyril bent over to make sure he didn't tumble into the water or the hold. They dragged him over to the main deck and tied and gagged him.

I found Eve standing beside me, peering over the side at the action. She turned to me and grinned through the cut-out mouth of her woollen mask. I grinned back but raised my hands with palms open towards her and signed for her to sit down and stay where she was. The grin left her. But she nodded and sat down, leaving our boat trembling in the water. I picked up my cudgel, stuffed it into my belt and pulled myself up on to the barge. Stan was right with me. We had to move fast.

We slunk round the lip of the hold. Midge was already monkeying up the rope. Cyril held the end steady, then when Midge was level with the open door he swung him backwards and forwards twice. The second time, Midge grabbed the opening and pulled himself in. Stan shinned up after him and I followed. I felt the rope burning my hands, and my lungs were panting as I was pulled in through the open door. But my arms felt good and strong; my workouts at Les's gym were paying off.

Cyril was already on his way up. He did a bad pantomime of Tarzan swinging on his liana. I reached out and dragged him in before he started to beat his chest. We freed our cudgels from our belts and tiptoed into the darkness of the warehouse.

I heard the cart trundling nearer. We settled into the dark, against the wall and part-hidden by wood pillars. We waited. Gradually shapes took on definition as my eyes adjusted. The big room seemed to stretch forever into the blackness, with beams in serried ranks. The cart was coming from our left but I couldn't make it out yet.

Suddenly there was a noise from the right. It was the same sound of wheels creaking. We were facing two teams. I should have waited longer to see what was happening before sending us over the top. I tried to be positive. Maybe it was just the two of them, with one man per cart? Maybe they would roll over and not fight. We still had surprise. I couldn't contact the others now but I knew they would have heard and understood. I saw small waves from each of them.

The cart from the left took shape, and I could see two heads pushing it. Damn! Turning, I was in time to see the one from the right come into view. I signalled to Midge and Cyril to take the left one; Stan and I would attack the right. We waited and waited, until both carts were within twenty paces. Surely they would see us? Closer, closer, then I acted. I gave a great roar and ran at the right hand truck. My voice was echoed by three others as the lads went in.

The two behind our cart looked stunned. But my man's reflexes were still working; he ducked my club and I caught him a glancing blow on his shoulder. I followed through with a tackle that brought him down. He was wriggling and kicking like a lassoed bullock. Stank like one too. I'd lost the club, and we fought in silence until I could hold his arm and get a clean punch in. I got him on the side of the head and drew blood over his eye. It slowed him. I hit him again and his head fell back with a crack on to the floor. He lay still. One down.

I got to my feet; Stan was standing panting over the flattened body of his man, ready to hit him again if he moved. He didn't look like he was going to any time soon. I dragged my bloke over to Stan and told him to guard them both. I ran over to the others. Midge had nailed his man, but Cyril was lying flat on the floor. There was no sign of the other. Bugger! We pulled off Cyril's balaclava. He gave a groan and stirred, and we helped him sit up. We all removed our masks. It was good to scratch.

"You big jessie," I said. "You all right?"

"Yeah, skip. Sorry. He ducked. I didn't." Cyril touched his head and came away with blood. I pulled a hankie from my pocket and gave it to him.

"What do we do?" hissed Midge.

"Nothing. We'll never find him in this rat run. Forget him. This is a good haul. Tie them up and bring them over to the door. We'll sit it out till Tommy gets here in the morning."

"What about the bint?" asked Stan.

"I'll go get her and bring her up here. We'll leave the other one where he is. He's not going anywhere."

Shortly we had the three of them trussed up and moaning

gently by the doorway. I reached out, grabbed the rope and slid down to the barge. I checked the man we'd left: he was well held. And awake; he glowered at me over his gag. I glanced over and saw Eve watching me. I walked over and gave her my hands. She clambered up swiftly and neatly. I held the rope and watched in admiration as she hauled herself up to the door. All that swimming must have developed her arms. One of the boys pulled her in and I followed. I found her shaking her hair loose and being admired by the boys who were preening in front of their prisoners.

"Get your fucking hands up!"

We whirled and stared into the dark chamber. The missing man was standing not ten feet away. He was a skinny little guy but he was holding a big fat gun. Slowly we did as he asked. I noticed Eve slipping back behind me so that I would shield her from the gunman. Smart girl.

He came towards us. I recognised the huge set of teeth in the little face. Sid the foreman. It figured.

"Now get over there, you bastards! Away from them." He waved his gun towards the doorway. We shuffled until he had us set up with our backs to the river. Eve was cowering behind me, holding on to my jacket at the back. His mates lay between us and him. They were stirring and ready to be freed. I felt a complete fool. I also felt vulnerable standing so close to the lip of the doorway.

Sid bent down and pulled the gags off the three men.

"Thank Christ, Sid!" said one of them. "Don't just stand there. Finish the fucking job. Shoot the fuckers."

Sid stood up, and looked at us. A grin came over his weasel face.

"I seen you in the yard. You'se fucking coppers?"

I shook my head, wondering about stepping back and jumping. But Eve was between me and the exit. I hoped one of the others would make the jump. Better to risk a broken leg than a shot in the belly.

"Well, that's all right then. You ain't gonna be missed."

"Shut the fuck up talking, Sid. Shoot!"

Sid raised his gun and took aim at my chest. He could hardly miss from six feet away. I braced myself. I suppose I shut my eyes. A gun went off and I heard a scream. It wasn't me. Sid was writhing on the ground, clutching his shoulder. Eve's right arm stuck out under mine. Smoke was clearing from the little gun in her hand. I didn't waste any more time thinking. I dashed forward and kicked the gun away from Sid. He was squealing in pain like a skelped pup. I retrieved his gun and walked back to Eve, now the centre of attention and congratulatory hugs by my lads. She wasn't looking joyous. Her face was strained and tight, like a kid who knows she's done wrong but won't admit it.

"I said no guns."

"Not to me you didn't," she said fiercely.

"I didn't expect you to need the warning."

Midge butted in. "Fuck's sake, Danny. She saved our skins."

I sighed and nodded. "You're right. Eve, thanks. Thanks a million. Now I suggest you use that journalist imagination to think up a good story for the boys in blue tomorrow." She looked at me warily. I smiled and stepped forward and put my arms round her. My turn to hug. Through her thick worker's clothing, her curves pressed against me. She felt good in my arms.

"Thanks. I mean it. You were amazing. You all right?"

She looked up and nodded, and this time she smiled and I

could feel the tension leave her and the shakes begin. I gently prised the gun from her. It was a toy, a Beretta 0.25. I'd ask later where she got it and how she learned to use it.

"Let's get Sidney here as comfortable as we can. It won't be serious. It was only a pea-shooter." I held up the gun. The boys laughed and bent to work. When we were done, we settled down for what was left of the night. That's how Tommy Chandler found us come daylight.

SEVEN

ommy almost wept when he found what had happened –
whether in gratitude to us or anger at being betrayed by
his foreman was hard to tell. We only just managed to stop
him from kicking the lot of them into the river, still tied. And
Tommy would have added a couple of bricks to help them on
their way to hell.

It took half a pack of Craven A to calm him down. I asked
him to get some of his boys up to mind the prisoners, and
pointed to the remaining one down on the barge. I wanted my
men well away from the scene when the rozzers got here. Same
with Eve. I especially didn't want her having to explain what
she was doing with a gun and why she was so handy with it.

Tommy was so grateful he would have agreed to lying to
the police on a warehouse full of bibles. There was no love
lost between the East End and the law at the best of times.
So an hour later, when the squad cars squealed up outside,
Tommy and I were alone, ready with a slightly tailored
version of the facts.

"You say you were the night watchman, Mr McRae?" the
inspector was asking. We were in Tommy's office and Inspector
Austen was tugging at his thick bottom lip. A sure sign that

he was weaned too early. I imagined him in private having a really good suck of that thumb.

"Temporary watchman, inspector. Mr Chandler asked me to help him stop the thieving. I'm a private detective – Finders Keepers."

He didn't like that. They don't. Private dicks are seen by the boys in blue as only one shade lighter than the crooks themselves. I think it's professional jealousy.

"And the gun? This is your gun?" Now he was mauling his mouth, trying to rub out his lips. No wonder his hair was thin and his skin so pale; this man needed a holiday, or a new job.

I looked at Eve's Beretta lying between us. "That's mine all right. I have a licence." That was a risk; I was guessing they wouldn't check it out. Why would they?

"You don't have a licence to go round shooting people."

"Self-defence. Look at what *he* had." I pointed at the other weapon lying on the table. It was a .45, and looked like a Bazooka alongside mine.

"Where do you think you are? The Wild West? Beat him to the draw, did you?"

Just then I saw some commotion outside through the glass panels of Tommy's office. The sound carried through. Inspector Austen looked pissed off, as though his brilliant interrogation had been on the point of forcing an unwitting confession out of me. He got up and went to the door. He opened it and shouted out.

"What's going on? I'm in the middle of taking a statement here."

Then I saw her. Eve was standing in the middle of the warehouse in her normal clothes – beret, belted coat and shoulder bag – arguing with a policeman and scribbling in her little black notepad. The constable was clearly past the point of being civil. His face was red and his collar looked two sizes too small as he ran his finger round it, trying to let blood through to his small brain. Eve saw the inspector and her face lit up as she strode towards him.

I heard a soft "Oh Christ" from him.

From her: "Inspector Austen! I should have known you would be the one to nab these crooks! I'd like a few words for my readers."

Apart from a hectic flush on both cheeks, which accentuated the dark pools below her eyes, Eve was the innocent but far from retiring professional reporter. She saw Tommy and me, but there was no recognition for either of us. Tommy reached for his fags, then realised he had one hanging from his lip.

"One of you two must be the owner. Mr Chandler?"

Tommy stuck his hand up like a school kid. Eve thrust hers out and shook his roughly.

"And you are…?" She stood in front of me, her eyes bright and challenging.

"Who's asking?" Two could play her game.

"Eve Copeland, reporter from the *Daily Trumpet*, Mr…?"

I took a risk that Inspector Austen would play along with a wind-up of the press.

"Hamish MacTavish, night watchman."

She squeezed her lips together to curb the grin. She shook my hand, and dug the nail of her pinkie into the palm of my hand. I don't know if it was tiredness, or after-effects of the fight, or too long without a woman, but I had a sudden and overwhelming wish that we were alone and I was biting those compressed lips.

The rest of the scene became an all-round farce: Austen trying to get rid of Eve and Eve trying to get the story she already knew from the inside. Tommy and I played along as best we could. Behind us, the sorry-looking gang were marched off, glowering at me with a message in their eyes that I had just bought myself a heap of trouble. The wounded foreman was carted off moaning on a stretcher, chest bound and face blanched.

Eve caught the late edition with enough tantalising hooks to ensure that the main morning run would sell out in minutes. It painted a picture of a plucky night watchman – one Hamish MacTavish – and a few doughty storemen besting an armed gang intent on plundering a treasure house piled high with exotic silks. She even hinted at having witnessed the shoot-out herself after a tip-off by underground contacts. This fearless reporter scaled the warehouse river-wall just in time to see the tail-end of the tussle. She referred to Hamish as the 'humble hero of the waterfront'.

The boys and me laughed about the first article that evening over a few drinks in the George. I'd come with their wages from Big Tommy. He'd been so pleased he'd added a bonus tenner to each of us, and the way Midge and Stan were putting it away, they'd have nothing left in the morning except the mother and father of all hangovers.

"I thought you was a fucking magician, Hamish, the way you drew that gun," Stan was slurring. "A fucking magician. Didn't even see you move."

Cyril butted in, slopping his pint over the already sodden table. His beard glistened with beer. "Then we saw it was the bint! Could hardly believe it. I know it was a pop gun. But what's she doing carrying it? And where did she learn to shoot like that? Have her in my unit any day, so I would."

We were in a little corner of the lounge bar, a bit away from other customers but the lads' voices were getting louder with every round.

"Keep it down, will you?"

"What's it matter, Danny?" asked Stan, who'd chosen the tallest seat at the table and managed to look like an elf on a kiddie's high chair. He could have done with a bib as well, the state of his shirt.

"I just don't want the world and his wife to know. You get names and photos splashed around and next thing the rozzers' eyes are on you, or some prat decides to take you on to prove he's a big guy. Low profile, that's best, then we can get more work. If you're sober enough!"

"What? Us? Don' you worry your pretty head, Danny boy," said Midge through his thickening tongue.

I was suddenly aware of someone standing nearby. I turned. His shoulders were as thin as a rail and his spine humped under his shiny jacket. Sparse black hair was slicked down with too much Brylcreem, and he kept passing a fag from one hand to the other taking a short suck in between. It was Fast Larry, a bookie's runner of my acquaintance. When he saw I'd noticed him, he smiled and edged a couple of feet closer. They can smell the money, these boys.

"No nags tonight, Larry. We're just having a quiet drink." Quiet? I glanced round at the ever-louder trio. Fast Larry was shaking his head and was now within three feet. He signalled with a finger to his lip and pointed at me. I let him come right up. He bent over. I could smell his sour breath. I turned my head.

"The word's out, Danny."

"What word is that, Larry?"

"You and the boys, here. You done over the gang in the paper there." He pointed at the evening version of the *Trumpet* soaking up the spillage.

"Not us, mate."

Larry rubbed his oily nose. "Gamba put the word out."

My blood started running faster. "Gamba?"

"Gambatti. Pauli Gambatti. He's looking for you. Those were his boys you got nicked this morning. He's not 'appy."

The underworld grapevine never ceased to impress me. I looked at Fast Larry and wondered why he was telling me this. Loyalty to his regulars? Larry was only as loyal as the last bet. Ordered to by Gambatti? A strange instrument. Or just malicious? His eyes were flicking all round the room. He was one of life's parasites. Always on the edge of a crowd looking in. Seen as a go-between, not a person in his own right. Breaking the news to me got him into my life stream, gave him existence. But I couldn't, wouldn't acknowledge it.

"You've got it all wrong, Larry. If you bump into your mate Pauli, tell him we had nothing to do with it." I was conscious the others were listening now.

"Yeah, piss off, Larry," called out Stan, who felt he could lord it over at least one bloke who was in worse shape than him.

Fast Larry winced like he'd been struck. He turned and shuffled off. But he'd left behind a small cloud. I didn't have to explain to anyone at the table who Gambatti was.

EIGHT

Neither did I have to explain to Eve. I found her the next night celebrating her scoop with her fellow hacks in the Coal Hole in the Strand. The pub was just far enough away from Fleet Street to avoid bumping into the editor, but close enough at a slow stumble to put the evening edition to bed. Eve saw me and pushed towards me. None of her flush-faced cronies seemed to miss her. Her face was rosy with drink and success. It was a big transformation in thirty-six hours.

She waved the front page of the *Trumpet* at me. "Read all about it! Fearless reporter scoops gang-bust!"

"I've seen it. A great story. Almost wish I'd been there."

"It's what we agreed, isn't it?" Her voice dropped. She looked anxious, as though I was upset.

"I don't need the publicity. Not with Gambatti out for blood."

"He's going to be my follow-up piece."

"Are you daft?" I exclaimed. "Why get Gambatti even more upset than he already is? You can't name names without proof."

She drew me further away from the rabble at the bar. We were standing by a shelf running along the smoke-blackened wall. Her face was close enough for me to smell her scent. She pressed a hand to my lapel and fingered the cloth. We got a hoot from her friends at the bar. She ignored them.

"Danny, this is my biggest scoop in years. I need to milk it for all it's worth. I'm too public for Gambatti to do anything to me. He'd be the first suspect."

"From what I've heard, that wouldn't matter a toss. He's a complete nutter. He had a waiter's fingers chopped off for slopping soup in his lap. He made a fortune out of the war. While the good folk of London were cowering in bomb shelters he sent his lads out on looting sprees. Lost a few of his gang in the air raids, but he never worried about it. Plenty more deserters to chose from. Cleaned out whole streets, they tell me. Even nicked the poor blighters' blackout curtains. Flogged them back to the owners on Saturday at the market. He's an all-round villain."

"That's what makes him so newsworthy." Her eyes shone provocatively. And something in them – maybe a recognition of what we'd just been through – told me that if I leant forward to kiss her she wouldn't slap my face. Her smile grew and she shook her head.

"Not here. Meet me in an hour, Baker Street tube. Unless you're too tired?"

I wasn't. Nothing would make me too tired for a date with Eve Copeland. Which I guess this was. Forty-five minutes later I was pacing around outside Baker Street station checking each entrance in case we missed each other. I stamped out my third cigarette, turned and saw her. She was standing looking at me, her face quizzical, as though she was wondering why I was here. Or maybe why she was. Then she seemed to remember she'd summoned me but couldn't decide what she was going to do with me now. I wasn't sure myself. She switched on the smile and walked towards me. She thrust her arm through mine, leaned up and pecked me on the cheek and led me off towards her flat in Marylebone.

We lay on our backs, gazing at the ceiling, hips and legs touching in luxurious intimacy. I'd lit two cigarettes and given her one. Bergman and Bogart in *Casablanca*. It was the best cigarette in the world. We'd been clumsy and urgent at first; she seemed as deprived as me. Maybe she'd been telling the truth about boyfriends. Maybe the dragon who rented the room to her usually did a better job of blocking visitors. I hoped so. Eve made me take my shoes off to climb the creaky stairs. I felt like a burglar sidling up the edges of the steps in time with her. Halfway up she'd given me heart failure by shouting out, "Early night, for me, Mrs Gibson." And got the reproving response above the sound of the wireless, "Just as well, Miss Copeland, after last night! I don't know what sort of job that is for a young woman."

We swallowed our giggles. Fortunately we didn't need much verbal foreplay when we sneaked into her room. We tossed our clothes on to her one chair and dived under the blankets. Her mouth was everything I'd anticipated: an erotic concoction of mint imperial, cigarette and alcohol. I couldn't get enough of her full lips and tongue. Her mane of hair smothered me in smoky, shampooed coils. I nuzzled the soft angle of her neck and under her chin and wanted to leave teeth marks all over her skin.

I would have kissed and held her for hours. Nothing more. It was all I thought I needed. But her demands overwhelmed us. OK, mine too. Our only constraint was the bed; its old springs kept us in check, made me gentle, more careful. I wanted this to be the best for her. As it was for me.

Ages later when the house was asleep, she led me back down the stairs and pushed me reluctantly into the night with a final finger kiss to my sensitised lips. I slid my shoes on outside and walked off in a state of grace down the quiet streets of Marylebone.

Where there's food or romance, the French have a phrase for it. In the case of love there is *coup de foudre*. I'd felt it the day she walked into my office, but ignored it. It was stronger after our first dinner. The warehouse raid had underpinned it. Now I was hunched over burnt toast and a cup of cold tea, worrying if we'd gone too far too fast. Wondering if she felt the same way or if it had just been that great charge, that release of tension after shared danger. All that adrenalin swilling about. Like me and one of my more volatile girlfriends savaging each other after one of our shouting matches.

We weren't seeing each other till the next day and I spent the next twenty-four hours oscillating between elation and panic. We met at the Lyons House in the Strand and when I saw her face my worst fears flooded through me. She was flushed and jumpy. I took it for embarrassment and regret.

"Danny, about the other night…"

"It's all right. You don't have to explain. It was daft. All that excitement…"

"We can't do it again…"

"I know, I'm sorry. It was great but I understand…"

"Danny, will you shut up and let me finish!"

The girl bringing our tea gave us a look and left us in resounding silence.

She started again. "Danny, we can't meet again like that. Not at my place. My landlady must have heard something. She gave me such a hard time yesterday. Came into my room unannounced last night. Sniffing the air like a blooming bloodhound."

I burst out laughing.

"It's not funny, you know! Rooms are hard to come by."

"My place is no palace. You've seen it. But it's snug."

Her neck flushed again. "We need to go slow. We've got work to do. It'll just get in the way."

"What will?"

"This! Us. I told you, I don't have time for men."

"We could read to each other."

"Shut up, Danny."

It wasn't till the day after we'd gone looking for trouble at the White City dog track that I could persuade her back to my place. I'd scrubbed my bedroom and changed the sheets just in case, but it still seemed cheap and tawdry when I showed her in. I wanted an Arabian tent filled with cushions and wafting silks for her. She didn't seem to mind brown lino and faded carpet. Or that I kissed her and helped her off with her clothes.

Afterwards we lay together with my arm under her head, nearly asleep.

"You must think I'm easy," she said.

"I think you're beautiful. I think you're funny and brave."

Her head shook in denial. Her shrub of hair tickled my nose. I calmed it down.

"I don't do this."

"What, go to bed with Scotsmen?"

She punched my chest. "With anyone."

"So this is special?"

She shifted her head so she could look at me. Her eyes were anxious. "This is lovely, Danny. But it's just fun. It's not anything else. Right?"

"Sure, Eve. It's whatever you want it to be."

Suddenly she sat up, supporting herself with her arm. "Danny, listen. This isn't anything. It's not going anywhere." She was fierce.

"OK, princess. Message received."

She studied my face, looking for the truth. I don't know what she saw, but she lay down again, and we held each other tight. Just for fun.

A pattern emerged over the next few days. We would keep up the professional façade while I helped her find new stories, but when the work was done – or sometimes when we couldn't wait a second longer – we'd make for my place. There, the only guardian we had to contend with was the moggy, and Eve soon had her purring round her legs. Me too for that matter.

Each time Eve would try to resist the temptation and each time she'd give in. And after each time she would say we had to stop. And we did, till the next time.

Guilt that we might be using her column as an excuse to leap into bed spurred us to put more effort into her work. Of course it would take something special to top the Tommy Chandler story, and I had nothing lined up that needed the unique skills of Midge, Cyril and Stan. So we began to frequent the seedier dives and haunts of the underclass looking for trouble. Sniffing around and catching the mood. So as not to kill the golden goose, Eve made it clear to anyone who asked that names and addresses would be changed to protect the guilty. Just as well, for she wrote about the dog fixers at White City, the protection rackets in London restaurants, and the stolen goods for sale in every open market in town. To read her exposés was to imagine a London corrupt from top to bottom, a festering swamp of thieving and cheating. She wasn't far wrong. It sometimes made me wonder how I kept myself clean. And why.

She took me into her newspaper one day when I showed interest in the process. I'd thought about becoming a journalist after uni, but there was more money in the police. She started me in a room swamped with papers and reporters. A haze of smoke swirling above the jumble of desks. Journalists sat talking together or pounding at typewriters. It was late in the afternoon and there was a sense of mild desperation in the hangar-like room as they fought to put the next edition together. We passed an office just as the door crashed open and a grey-haired man with broken veins on his pock-marked face emerged shouting.

"Where's the bloody lead? That lead was to be on my desk twenty minutes ago." The sheer volume of his voice was offset by the clean vowels of northern Scotland. I placed him from Inverness.

A shout from the depths of the hubbub came back: "Coming, Jimmy! Just coming!"

The man turned his glowering eyes on us, and his face softened. "It's yourself, Eve. Nice piece today. We'll run with that. But a wee bit too much alliteration. We're not a poetry magazine. Who's this?" he demanded, scrutinising me.

"Jim, this is the man who's been helping me with those scoops. This is Danny McRae. Danny, this is my boss, the editor, James Hutcheson."

"You've been costing me a wee fortune, Mr McRae. But so far it's been worth it. Any more adventures like that warehouse job in the offing?" He raised one of his huge grey eyebrows in inquiry and reached out a hand to shake mine.

"Not this week, Mr Hutcheson."

"In that case my expenses will be lower, eh?"

There was more than a hint of seriousness in his comment, but he suddenly softened.

"Look, come on, Danny. Call me Jim. You're an interesting character. Come and have a dram. You'll take a malt, I trust." His back was already retreating into his den as he said this. Eve shrugged and smiled, and we followed him into his nicotine cave. He cleared a two-foot pile of old papers off a chair and dumped them on an already tottering stalagmite of newsprint. He unearthed another chair and dipped into the top drawer of a dented filing cabinet and triumphantly hooked out a whisky bottle. His desk drawer yielded tumblers of uncertain cleanliness and we were off.

It was an entertaining half hour punctuated by bellows at his staff and splashings of Scotch. But no matter how much he drank, it didn't seem to affect his ability to scan a draft. He flourished his blue pencil with deadly skill and loud scorn for the English education system.

The rest of Eve's tour was thankfully less whisky-fuelled. My head was already buzzing by the time we reached the bedlam in the foundry. It was like a blacksmiths' convention: benches lined with men hammering lead type on to metal sheets and feeding discarded slugs back into the melting pot for re-use. I wondered what it did to your brain to be writing backwards and upside down all the time.

In the next room, they slid the still-hot plates into the presses, and inked the typefaces before feeding through the first of the sheets from the giant rolls.

Eve handed me the first edition, still hot and wet. I glanced at the headlines and the cartoons, then up and around at this Vulcan choreography. I shook my head – metaphorically; I didn't want to hurt Eve's feelings; such industry and effort for something so slight.

NINE

Eve announced she wanted to move upmarket. In the three weeks we'd been working together she'd written about warehouse theft and dog doping at White City. Now she wanted to tackle corruption among the toffs, bearding them in their fancy gambling dens.

"The one in Mayfair," she said. We were walking in her lunch hour through Lincoln's Inn, sidestepping blokes in wigs and winged collars. It was like the movie set for *David Copperfield*.

"Carlyle's? Start at the top, why don't you? How do you know about that?"

"Danny, it may be illegal but any cabbie will take you. All I need is an escort." She took my hand and gave me her most winning smile. She knew that I knew she was conning me. She also knew I was a sucker for her smile.

I tried to be practical. "You also need a sponsor. It's a very private club. No coppers, no press. Especially no press."

"Jimmie Hutcheson has it all arranged," she said gaily. "A friend of a friend who didn't want her name in the papers. Divorce can be *so* messy."

"You folk have the morals of an alley cat."

She waved the notion away. "As Jimmie says, it's all bread

and circuses. The baying crowds want blood. And if it's the blood of wealthy spivs or the ruling class so much the better. It makes our fellow citizens feel less guilty about buying that extra sausage without a coupon."

I laughed and agreed we'd put on the glad rags and enter the den of iniquity on Thursday night.

In honour of the occasion I spent an hour at the slipper baths in Camberwell and came back glowing and gleaming. As I scraped my face with my razor I thought of the night ahead with a mixture of excitement and apprehension. The fact that everyone had heard of Carlyle's should have meant the place was closed down years ago. But everyone also knew of the existence of two laws in this country: one for folk who take the bus and one for those who ride in the back seat of a Rolls. Places like Carlyle's existed in a parallel universe in which the police wore blinkers and the judges were kindly old men with unlimited reserves of tolerance and compassion. But only for the weak and foolish members of the moneyed class. Or blokes they went to school with. Usually the same thing.

It was also said that in the case of Carlyle's, illegal didn't have to mean squalid. Behind the reinforced doors was a set-up as lavish as anything this side of Monte Carlo. Which meant we had to dress the part. I was renting a tux for the first time in my life. I plastered my hair down, crammed my neck into a winged collar, and spent ten minutes wrestling a bow-tie into submission. I felt both an idiot and a prince as I sauntered into the American Bar at the Savoy where we'd agreed to meet. It would put us in the right mood, Eve said.

My mood was controlled panic. This was a different species of watering hole from the George. The floors had carpets, not sawdust. Smart waiters in white gloves served you, not a fat-chested blonde with black roots and a fag in her mouth. The pianist was playing Irving Berlin, not *Knees up Mother Brown*. And I was supping a Tom Collins, not a pint with a chaser. If my dad could see me now, or his pals from the working men's club.

As the alcohol hit and my panic subsided, I began to speculate how I could live like this on a permanent basis. Then a vision walked in and stole a dozen men's hearts. Mine had been purloined weeks ago. I got to my feet, collar suddenly too tight, as she walked down the four stairs into the lounge bar. Two flunkeys were at her side in a flash, taking her cape and throwing rose petals in her path.

The dress was silver and ankle length. It clung to every curve like the skin of a salmon. Her neck and shoulders were bare except for a silver chain with a small amulet pointing into the magnetic groove of her bosom. Fine white gloves clothed her hands and arms up to above her elbows. How does a reporter afford such finery? Her jungle of russet curls had been twisted and tamed into a soft crown of red and gold. For a second I was jealous; other men's eyes could make out the lines I had grown to love so well. Then I felt fear; how could someone this beautiful and smart want someone like me? Then she was with me and I could tell the flunkeys were disappointed in her choice. Her eyes – wider than I ever remembered them – looked hesitant and anxious.

"Is it all right? Do I look all right? Not too...?"

"... lovely? Absolutely. You are far too lovely for this shabby place and this poor suitor."

Her face broke its serious mask and she grinned. "And you look very distinguished."

"I feel a prat. What will you drink?"

"Same as you, darling."

My insides melted at the word. I nearly called for the bill and a cab to whisk us straight back to my hovel, but this lady deserved to be on show. We took our cues from the other smartly dressed drinkers and reclined gracefully in our chairs, pecking at our drinks and smoking, as though we did this for a living. I tried not to look too smug, or to catch the eyes of the men that kept staring at her.

"The *Trumpet* pays better than I thought." I indicated her ears. "Are those real pearls?"

She touched the little clusters that hung from her lobes. Her neck coloured again.

"Family heirlooms. My mother's. I'm sure they're artificial."

"And the dress? A jumble stall in Petticoat Lane?"

"Mum again. I had it taken in."

"I hope Carlyle's has polished the silver."

We left after our second drink and before our heads became too fuddled. I need to approach gambling sober, before I start believing a three-legged nag is a sure-fire bet just because it's called Scottish Warrior or Highland Miracle. The flunkeys grovelled all the way to the door and into the cab.

As we moved off into the Strand I glanced casually around. I let my eyes slide off him. He was reading a paper on the corner, and in the wing mirrors of the cab I saw him fold it and wave to someone behind him. A minute later a car settled behind us, not too close, but not so far away as to lose us.

"Anything wrong, Danny?"

"What could be? Just watching your loyal subjects out there. Wave to them, princess. They expect it."

She laughed and took my hand and I wished to God that my

mind was playing tricks. But I knew better. There had been watchers on us for two weeks now. Correction: not us; her. I never saw them when I was alone. They were tailing her. A team of four. They were good, but I was better. I tried to put it out of my mind. I didn't want to spoil the evening. And for a while it worked.

I was prepared to be turned away at the door, but old Hutcheson's blackmail had worked; that and the five guineas a head. They checked us off a list at the door and we passed through into what must have been an old ballroom. Now it was aglow, with chandeliers sparkling in resonance with the diamonds on the women's throats. Short-skirted cigarette girls wound their way through the crowds at the tables, dispensing free cigars and cigarettes. Waiters offered a constantly refilled tray of cocktails and champagne. Our entrance fee began to seem less exorbitant; it covered everything except the chips on the tables.

My initial sense of being out of my depth soon left me, and it wasn't just the booze. A closer look at the gamblers, and some eavesdropping, made me realise what a motley group this was. The men were all in tuxes, but some wore them easier than others. The accents strayed from Chelsea to Stepney. And there was a coarseness and a flashiness to some that suggested that the money they were throwing around hadn't necessarily been the result of twenty generations of careful husbanding of the family heirlooms. Mind, even the best families started out through some act of skulduggery. On which subject, one or two of the faces were familiar from dodgier venues I'd dragged Eve to. Villains rubbing shoulders with stockbrokers. Gambling: the great leveller.

We could have left within half an hour having got what I thought we came for: Eve had all the material she needed to describe the workings of the flashiest illegal gambling den in town. But she seemed in no hurry to leave. She bought some chips and I lost them at baccarat. She didn't mind; the paper was paying. We strolled about watching others at play, but I could see she was looking around, looking for someone.

It was nearly midnight, way past my bedtime. I didn't begrudge Eve her night of glory, but she ignored my warnings of pumpkins and abandoned glass slippers. Just as the clock struck the hour, there was an eddy at the door. A party of three entered: two hulking outriders shielding a smaller character in a white dinner jacket. A big cigar was clamped in his jaw. The trio walked straight across the floor, parting the crowd like a spoon through porridge. They disappeared through a door on the far wall. I caught a glimpse of a room, softly lit, with a card table and expectant croupier. A private room within a private club. This was for high rollers. Eve had seen him too. Her eyes were alight and she gripped my arm hard enough to leave a bruise. This was what she'd been waiting for. Or whom.

Next thing, she's walking away from me, fast, following the man in white. I charged after her, but got involved in a quick-step with a waiter and a cocktail tray. By the time I was on the move again, Eve had reached the door and was sweet-talking the six-foot thug in a too-tight tux who stood guard. She must have been convincing for he leaned down and opened the door. She slipped through and for a long few seconds she was inside. I stopped my headlong rush and sauntered casually towards the door, lighting a cigarette as I went.

I was within ten yards when the door shot open and Eve was

bundled out by a muscleman with her hand rammed up her back. Her face was contorted. They were closely followed by the man in the white tuxedo. The thug at the door grabbed her other arm and pulled. She was stretched between them, two heavy paws on each slim wrist. They looked like they were going to make a wish. I closed the gap in a heartbeat.

The SOE taught me how to disable an opponent. It's easy, one on one, in the dark, coming up behind with a knife in your hand. This time there were two of them, facing me in the full glare of the chandeliers. Fortunately Eve was making enough of a fuss to distract them. But the odds were still worse than on any of the card tables around me. This was no time for Queensbury Rules or the variations thereon at Les's boxing academy.

I went for the one on the right. He was standing feet well apart and legs straight to take the strain of holding Eve. I ran directly at him, got within three feet, pivoted on my left leg, drew my right up towards me and lashed out low and hard. My heel drove into his knee cap and I felt it give. Knees don't normally bend backwards. The big guy squealed and fell like a tree hit by an axe.

I followed through on my pivot to end up facing the second goon. He'd dropped Eve's arm and moved into a crouch. His right arm was already digging inside his jacket. I didn't think he was reaching for his fags.

I kept my momentum going. His head was now level with mine and I took one big step forward and lunged. The human skull is a helmet coated in skin and hair. It does a great job of protecting the brain, as my own scars can testify. The strongest area is where the forehead rises to the hair line and slopes back. The most vulnerable point is the nose. It juts out, bone and gristle, just asking for trouble. It's why the Normans and their ilk had a flap of steel hanging down from their helmets. This bloke wasn't wearing one.

My forehead hit his nose with the power of a mallet. I felt it burst and explode, and he went down with blood erupting from his face. Adrenalin made the whole action take place in slow motion. I bent over, slipped my hand inside his bloodied jacket. and pulled out a smart little Beretta M1935. Semi-automatic. Fires .32 ACP ammo from an 8 cartridge magazine. Has the stopping power of an old lady's handbag beyond twenty feet, but it's easy to conceal and deadly up close. We captured thousands from the Eyties and Jerry.

I stepped back panting, surveying the havoc and only now hearing the first screams of women behind me. Why do women do that? Though not all women; Eve was staring at me as if she was curious what I'd do next. She was rubbing her wrists thoughtfully.

The bloke with the knee problem was writhing around, clutching his leg and cursing. I hoped he didn't have an England trial the next day. The other one had pulled himself back against the wall and was trying to staunch the bleeding with a red-soaked hankie. He seemed to be having trouble breathing. I held the gun steady in two hands but aimed at the floor. Didn't want to cause serious injury.

The man in the white tux was looking like he'd explode. More goons were running towards us from the front door. I moved to put my back to the wall, dragging Eve with me and tucking her behind me. I lifted the Beretta up and aimed it steadily at white jacket's head, looking straight into his mad eyes. He was plump and sleek with grey streaks contrasting perfectly with slicked-back dark hair. There was sweat on his brow. His mouth was snarling like a wolf eying a pet rabbit that had miraculously strayed into its den at dinner time.

Keeping my eyes and gun on him I turned my head to the crowd and called out, "Touch me and he's dead!"

The rush towards me stopped. I glanced round. It was like a firing squad. Five of them. They must have bought a job lot of Berettas. I could see the gears of their peanut brains grinding round. They'd been trained in a limited range of actions. They were trying to decide whether their boss was in worse trouble if they shot me or if they didn't. Their preference was to shoot me anyway, then beat my corpse to a pulp.

"Easy, boys. Easy," I shouted. "Fight's over. These blokes were manhandling my girl. I don't like that. But it's over. OK? We're going to leave here quietly. No one else gets hurt." I turned back to white jacket. "OK?"

Out of the corner of my eye I saw one of them step forward, the one from the door. He flexed his shoulders and I could see his trigger finger going white. I straightened my gun arm so that the barrel was two feet from his boss's head. White jacket's eyes widened. He got the message.

"Enough, Len! Put the bloody gun down!" White jacket sounded for all the world like the man who ran the Italian chip shop in the Gallowgate. "All of you!"

Eve took her chance. She stepped out from behind me and took my arm, my free arm, not the gun arm. Her accent was pure upper class. "Oh, darling, there's been a terrible mistake," she gushed in her ritziest tones. "I thought I was going to the loo. Silly me! These men were having a private game of cards or something and I must have broken their concentration."

It was such an outrageous speech that I nearly laughed out loud. No one else seemed to think it was funny, especially not the two groaning heavies on the floor. I looked round at the ring of muscle that surrounded us. I could see doubt appear on some faces. They were having to think so much I feared their brains would seize. But they lowered their guns.

"But she said she was with Mr—" the door-guard began.

"Shut it, Len!" white tux cut him off. He looked us up and down. "I know who she is. I seen her face enough in that rag she writes for. Lies, all lies. But who are *you*, pretty-boy? And who gave you the side parting?"

Eve cut in. She dropped the accent and the attitude. "He's hired for the evening. He watches my back, Gambatti."

The name was no surprise to me. Eve had planned this all along. How did she know he'd be here tonight? Maybe Gambatti was always here.

"Better mind the front too, missy." He leered at Eve's cleavage and got a reverential chuckle from his boys.

"That's enough, *Mister* Gambatti," I said moving between him and Eve and sliding my hand under her arm. "We're leaving now."

"Good. Saves having you thrown out. Len, see them to the door. Find out how they got in. Make sure it don' happen again. And get these idiots out of my sight." He pointed at his disabled men.

"Smile and walk," I said to Eve. I slipped the Beretta into my side pocket.

We began to move forward, slowly. The circle of goons parted and we stepped between them, like an honour guard. The hushed crowd moved back as we made to the door. The bride and groom. Though no one was tossing confetti and no one was smiling. Except us, in a forced sort of way.

"What a story!" she hissed.

"You are a mad woman."

"*You* did the violence!"

"You *knew* he'd be here. Why didn't you say?"

"You'd have gone all pompous and talked me out of it. I'd have missed a story."

"Pity you can't use it."

"Don't be crazy. This is front page."

"What exactly?"

"Look around." She had a point. The room was awash with money. Until we'd interrupted play these chattering socialites were bent over spinning wheels or sitting at green baize tables studded with cards.

"Eve, we've just poked a tiger with a stick. He'll rip our heads off!"

"He wouldn't dare. I'm too public."

"I'm not. And I have to work in this town. I have enough enemies."

We reached the front door. Two big men held it open for us and glared at us as we sailed past. I thought about tipping them but they might not have seen the funny side. I felt my back itch all the way down the stairs and out into the road. I prayed they wouldn't think it smart to put a bullet in my back. As we made our leisurely getaway I turned to her. She had to know.

"Speaking of enemies. Someone is having you followed."

It got no more than a tightening of her lips but it was enough to tell me she wasn't as surprised as she now made out.

"Don't be silly. People don't like my column, but it doesn't make them my enemy."

"They've been following you for at least two weeks."

She stopped and shook her head. "Don't be so melodramatic, Danny."

I stood in front of her. I took her hands. "Princess, they could have been around long before that, but I was so... well, let's say I had my blinkers on." I smiled at her. "I could have missed them."

"You *are* crazy, Daniel McRae. Why would anyone follow me? Where are they, then?" She swivelled her head round looking for them. "Yoohoo! Come out, come out wherever you are!"

The sarcasm surprised me. Why was she being so perverse? After what we'd just been through? "You won't see them. They're good."

She poked me in the chest. "I think *you're* seeing things. But if you want to play big brave protector, that's OK. Take me home, my hero."

I did, and we made love, but something had changed. She clung to me in the night as though tomorrow was D-Day and I was leaving for France. And over scraped toast, marge and meat paste in the morning she was cool. As though she'd stepped back from me and was watching from a distance.

"What's wrong?" I asked.

"Nothing. I'm fine."

"Is it the story? You want to splash Gambatti's name around? Go ahead. It's your skin. But I'd rather it stayed on your back. I love your back."

"It's not Gambatti."

"Are you worried about being followed?"

"Danny! Let's stop this! I am not being followed. All right?"

"Why are you so angry? I've never seen you like this."

"You're upsetting me with all this stupid detective talk." She saw she was getting to me and her face softened. "Just a bit hung over, I expect."

It was a hangover that didn't improve. Over the next few

days, she made excuses and wouldn't even see me, far less make love to me. When we finally met I couldn't get through to her. She would smile but not with her eyes. It was as though a sadness had settled on her that she couldn't share. We still had the watchers but she wouldn't believe me. Didn't even want to talk about them. I guess that's what made me do it.

It had been a week since we'd made love and we were walking towards her office after a desultory sandwich and tea at the coffee house on the Strand. I had used up all my weak attempts at humour and we were quiet with each other. I wanted to shake her and find out what was going on in her head. But I was scared what I'd hear. Then I saw one of them. He was keeping pace with us on the other side of the street. I waited till a bus came between us. I scuttled round the back of it, sidestepped a car and grabbed the man by his lapels as he turned to face me.

"Who are you! Just who the fuck are you, pal? Why are you following us?" My face was an inch off his. I watched the shock turn into amusement.

"What the hell's going on, buddy? You limeys drink too much at lunchtime, you know that?"

His American accent threw me. I began to loosen my grip. "You've been following us for weeks. Don't give me that phoney Yank stuff!"

"I don't know what you're talking about, buddy. Now, unless you take your goddamn hands off me, I'm going to call the police."

"Danny! Danny! What the hell are you doing?" Eve was running across the road, careless of the traffic. She reached me. Her face was red and angry. She dragged me away.

"Sorry, mister. Sorry. He's OK. Just had a bad day." She

hauled me along the pavement. "What are you doing? You've gone mad, Danny. I don't know you any more. This is crazy."

"*I'm* crazy? What's happened to you? We had it all. We were good. *Are* good. But you're in trouble. Don't you see it? I know what I'm doing. This is my job, Eve! Trust me!"

"Stop it! Stop it! There's nothing!"

We were shouting at each other. Tears were running down her face. I scraped them from mine. I knew I had to shut up or lose her. But all I could do was go on and on about how I needed her and how I feared for her. Every word I said was killing us, sending me further from her. Her eyes were full of pity. I rambled to a halt, my chest heaving and my tears blinding me.

She spoke softly now. "Danny, we need a break. From each other. Just let it go."

"No, oh, no. Please…"

"We must…"

"We mustn't. Don't do this." I gripped her arms. I couldn't let her go. If we parted now, it was for good.

"I have to. I have to go. Just give it a few weeks. Don't call. Don't come round. Just give us time." She pulled free and was already turning away. I should have held her, hugged her to me till the madness left us. But all I could do was stand like a dummy, watching her go. Watching the best thing in my life walk away from me.

I don't know how I got home, but I picked up a bottle of Red Label on the way. I threw my jacket off and loosened my shirt. I got a jug of water and a glass and sat them beside my chair. I took the first gulp without water and felt it rip my throat. I gazed at my bed and saw us, saw her, tumbled and lovely on the cover. I couldn't accept this was the end. I'd find a way. I'd drop all this shit about followers. She thought I was mad. Maybe I was. Maybe this was one of the side effects of the head wound. Prof Haggarty would know. That's it; I'd call him and ask his advice. But that would be tomorrow. Right now there was nothing more I could do than wait to get drunk.

TEN

Either I hadn't drunk enough or drank too much, but it didn't make me happy. And for a guy who once had problems with his memory, I found it pretty hard to forget every turn of her body and every shift and shadow of her mobile face. I slept, but the dreams were bad; some of the old camp ones crept in and scared the shit out of me. I felt the big boulders piling up all round me and I couldn't get past them and they kept moving slowly on top of me to hem me in and smother me. I kept waking up gasping for air, and retrieving the quilt that seemed to be having nightmares of its own.

I was glad of daylight, though it brought a mighty headache. I had a raging thirst and gulped at the water pouring from the tap. I threw more water on my face and fought back the nausea. I needed to do something, anything, but it was too early to try Haggarty. I made a big bowl of my father's patented hangover cure: porridge. Still in my singlet and pants, I cleaned the flat from top to bottom, realising as I did how long it had been since the linoleum had seen a mop. I played the wireless as loud as it could go until the pips went for nine o'clock, then walked through to my office on the still-damp lino to place a call to Professor Haggarty.

"Vivienne, it's Danny McRae. I need to talk to the Prof. It's important."

I could hear her sucking her teeth at my use of her first name. "Professor Haggarty is with a client. He couldn't possibly be interrupted. You have an appointment next week. I'm sure it can wait."

"Viv. I said it was important. Can you please get your boss to call me back? I must talk to him."

I swear she sniffed. "I can't promise. It's most unusual. I will speak to the Professor when he has a moment and see what he says. But his diary is very full."

Full of more important people than me. I retreated to my bedroom. It was tidy but it still held after-images of her. I scrubbed myself raw over the sink, using the nail brush like a scourge as though I could rub her impression off my skin. I banged around making tea and toast, though I had no appetite for either after the porridge. I went hunting for the cat with a slopping bowl of milk, but even she had abandoned me.

Finally Haggarty called back. The lovely Vivienne put me through, but she sounded as though it was costing her blood.

"Right, man. How the hell are you? Are you in bother, now? Tell me about it. Do you want to come in? I can fit you in, no bother." There was a side comment in a strained female voice, then, "Sure we can, Vivienne."

"Prof, thanks. Maybe we can do this on the phone. I just wanted to know…" I began to feel stupid. What the hell was I going to ask him? "Look… there's this girl I've been seeing."

"And you want to know if you really have been *seeing* her, Daniel?" He said it with a bit of a laugh but I didn't see the funny side.

He meant Valerie, the girl my beat-up brain had conjured to help me through the Caldwell case. "Others have seen us, talked with us. I've touched her. She's real enough, Prof. But here's the thing; I think Eve's being followed. In fact I know she is. They're pros. Four of them. They aren't easy to spot but I know what I'm looking for." Just as I had been certain about my ghostly helper.

"Go on." There was no hint of scepticism, so I pressed on.

"She's a reporter. A crime reporter. She's upset some people."

"Why doesn't she call the police?"

"She doesn't believe me. She says... she says I'm crazy. That I'm seeing things. That's what I wanted to talk about. Is it possible? I mean with my history. Could I be imagining these men?"

"I see. Well, you know I've always said what a mysterious thing the mind is..."

"Spare me the philosophy, Prof. You're the expert. What's your opinion? Am I having a relapse?"

His voice firmed up. "Based on what I've seen of you, Daniel, I would say no. The Valerie figure is explainable. She was your inner mind trying to get through to the damaged surface. As your brain mended, so Valerie appeared and helped you to solve the crime. But I don't see your current mind *needs* to conjure up these... these stalkers or whatever you might call them. Unless they're figures from your past. When you were an SOE agent, a spy. Are any of them familiar?"

"No. And one of them... I confronted one of them in the street this week... that's why I'm calling... Eve thought I had completely flipped. One of them had an American accent. It sounded genuine enough, but so what?"

"An American, you say? Wasn't it the Americans who liberated Dachau? Who saved you?"

Shit. I hadn't thought of that. Was that the connection? Was I getting my past all mixed up with my present? Was this my subconscious trying to make sense of more buried memories? Or was I just mad as a hatter?

"Is it time for the straitjacket again?"

"You know, man, it's a blooming miracle there's a sane mind left in this country after what we've gone through. And you fellas working behind the lines, in disguise and cut off from home, had it harder than anyone. It does dreadful damage to the psyche."

"So I *am* nuts. But it's OK, 'cos everybody else is?"

"Not a bit, Daniel. Not a bit. You show none of the signs of delusion. Your girlfriend saw this man you tackled, didn't she? It's not as if he was imaginary. And you haven't been having conversations with yourself, now have you?"

"No. And she did see him. She dragged me off him."

"Well, fine. I suppose. But all the same I'd avoid tackling strangers in the street for a while. Is there no way you can get some corroboration on these chaps following your lady friend?"

"Not from Eve, that's for sure. That's why she's called it off. But you've given me an idea, Prof. Look, you've set my mind at rest. A wee bit, anyway. Let me see if I can get a second opinion on this."

We hung up and I had the operator make another call, to Finchley this time. It rang for a long time.

"Hello." It was a suspicious voice, high pitched, nasal and calculated to make your ears bleed unless you too had grown up in Birmingham and were immune.

"Mrs Witherham? Is that you? And how are you this fine morning? Could I speak to Midge, please?"

"Oh, it's yow again. I've told yow before, I don't run a telephone service for my lodgers." She made Glaswegians sound couth.

"It's an emergency, Mrs Witherham. Honest. I need to speak to Midge urgently. It's about some money I owe him. I need to give it to him."

I knew that would get her. She bellowed up the stairs. "Mr Cummins? It's that Scotch man again. Something about money. Maybe yow can pay my rent now!"

It took a while. Midge wasn't an early starter. He took the phone from her grumbling hands, "And a pleasant morning to you too, Mrs Witherham." There was a pause. "She's gone. I need to move. Danny? What's happening?"

"I need you and the lads to do some tailing for me. It's my own money. Ten bob a day. A week at most."

I explained what I wanted and overcame his objections by explaining that it wasn't *her* I wanted followed but the blokes that were tailing her. I hung up and looked round my bare office. But all I could see was the image of her marching through the door on that first day like Miriam Hopkins in *Lady with Red Hair*.

I met them exactly seven days later in the George. By then I was a wreck. There were more bottles in my bin than in the backyard of the pub itself. This girl had got under my skin. Every morning I woke hoping it was a bad dream, and every morning I felt the world drop away at the thought I wouldn't see her again. I picked up the phone a dozen times and replaced it without calling her. Once I couldn't help myself and got put through to her number. She answered: "Hello? Hello? Who's there? Danny, is that you?..." But I had nothing to say. I replaced the phone in the cradle as her voice trailed away.

I even sloped down to Fleet Street to see if I could spot her. Then I realised I might run into the lads, and that I would just be swelling the ranks of the spies on her tail. It was getting to be a circus.

I had three pints of beer sitting waiting for them in the cubby-hole. They arrived in dribs and drabs. When they were all settled I looked round their faces trying to judge what they'd found. It didn't look good.

"OK, what have you got?"

They looked bashful. Then Midge spoke up. "Nothing, Danny. We saw nothing. Maybe you scared them off. You know, when you grabbed that Yank?"

He was throwing me crumbs, and he knew that I knew it. "Nothing? Not a sniff? How many times did you spot her? Sure you didn't lose her?"

I looked at them. They hadn't lost her. The followers – if they ever existed – had gone. I hadn't the heart for a session with the boys. I was bored with getting drunk. I left my beer unfinished on the table together with the money I owed them, and headed for home carrying my delusions with me like a pack of Furies. I'd lost the girl I loved, for nothing.

I needed to get hold of myself. I wasn't the first bloke to get chucked, though it felt like it. I was weary, as though someone had drained my blood. Or replaced it with Scotch. So I laid off the booze for a couple of days and began to feel a little saner, if not happier. There was a thin trickle of enquiries coming in so I threw myself at them, even the adulterers.

Usually I find no joy in setting up the evidence to let two poor saps get a divorce. But I was positively enthusiastic in booking the hotel, getting one of Mama Mary's girls to pretend to be the *femme fatale*, and bursting in on them to catch them *in flagrante delicto*. My enthusiasm left me when I found this small adulterer sitting on the end of the bed looking sad and embarrassed, as though his world was ending. Maybe it was; I had the impression it was the wife who wanted rid of him.

I had to encourage the bloke to show a little more interest for the photograph. I even thought of suggesting he availed himself of the opportunity of one of Mama's kindest and cutest, though he was closer to tears than seduction. But I got enough material to lay before the judge. It was a messy way of getting out of a loveless marriage, but if these were the rules, I was ready to play by them.

In between cases that week I kept fingering my phone. She hadn't said never, had she? I'd let things cool off. And now I'd got over my obsession about her being followed, what was the problem? It had been a fool's logic, or a kid's. But I never got the chance to test my flimsy theory. The phone call from Eve's boss threw my world upside down.

"Danny McRae? Is that you? It's Jim Hutcheson here. The *Trumpet*." His soft Inverness accents trilled down the line, and I could see his great eyebrows twitching at me from afar. My heart picked up pace. Was Jim interceding for her?

"Hello, Jim. How are things?" I wanted to shout, *How is she? Does she still love me? Does she want me back?* But I thought that might make him hang up.

"Look, Danny, I'll come straight to it. Is Eve with you? Have you seen her lately?"

I felt the blood congeal in my veins. "No. Not for a week or so. We had a bit of a tiff…"

"Damn. Look, she hasn't come in all week, and her landlady

says she hasn't seen her. She said she might try you. Has she moved in with you, then?"

"No. No, of course not."

"I think I'd better get the police."

"Jim, could you wait a wee while? I'll come straight round. I'll be there in twenty minutes."

I grabbed my jacket and was out the door in two, fear clawing at my belly like a tiger. I kept telling myself there was no connection. Nothing to link my sightings of men following her with her disappearance. No follow-up revenge by Gambatti. She was off visiting some friend. Or she was chasing a lead and would pop up any time.

But after I'd talked to Jim Hutcheson, I knew something had happened. I asked if he'd let me look around before calling the coppers. There might be something I'd spot before a bunch of clodhoppers started throwing everything up in the air. He led me to her corner and left me to pick at the papers.

I sit at her scruffy little desk and stroke the arms of her chair. Her typewriter has a sheet of paper in it, ready for her blizzard of thoughts. Scraps of newspaper clippings stud the facing wall. All her own articles, the best of her war years. Several are topped with her face in that cheesy smile I used to tease her about. I smile back and feel a stone lodge in my chest. A further pile of cuttings and draft articles spill from an in-tray. It's like she's just stepped out to make a cup of tea; she'll be back in a minute.

I pull open her drawer and rifle through the bric-a-brac. Something solid comes to hand: the black notepad she always carries. Now I know it's bad. She went nowhere without it. It was her life. I heft it and run my finger round the edges. No one is looking, so I hold it up to my nose to see if I can catch a whiff of her, that particular scent that she said was cheap and anyone could buy from Woolworth but smells only of her. There is something. A hint. A distillation of the past hectic two months. I can't be sure. I put the notepad back on the desk, ready to open it. Ready to see if something in it could be a clue about how to find her. Dead or alive.

I open it and find a journal, part written in English but mostly in hieroglyphs. Shorthand of some sort that I couldn't decode. I flick to the end – her last entries. Some are in code, some in clear. Clear enough. She'd been lying to me.

ELEVEN

What I learned convinced me I didn't want the police trampling over her life – or mine. Not yet. I slipped the notebook into my pocket and gave my farewells to Jim. He eyed me suspiciously from under those great grey brows but didn't probe. I left the building just as a squad car drew up. I pulled my hat down and walked up Fleet Street and into the Strand with the book burning a hole in my pocket. I crossed Waterloo Bridge, not pausing as I normally do to watch the coal barges trundling up and down river. I should have got a bus. My leg was aching. But I needed to walk. And the physical pain was oddly comforting. It took my mind off the one fact: *she knew she was being followed. Why did she keep it from me?*

I reached home in a lather. I threw off my jacket, undid my tie and made myself comfortable at my desk. I guessed it wouldn't take long before I had visitors, and I needed to read enough to decide if I was keeping the notebook or handing it over.

The inside page had her name on it: Eve Copeland. She'd underlined her first name and written her office address underneath. The ink was black and was already fading to brown in the early entries. I had seen the fountain pen she used: a gold-nibbed, green lacquered tube, capable of producing elegant calligraphy in the right hand. A present, she said.

She seemed to be using three different scripts: plain English, some kind of jagged scrawl which included some English lettering, and a type of shorthand.

In the early pages – the pages in clear – Eve had jotted her thoughts down in a fine script, all leaning neatly to the right in flowing loops. My old teacher would have given her five gold stars. It was a feat beyond my talents; somewhere between dipping my nib in the inkwell and transferring it to the page, my hand would be taken over by the school poltergeist. Even the threat of the belt across my trembling palms was never enough to stop the inky havoc.

Eve's pages were lined but unnumbered. She'd turned it into a kind of diary by putting dates at the start of every new item no matter where it began on the page. The entries began in mid '45. Some pages had several short notes; some in plain English, some in "squiggle" as I called the indecipherable scrawl, and then the coded shorthand. Some items went on for several pages as she drafted a column or took down notes of a long interview. It also seemed to serve as an appointments book, with follow-up observations about some event or person she'd met: *no doubt he's a con man… mind like a sewer* (I hoped she wasn't talking about me!)*; sweet gentle lady… love to be friends; big disappointment compared to voice; great picture… wish I had legs like Cyd Charisse!!*

It was uncomfortable; like dipping into her mind. But how else was I going to find out what happened to her? That's how I'd explain it when we next met. When. *If* had no room in my thinking. I was chewing my nails as I got to the later stuff covering the last few weeks, our weeks. What would I find about me? My anxiety rose when I identified the dates, but found the comments themselves in squiggle or shorthand.

I should have been able to read some of the shorthand, albeit slowly; it had been part of our SOE training. There were many forms but usually enough of an overlap to get the gist. But I was stymied by hers. The secret of Pitman is it's phonetic; there are hundreds of symbols each with its own sound. The thickness of the strokes distinguishes vowels and consonants. All you have to do is memorise them and put them together in your head to make words. With daily practice you can become competent – in a year or two.

I tried saying some of the shorthand out loud, the ones that bore a vague resemblance to what I'd learned. Nothing. Gibberish. In fact with the ochs and achs I was making they sounded a bit like the Ayrshire dialect – Lallan Scots, the language of Burns.

The idea hit me. I grabbed the notebook and a pad and a pencil from my drawer. I ripped my jacket from its peg and ran down the stairs. The cat exploded at my feet.

I was out and running, gammy leg forgotten. A double-decker was trundling away from the stop. I sprinted and caught the pole and hauled myself inside, vowing to give up the fags sometime soon. A change at Elephant and I was in Bloomsbury within half an hour.

I'd never been inside the British Library but had once stood outside peering through the glass doors. To me it was a sort of shrine. Kilpatrick's old Victorian library and museum, with its stuffed lion guarding the top of the stairs, held what I thought of as the world's biggest collection of books. I would raid its shelves every week. But the British Library! Where Marx and Dickens sat. Too much for me before. Now, I needed to get in.

I explained my errand to the girl behind the desk. She said that it was impossible. I said I was a private detective. She said she shouldn't. I said my girlfriend had been kidnapped. She said only if you're quick and don't let the Super see you. She led me to a little seat in front of a long brown desk. High overhead soared the great dome, and under it the wooden gallery that followed its curve. Around me and above me were miles of aisles holding books from every corner of the English speaking world. It was better than the echoing vacuum of St Paul's. This was religion enough. A few minutes later the girl came back with a small heap of books. She laid them on my desk, gave me a stern look from behind her glasses and then a wink. I blew her a kiss and she shot off, red as a tomato.

I took the first book; it was Pitman's standard shorthand dictionary. That was my benchmark. I then set out in front of me the other three books: versions of shorthand dictionaries for the German language. In the Lallan Scots and north of England dialects you can hear the last throaty vestiges of the language roots. I placed Eve's notebook alongside and opened it at the first page of hieroglyphs. I propped up the three German dictionaries in front of me and began to scribble on my pad. It took me five minutes to be certain: Eve hadn't been writing in English shorthand. It was Gabelsberger's system, which looked a little like proper writing with its flowing cursive style. Simple. But why?

Then I noticed something else. In the appendix of one of the dictionaries, was a set of squiggles that looked remarkably like the third form of entry Eve had used. The heading explained that I was looking at Suetterlin script, the standard form of German handwriting taught in all their schools until just before the start of the war. How did my ace reporter come to be able to write like a German and use a German shorthand? I put the obvious conclusion to one side while I grappled with the problem of turning both scripts into English.

I decided to tackle the shorthand first. It was closer to what I'd learned in spy school. The trouble was that the shorthand would translate into German words. Prof Haggarty had tricked me into revealing that I'd picked up some fluency in the language while I was sunning myself in Dachau. I'd developed a workaday if specialised vocabulary. The camp held some pretty bright people – doctors, engineers, teachers, musicians – and conversations sprawled across culture and philosophy as well as the mundane details of living and dying behind the barbed wire. But I never saw written material except on official signs. *Arbeit Macht Frei* for example. It wasn't the sort of place to order your copy of *Die Zeitung* to be served with breakfast.

At the rate I was going it would take me a month to translate all her codes. But it didn't take me long to spot the sign that meant Danny, a sort of lower case d with a tail and circle. So I confined myself to the last two months and wherever I saw my name.

Translating shorthand is an inexact science at the best of times. But now I was having to rely on getting a set of sounds and symbols on the page then listening in my head for the German word to pop up that most closely resembled it. I couldn't write down the word because I didn't know how it was spelled in German. I had to make the leap straight to English, and see if some meaning emerged from the jumble.

As I struggled with my silent battle the receptionist came over looking anxious. She asked me in a whisper if I was all right as someone had complained about me making faces. I pointed at the dictionaries and made some mouth shapes. She seemed to get the message but gave me a frown to keep my funny faces to myself. Like other women in my life, she was already regretting her kindness.

I worked away for an hour or two until I had a page of jottings. Some of it was guesses, some inspired analysis, but sitting back and taking it from the top, I could get the gist of recent events from the day she invaded my office and my life:

22 May: d very red very scot, funny sarcastic, hates my paper, bastard, d needs money, hook?

23 May: d called, caught fish!!!!

25 May: mary prostitute, d very close ????, first mention PG, d offer more? / deeper? action for me, d interest me / him?

28 / 29 May: tommy chandler warehouse job, big thrill, big time, big risk, showed? / revealed??? gun, no choice, PG upset?

29 May: d bed, tired lonely excuse? not love just warmth, stupid stupid

3 June: love? D soft hard, funny sarcastic, why not? Stupid time

There were several more entries along these lines, each a seeming debate with herself about how to avoid falling in love. In three of them the word *watcher* or *follower* appeared with a query after my name. She knew, didn't she? Then...

15 June: mother dress, Savoy, mother!!! Big night, big mess, beautiful couple, wrong time!!!! PG gate crash, mad, mad. D saw watcher, too late, always too late, must stop!!!

Then in clear English a week later:

23 June: Horrible day. Danny saw the watcher again and attacked him. I pulled him off and denied everything. Told Danny we had to break for a while. But it's over, has to be. How did we get here? What am I doing? So sad...

Then back in code again except for the Latin:

25 June: saw midge saw stan, d watcher now!!! Quis custodiet!!!

30 June: all gone. All quiet, waiting. Alone again. Waiting for them.

That was her last entry a week ago. She knew something was about to happen to her. I could see her sitting in her room in a period of quiet before the storm hit. It tore my heart out. Why did she hide it from me? Why couldn't she turn to me? All her notes seemed to be telling me she was trying not to fall in love with me, but she wasn't succeeding. So why did she lie about the watchers? I could have helped. I could have saved her. Maybe.

Did she want to be taken? Was she protecting me? I'm certain the reference to PG was to Pauli Gambatti. That was more than coincidence. I flicked back through her notes. I was right; there were other PG references before my time. She'd feared him and decided that he was having her followed. But why would he? An East End thug? If he wanted to harm her, why didn't he send one of his hoods round to her flat and pick her off there? And why did she walk into the lion's gambling den? Did her nerve snap and she had to confront him, face her fears? Like the mad bastard who storms a machine gun nest?

My head was reeling. I'd had enough. I needed time to digest it all. I handed back my books to the librarian and made her blush just by smiling at her and saying how sweet she'd been. I needed her on my side; there was more to uncover in this book, much more. For the moment it was time to act. In the absence of any better target, I wanted Gambatti in my sights. But before I could pull the trigger I had to flush my bird. There was no returning to Carlyle's; they wouldn't let me within a hundred yards.

Over the next three days – more exactly, nights – I put the word out. It was easy enough. I went on a pub crawl. I was careful to drink only in the East End and only in Gambatti's patch. Wherever I went I bought a half of bitter and began asking questions. I would smile at the landlady and ask if Mr Gambatti ever frequented her fine establishment, and watch her face crumple in fear or irritation. Sometimes they flat out denied everything. Never heard of him. Sometimes I was told to drink up and piss off. Sometimes they asked why I wanted to know. When I explained I had a bone to pick with him, they were as likely to laugh in my face as to tell me to clear off. Whatever their reaction I made sure they knew my name and I always used my loudest voice. Drunks have big ears.

I made a particular point of buttonholing Fast Larry when he slid into the George on night three. The lads were as startled as Larry was when I called him over to our corner of the snug.

"Let me buy you a drink, Fast Larry."

He looked at me like I was dispensing hemlock. "I'm fine, Danny. You want to place a bet?"

"Sit down. I want a word in that shell-like of yours." I ignored his protests and made the boys move over so that he could sit by me. He was twitching like a diviner's rod, his eyes rolling everywhere except near mine.

"I want to talk to Pauli Gambatti."

Fast Larry's eyes stopped swivelling and he looked at me. "You're fucking mad, Danny. Why d'you want to get your balls cut off?"

"I'm mad all right. Mad as could be. It's his balls I'm after unless he has a cast-iron alibi for his whereabouts at the time of the disappearance of a dear friend of mine."

Fast Larry's eyes were whirling again. "This bint of yours?"

"How do you know about that?" I asked sharply.

He shrugged. "It's in the paper." He tapped his shiny jacket pocket.

"Show me!"

He drew out a distressed copy of today's *Racing Mirror* rolled inside a copy of the *Trumpet*. He disentangled them and laid the *Trumpet* out on the table, trying to flatten its folds in the pools of beer.

"Give me that!" I grabbed it from him. Her photo was on the front page. TOP REPORTER MISSING! was the headline, and underneath glowing words of praise and speculation about a gangland kidnap. Fearless reporter Eve Copeland abducted by very men she'd named and shamed. I read it twice. It said nothing I didn't know, except they were offering a reward for news of her. I prayed someone was already phoning in to collect. In the meantime...

"Fast Larry, I want you to get a message to your mate, Gambatti. Tell I'm coming after him, and I'll wreck his whole bloody organisation just like I wrecked his team at the warehouse job. Got that? Now bugger off and tell him."

Fast looked at me pityingly for a long moment then got up,

refolding his papers like a bad example of origami. "You're round the twist, Danny McRae. Fucking doolally."

The lads thought so too when I explained my plan.

A couple of days later my madness paid dividends. Of a sort. I walked into my office, wiping my forehead from the heat and the climb, and found a man sitting at my desk with a gun trained on my belly button.

I didn't think he was going to kill me. Not right away. In my experience, if someone sets out to shoot you, they just do it; they don't hang around and discuss it. That only happens in movies when they want the killer to reveal why he stole the falcon. And killers don't usually sit in your chair with their feet on your desk, drinking beer from a bottle. Your beer. They wait behind the door and shoot you from behind. Much smarter and safer. For the killer.

But that didn't mean that this guy *wouldn't* kill me; it just wasn't the first thing that was going to happen. I stuffed my sweat-stained hankie in my trouser pocket. My jacket was over my arm – the hottest day of the year, they reckoned – and I reached out and hung it on the coat rack behind the door. I turned and waited for him to get round to telling me why he was here and why the gun. Though I had an idea.

"Comfortable?" I asked.

"In a shit hole like this?"

He waved the gun round my room. I wasn't hurt or offended. No one would mistake the offices of Finders Keepers for a palace. But then why would you need fancy décor if most of your work took place on the street? And my customers weren't the sort to be impressed with pictures on the walls or Persian carpets; they wanted results, fast, and as cheaply as possible.

"It may not be what you're used to, pal, but it works for me. And unless this is a takeover bid, that's what matters."

I walked towards my desk as nonchalantly as a man can with a gun on him. I did it smoothly, no rush, hands well in sight, holding his eyes and smiling my best I'm-harmless-don't-kill-me smile. I gingerly pulled the chair back – the one in front of my desk for clients – and sat down slowly in it. I sized him up. He was the heavy type, dark suit tight round his thick shoulders and biceps. The hand was steady and experienced holding the gun – a familiar gun, a Beretta M1935. Out of Gambatti's armoury. The goon's face had been roughened by better men than me. And his eyes wouldn't have looked out of place on a fishmonger's slab.

"They said you'd be a funny guy. I don't like smart-arses."

"Then maybe you've come to the wrong place."

"An' I don't like what you did to my pals."

"Then don't get in my way."

He rubbed his face wondering if he could get away with killing me and saying it was an accident. "The boss wants to see you."

"Oh, and which boss would that be?"

"Mr Gambatti. Pauli Gambatti."

"You see that thing on the desk?" I pointed at my phone. "Doesn't Pauli have one? All he had to do was lift the other end and ask me to drop by."

"In your own sweet time. And it's Mister Gambatti to you."

"Can we put the gun away? I get the message. Tell Pauli I'll come by tomorrow."

The muscle sighed. "You're not getting the message. Mr Gambatti wants you *now*."

"I'd planned to have a beer first."

"Too bad, jock. It's drunk." Muscles picked up the bottle that I'd been keeping cool in a basin of water and drained the last mouthful. He burped and slammed the empty down on my desk. "Now you've got no excuses."

"Put the gun away and I'll get my coat." I waited.

He wiped his lips and reluctantly lowered the weapon. London was flooded with souvenirs brought back by our boys. He gazed at it briefly, sorry it hadn't been used, and slid it inside his jacket. A fancy holster under his arm. James Cagney had a lot to answer for.

"Let's go."

"I hope you've got a car. My feet…"

"It's waiting. Let's go. And no fucking tricks."

I had no intention of attempting tricks, not with a gun in my side and a second muscleman driving. Especially when the driver turned round and showed me his face. The eyes were still black and blue and the nose looked as though it had gone ten rounds with Joe Louis. He grinned at me, not in a friendly way.

We cut down the Old Kent Road and then picked up Jamaica Road. Once through the Rotherhithe Tunnel we were in the badlands of Stepney. Everywhere we drove I could see how they'd taken a hammering. Goering sent his planes into the docks night after night, and it showed. Wide areas flattened and cleared. Plenty of football pitches. England should have a fine team in about twenty years.

"Here. Put this on." The thug beside me had drawn a thin scarf out of his pocket and was holding it out to me.

"I'm not cold. It's summer."

"I told you I don't like smart-arses! Put the fucking blind-fold round your fucking eyes!" This time he backed up his request with the Beretta jammed into the side of my head.

"This isn't the bloody pictures, you know. Who am I going to tell?"

He pulled the gun back an inch then jabbed it into my ear. It hurt. And at that distance he wasn't going to miss. I stopped arguing and tied the scarf round my head. He made me slouch down in my seat so that no passing copper would think it funny and pull us over. We drove for another five minutes, past a railway line, twice. I gave up trying to map our route in my head. At last we came into a yard; the traffic sound got cut off and our own exhaust note bounced back at us. My door was opened and I was hauled out still unseeing.

I heard big doors creaking open and was shoved forward. I sensed we were inside a big enclosed space. A warehouse of some sort. I could smell a burning cigar. The blindfold was ripped from my head and I was pushed forward so fast I stumbled and fell on my hands and knees.

"That's where I like to see shit like you." The familiar voice was dead ahead. Introductions weren't going to be necessary. I got to my feet, brushed the dust and gravel out of my trousers and wiped my hands. I looked at the man who was sitting on a crate in front of me. He had nicked a cigar from Winston's personal supply and puffed away on it as though he was in his private club. His black grey-flashed hair was so heavily greased it would deflect an axe. The double chin and chubby cheeks didn't soften the face one bit. It was the eyes that threatened, dark and feral either side of a long shaft of a nose.

Beside him, on another crate, with his crutches leaning against the wood and his leg heavily plastered, was my other pal from the casino. He looked pleased to see me. Like a hyena finding a baby deer with its hoof caught in a trap.

Gambatti spoke again. "If it isn't the geezer who upset my card game? You're a bit of pest, sonny."

"Nice to meet *you* again, Mr Gambatti."

"It's not mutual, *Mister* McRae. Who the fuck do you think you are, putting the word out on me?"

As he said this he nodded at the muscle who'd brought me here, each cast from the same mould: Gog and Magog. Gog leered at me from behind his broken nose. The pair of them stepped towards the crates behind Gambatti, took their jackets off and rolled up their sleeves. Suddenly I began to feel hot too. They came towards me and helped me out of my own jacket and flung it away. They pushed me down on the ground again and unceremoniously removed my shoes and debagged me. They grabbed my arms and began wrapping rope around my upper body and my ankles so that I was tied up like a Sunday joint.

I heard clanking and looked up to see a hook descend from the rafters above me. Gog held my body while Magog twisted the hook into my ankle ropes. He walked away and I heard the pulley cranking again and felt the rope begin to tug at my feet.

"Pauli! I wanted to talk! That's why I sent out those invites. That's all!" I cried out desperately as my legs were pulled from me and my weight was held by muscle boy for a few seconds until the hook had my ankles well above my head. The pulley went on cranking until I was suspended upside down with my head at face height to the grinning thugs. My shirt was falling over my head until he ripped it open and let the ends flap down past my shoulders.

They began to spin me and I started to feel sick. Maybe it was just fear. Maybe it was a throwback to the feelings of helplessness in the camp when all you could do was take the beatings. I tried to hold on to that thought: I'd had worse done to me. But it wasn't helping. Hanging upside down disorientated and semi-naked, in front of three villains with a reputation for chopping bits off people, leaves you feeling a wee bit vulnerable.

They stopped me spinning and when my head caught up with my body, I saw Gambatti strolling towards me. He got within two feet of me, took a drag on his cigar and blew it into my face. I coughed. It hurt. But not as much as the fist he rammed into my exposed belly. I jack-knifed up and felt my stomach heave; then I threw up, or in this case, down. Sadly, I missed Gambatti. I guess he knew what to expect.

I hung there feeling like shit, with a trickle of vomit running up my face and waiting for the real beating to start. It was not a moment to cherish. One of the thugs stood in front of me and I tensed. Instead he took the tail of my shirt and wiped my face. Gambatti stepped closer again.

"Now we talk, McRae. Yes?"

"That's what I'm here for," I croaked. "It's about the girl."

"Always a girl."

"Eve Copeland. The reporter."

"I know the bitch."

"Were you following her?"

"Why would I waste my fucking time following some bint who gets up my nose?"

That seemed too heartfelt not to be true, and fitted with my own view, even an upside down one. Now the big question.

"Did you take her? Have you... did you get rid of her? That's all I want to know."

Gambatti scrutinised me silently for a moment. "A girl like that, she makes a lot of enemies. I thought about it. After what she and you did in my club. In front of my friends. Showing me up like that. I thought about arranging a nice accident. Something painful. Something permanent. But I never got round to it. The filth would be round my door before breakfast."

"You didn't touch her?"

"You don't believe me, you little shit!" He punched me in the belly and stood back while I retched and convulsed like a rat held up by its tail. I believed him. Now all I had to do was talk my way out of here.

"I believe you, Gambatti. I do. I can see you're a man of your word. That's it. That's all I wanted to know. That's why I put the word out. I didn't know how else to get hold of you."

The blood was rushing to my head and made me sound like I was talking under water. I felt I was going to be sick again. I saw Gambatti smile.

"You shouldna bothered, shithead. I was gonna find you. I owe you one. Maybe several. For what you did to my business down by the docks. I had a nice little thing going there till you fucked it up. That's bad in two ways. One, I lose money. Two, I lose face. Every shithead in town knows you done us over. That's not acceptable."

"Pauli, I didn't know it was you. This isn't personal."

"Oh, no?" He stuck his piggy face close to mine. "Now it is, shithead. Now it is. I'm gonna let the boys get some exercise first. You owe them. Then you're gonna join the sewage in the river. 'Cept shit floats. So we've got some stuff that'll keep you down."

Gambatti stood back and pointed his cigar at a large pile of chains lying by the crates. My only hope was that the beating would be so bad the drowning would be a relief.

"He's all yours, boys."

Gambatti stood back. Broken nose helped his mate to get down and on to his crutches. Then he picked up two long crowbars used to break open the crates. He gave one to the guy with the knee problem. It didn't seem to inhibit his back swing. They were grinning like kids let loose in a toy shop. I closed my eyes, tensed myself and waited for the first blows. Already my skull was bursting where the plate was. It felt like one of my old fugues coming on me. It would be a mercy if it came quick.

Suddenly there was a crash behind me, and shouts. I heard running feet and saw three figures charging across the concrete. They shrieked like they were storming a Normandy beach with fixed bayonets. There was a brief clash of metal on metal, some solid thumps and then the three musclemen were on the ground nursing serious head wounds. It was no contest; combat-hardened soldiers versus spivs, one a cripple.

Someone grabbed me and lifted my head. Through bloodshot eyes I gazed into the ugliest, most beautiful mug I'd ever seen. My insurance policy.

"What kept you?" I managed. Midge just grinned.

"You said give it ten before interrupting. Maybe my watch is slow. Hang on in there, pal. We'll have you down in a mo."

He left me, then I heard cranking of chains and I was gently lowered to the ground. As Midge untied me, I looked up to see Cyril and little Stan poised with the crowbars above the groaning and thoroughly pissed-off gangsters. Gambatti, wisely, had his hands in the air and was chomping away at the cigar in his mouth. His minions struggled to sit up, trying to get their battered brains round this turn of events and what to do next. Midge helped them out. In his left hand he held the Beretta I'd confiscated at the casino. In his right was the crowbar.

"One move and you get another one!" He swung the heavy rod. "Hands on your heads."

Stan moved towards the thugs and deftly patted them down. He relieved Gog and Magog of a brace of flick-knives, then searched their jackets and confiscated two more Berettas and a fine- looking Luger. It had the six-inch barrel preferred by the German Navy. The Wehrmacht made do with four inches. Gambatti didn't seem to be carrying.

I crawled on to all fours then got slowly to my feet, head reeling. I found my trousers and dragged them on, then my shoes, and began to feel less like a human sacrifice. I walked over to Cyril and Stan and clapped each of them on the shoulder.

"Bloody heroes. Thanks, pals." I swear Stan blushed.

"What do we do with this lot?" asked Midge.

"There's enough chain. And it's a wide river," suggested Cyril with real enthusiasm.

"We could hang the bastards up one at a time like they did Danny and use those jemmies on them," offered Stan.

I walked over to the four of them. I was hurting and nauseous and generally disinclined to be magnanimous. It must have shown; I could see real fear in the hard men's eyes. I landed a good kick on two of them – not the cripple; I have standards. That made me feel better.

Gambatti looked sullen and nervous, and kept chewing on his cigar. I reached out. He flinched. I removed the stogie from his mouth and crushed it on the floor.

"Get your trousers off. Right now! All of you."

They danced and shuffled and finally stood in their shirts and socks. It's amazing how diminished a man looks without his trousers. "Down on the floor. Sitting. Back to back." I ordered.

They grunted and groaned, but got down into a clumsy huddle with their legs pointing out and their backs to each other. I picked up the rope they'd tied me with and made a loop in one end, slipped it over Gambatti's neck and pulled it nice and tight. Then I looped it round the others' necks and gave it a couple of turns round the body, pinioning their arms.

Gambatti was looking as though he'd self-combust with anger. When one thug moved, the other two choked. Perfect. I took the Luger from Stan and ran my hands over it. It was a fine piece, better to look at than to shoot. Better than the Beretta because of its longer barrel, though even then its accuracy goes to pot over about fifteen yards. But with the muzzle against his head, Gambatti knew I couldn't miss. Sweat dripped from his brow. And I noticed the black in his hair was beginning to run in rivulets down his neck and sideburns.

"OK, Danny, you've had your little joke," he said. "A hundred quid to let us go. No hard feelings. We wasn't really gonna do you in." He tried a smile, sounding more Italian by the minute.

I squatted in front of him with the gun on his chest. "We'll never know, will we, Pauli? The question is, should I be as charitable?"

"Let us go and call it quits, eh? Two hundred quid is yours." His eyes went narrow. "What about you come work for me, Danny, eh? A handy boy like you? And your men here. I need a new team. How much you earn? I give you hundred a week guaranteed. And always bonus. All my guys make bonus. Two hundred a week!"

"Worth thinking about, Danny!" called Cyril.

For a long second I was amazed to find myself seriously considering the idea. I shook my head. "This isn't about money. Tell me again, what happened to Eve Copeland?"

The rivers of black were melting down his face. "Nothing! On my momma's life! I never touched her."

I was inclined to believe anyone with a gun up his nose. "What do you know? You must have heard something on the street?"

He shook his head, looking desperate. "Look, I tell you what I do. Let me go and I find out. OK? I put the feelers out. I listen. Then I tell you."

I held his gaze. Was it worth the risk? Knowing Gambatti's type he'd as soon set me up as give me free information. Maybe the world would be a better place if we did drop this lovely quartet in the Thames wearing some heavy jewellery. I got to my feet. The lads were waiting. Say the word and they'd make these pigs disappear. I looked down at Gambatti. He looked pitiful with his hair dye dribbling and his thin knees knocking.

"You've got three days. If I don't hear from you, with worthwhile information about Eve Copeland, I'll come looking for you. Got that?"

He was all eagerness now. "Absolutely, Danny. Don't worry. Pauli Gambatti is a man of honour."

"Yeah, right. Let's go, lads. Here..." I dug out Gambatti's well-filled wallet and rifled through it. "Two hundred, you offered? Not enough here, Pauli. This'll have to do." I plucked out a dozen big white fivers. "Travel expenses." I gave each of the boys twenty quid and threw the empty wallet on the floor. I kept the knives and the Luger.

"Let's go. How did you boys get here?"

"Cab," said Stan. "This'll cover it." He waved his fivers with glee.

I turned back to Gambatti. "We're borrowing your car. You

can pick it up at the George, Camberwell Green. Keys behind the bar. And no torching the pub, unless you want a war."

We turned and walked out, leaving Gambatti cursing his hatchet-men for strangling him. But he didn't seem to hold a grudge. Two days later I got a phone call.

TWELVE

That was the call that led me to the Angel pub by the river that night. I met my contact and watched him go to the bar. Then, from the filthy floor with a man on my back, I watched them slaughter him like a sacrificial goat. Like the other cowardly clientele I fled into the night to avoid explaining my presence to the boys in blue. I got home at midnight, exhausted and deflated. My one chance of finding Eve, or even learning if she was alive or dead, was gone. All I'd gleaned was that my contact had an Irish accent and one of his killers had a foreign one. It was a set-up. It told me that an organised gang was involved in her abduction. And that someone had tipped them off about my rendezvous. Gambatti, to get me out of the way?

I took my only suit to the cleaners again, the second time in a week. I sat and I fretted, walked round and round my office till even the cat got dizzy. I hung a sign on my office door telling the world – if it ever chose to beat a path to it – that Finders Keepers was on holiday, and took to walking by the Serpentine, feeding the ducks and feeling sorry for myself. I hate inaction. I'd rather be doing something meaningless than nothing at all. Even a visit from the Flying Squad to grill me over Eve's disappearance would have been welcome. I was well enough known to her office mates, not to mention Hutcheson and her landlady. Surely they weren't that incompetent? Why the silence? There was nothing in the papers about the murder. A man dies in a pub brawl and doesn't even get a mention. Life is cheap in the East End, but not worthless. Had the coppers been bought off?

I needed a plan. I thought about finding Gambatti and beating his head in. But however satisfying that might be I doubted it would lead to Eve. If it had been his gang that had taken her, why go to all the trouble of setting me up? It would have been easier to bump me off than my mystery contact. And if Gambatti had put the word out about the meeting, he sure as hell wasn't going to admit it to me, far less tell me who he'd spoken to.

It got so bad inside my head that I began to think seriously about Gambatti's offer. My life was shit. I barely made a living. I was going nowhere. The whole world seemed bent and I was the only straight man left. What was the point? Principles, or just habit? Most of the time I worked in the gutter, and often enough it was hard to know who the bad guys were. Take my old sparring partner Detective Inspector Wilson: just as much of a thug as Gog and Magog. Worse maybe; at least those gangsters made no pretence about which side they were on. Why did I want to stay on the losing side?

But just when you think you'll go daft with inactivity, life kicks your door in. I came back from the park and found a parcel waiting for me. It hadn't been left by the postman. It just had my name on it. It was hatbox-sized, about a foot long on each side. Brown paper, tied with string and sealed with red wax. I touched it gingerly with my foot. It moved easily. It didn't look like a booby trap. But then – as any good SOE instructor tells you – that's the whole idea. I took the risk and lifted it. It was light. Maybe there *was* a hat inside.

I walked in to my office and put it on my desk. I sniffed it. Nothing. I shook it gently. Something moved inside but it didn't clunk or thud. I took out my scissors and sliced through the string and sealing wax. I opened the lid and for a moment my world dropped away. It was full of hair. Like the rich, russet mass surging from a black beret, or floating beside me on the pillow.

I lifted it out, in no doubt it was hers. I laid it tenderly on my desk and stroked it like it was alive.

There was a folded paper on the bottom of the box. I opened it up. A few words were scrawled in capitals:

NEXT TIME IT WILL BE HER HEAD. FORGET HER!!!

I checked the box outside and in. Nothing else. I walked round to my chair and sat down and touched her hair, clinging to the notion that she was still alive. Why else would have they sent the warning? Did it mean I was getting close? I picked up her curls in both hands and buried my face in it, inhaling her perfume and the faint tang of tobacco.

What the hell did I do now?

THIRTEEN

t was ten o'clock and the pubs were closing. Drinkers poured out of the bars, joshing and singing: displays of bravado before facing the wife with a schoolboy excuse for the dent in the pay-packet. I'd had a couple of pints at the King's Head down at the Elephant, and found myself wandering down towards the river. My empty flat didn't appeal. The pantry was bare and I hadn't eaten since lunchtime. I knew a good chippy, a van on a bomb site near London Bridge.

They had one cod left. It had my name on it, in a cone of newspaper with a mountain of chips all doused in salt and vinegar. Only a woman's nape smells better. I walked over to the railings by the river and gazed out over the water, thinking it was time to go the police. I wolfed down the sodden batter and salt-encrusted chips, chucked the paper in the river and watched it float off downstream. I licked my fingers and began to walk back towards Borough High Street through one of the many alleyways that ran round Southwark Cathedral. My shadow ran in front of me as I dipped between rare pools of light.

That's when I heard the steps. At first I wasn't sure. A drunk passing, the faint echo of high heels running for the last bus, a dog on his night prowl. I slowed and listened. The streets were quiet. I stopped, listened again. Nothing. I started again, this time walking faster. I suddenly did an about turn and walked smartly back the way I'd come. No one. I turned down a side street I hadn't intended taking, slid into a door well and waited. If he was following me he was good. I gave it five long minutes. Still nothing. I glanced down the side street and saw it led nowhere. I pulled my hat down over my face and tiptoed to the corner feeling daft. I peered round.

He was standing with his back against the wall, hands in his pockets, waiting. I didn't recognise him at first. He was big, but his coat hung loose on his frame like he'd borrowed it from a bigger brother. I walked up to him, slowly. I still didn't recognise him. Then he grinned, and bile choked my throat. He was the last person I wanted to meet down a dark alley, away from witnesses.

"You've lost weight," I said.

"Thanks to you."

"Any time. Why are you following me, Wilson? Revenge?"

He shook his head. "Why didn't you leave me to die?"

The last time I'd seen Detective Inspector Herbert Wilson, he was lying on the bare floor of one of Mama Mary's flats. I'd lured him into a confrontation with the lovely but spoiled Kate Graveney. Wilson was groaning. Hardly surprising. He was bleeding his life out from a wound in his stomach, clawing at the splintered leg of the chair on which he'd impaled himself. It seemed a fitting but unintended revenge for his bestial plundering of nameless Soho girls including Kate herself. Not to mention the pasting he'd given me in the nick. I've known bent coppers in my time, but Wilson's brand of bullying sadism made them look like wide-eyed cherubs.

"It wasn't for your sake, believe me."

"Oh, I believe you, McRae. I believe you."

"Is that all you wanted to know? You could have phoned me. Or ambushed me in my office like everybody else does."

"I can do you a favour."

I laughed. "In return for what?"

"Helping us."

I took out my cigarettes. I didn't offer him one. Bad for his health. I lit up and watched my smoke drift through the street lamp.

"Us? Who's us, these days, Wilson? Thought they'd pensioned you off."

His grin widened. Even in the poor light his teeth looked brown. "*Us* is the Yard. Scotland Yard. CID."

"God help us all," I said with feeling. "Why would the Yard want to help me?"

"Eve Copeland. She's not who you think she is."

Her name in his mouth was like a blasphemy. I flicked my fag away. It spiralled into the dark and kicked up sparks when it hit the pavement.

"Oh? And who might she be?"

He put his head to one side and looked at me for my reaction. "A German spy."

Can your whole body flinch? I laughed. "You're daft, Wilson. Off your trolley. They let you out of hospital too soon."

His face lost the steady smile. "As I recall, you're the one with the hole in your head, McRae. Are you going to listen?"

"Why the hell should I listen to a madman talking shit at midnight?" My mind was rotating like a whirligig. All I could see was her notebook with its encoded messages in German script and shorthand. But what did *that* prove? She was a linguist, OK?

"Prove it, Wilson. Bloody well prove it."

His smile widened. He was loving this. I should have let him bleed to death.

"Meet us at her flat tomorrow. Ten o'clock. Don't be late. You'll miss the party." He tipped his hat at me, turned and walked away. I could have jumped him, given him a good kicking. We were alone. Instead I stood like a dummy looking after him. Then I lit another cigarette and walked home, my brain numb.

I got to her flat at quarter to ten. A policeman was standing on the front steps. I walked up to him, my mind dragging me back to the first night she sneaked me in and up to her bed. German spy indeed!

"Sorry, sir. No one's allowed in today."

"I'm here to see Wilson. Detective Inspector Wilson." The title stuck in my craw.

The bobby's face changed. "Your name, sir?"

"McRae. Danny McRae."

"You're expected, sir. And it's Superintendent Wilson now, sir." He winked at me, turned and opened the door. "The Super and the other gentleman are with the landlady. Downstairs."

The Super? So if you really screw up you get kicked upstairs. I walked down the hall, not on tiptoe this time. Voices drifted through the open door, and I recognised the landlady's nagging tones.

"I knew she was up to something funny. I just knew it. All those late hours. Not right for a young woman. But who am I to say? It's all different these days. No respect and no morals neither. And as for—"

"That's fine, Mrs Gibson." A man's voice hurriedly cut in. Not

Wilson's, but familiar. It was a Kafka moment: my enemy and my friend allied against me. "I think we have all we need for the moment. We'll just finish our search upstairs, if you don't mind." I heard rustling and a clatter of teacups.

"I don't know what I'm going to tell the neighbours…"

"Well, actually, nothing for the moment, if you don't mind," went the familiar posh tones.

I stood rooted in the hall waiting for him. He still had the moustache and the floppy hair, but now he was in civvies like the rest of us. It made him seem lesser.

"Hello, Gerry," I said. My old boss, Major Gerald Cassells, SOE retired, had the grace to look sheepish as he emerged from the vocal clutches of Eve's landlady.

"Hello, old boy. Funny old world."

"Hilarious, Gerry. Wilson." I nodded to the smirking figure filling the doorway behind him.

"Shall we go upstairs, Daniel?"

"Oh, let's. After you, Gerry."

We trooped upstairs and straight into Eve's room. It looked tiny and shabby in daylight without her in it. Not helped by having the contents of her drawers and wardrobe tipped on to the floor. The bed itself was pushed against the wall and the covers were in a heap. The floorboards under it had been ripped back – or rather laid back; they'd clearly been made to lift up. Between the joists sat a metal box. I recognised it. It wasn't identical to the one I'd used in France, but radio transmitters have certain features in common, whether British or German.

I walked over to Eve's only chair, the one she flung her clothes over before she dived under the sheets with me in hot pursuit. I sat down, took my fags out and lit one. My hand was surprisingly steady.

"Shall we take it from the top, Gerry? Assume I know nothing. Like what you're doing here? And why you're with Wilson? And what you think happened to Eve Copeland?"

Cassells and Wilson exchanged looks, as though having brought me here, they were suddenly unsure about what to tell me. He took a seat on the edge of the bed. Wilson leaned his elbow on the mantelpiece and stared at me. I blew my smoke at him.

"It's like this, Daniel. I'm with the Security Services now. A natural progression, I suppose. Bert, here, is our link man in the Yard."

I couldn't resist smiling at Wilson. Bert, was it?

I thought back to my hospital bed, after Wilson gave me a serious going over in Charing Cross nick. I could hardly speak, and moving hurt – a lot. Major Gerald Cassells, who'd summoned the coppers after finding me rifling his files in SOE HQ, was bent over me, being very solicitous. Referring to Wilson's treatment of me as animal-like. His face then was full of contempt for someone so prepared to abuse his power.

He seemed to have got over that.

"So you and Bert are like that, Gerry?" I crossed my fingers to show how close they'd become. "Glad to see there's no hard feelings between you."

Wilson growled. "That's enough of the cracks, McRae." He turned to his new best friend. "I told you he'd play the smart-arse."

Cassells tugged at his moustache. "Look, I know there's no love lost between you two, but we have business to attend to. Shall I continue?"

I shrugged. Gerry took it as a yes.

"Very well. The girl you call Eve Copeland has been known to us for some time. She first came to the attention of the Security Services back in '42. We had a tip-off from one of our agents in Germany. We did some checking. Her real name is Ava Kaplan. She's German. She spent some time here before the war – college, that sort of stuff, so she speaks excellent English."

With a posh accent, I thought. I was going to make a stupid comment about that not proving she was a spy, but the transmitter sat among us like an unexploded bomb.

"If you knew she was working for the Germans, why didn't you pick her up?"

"It was before my time, of course, but apparently we found her useful. In her position as a reporter she got close to a number of senior chaps – civil servants and military – got them talking. We made sure that what she heard was duff gen."

"You fed her false info?"

Cassells nodded. "SOE did it all the time, if you recall. Worked a treat. 'Specially with D-Day. Jerry didn't know where the landings were going to take place till after we got there."

I needed to get away from that smug bastard watching me from beside the mantelpiece. I stood up and looked out of the window, pulling back the net curtains. It was any view in London; rows of straggling fences enclosing little allotments, some still with Andersen shelters, some with washing hanging out. How could Eve – *Ava?* – look out on this scruffy evidence of humanity and plot to bring it all down? I didn't believe it, couldn't believe it. I turned back to them.

"Is she alive?"

Cassells hesitated. "We think so."

"Do you know where she is?"

He shook his head.

"Were you the ones following her?"

"No. We didn't need to."

I raised my eyebrows. "We knew where she was, knew what she was up to," he explained.

"Why didn't you pick her up after the war?"

He shrugged. "It was a mess. Europe was in chaos. Still is. We had agents all over the place that we needed to bring back. Frankly, old boy, we had more important things to do than pick up a minor agent of a defeated enemy."

It all sounded rehearsed.

"Any idea who *was* following her?"

Wilson shifted his stance. "We thought you might have a better idea, *old boy*. You and your gangland pals."

I wished I had a golf club handy; a mashie niblick would do, with plenty of follow-through. He was still taller than me, but he'd lost a hundredweight or two. I reckon I could take him now. I spoke to Cassells.

"She upset people. Bad people. It goes with the job. The reporter job, that is. But I guess her disappearance had nothing to do with East End villains." I pointed at the transmitter. "What have you found?"

"That she was still using it up till a month ago. We picked up her signal. Part of our routine sweep."

I was stunned. "She was still operating? Who with?"

"We don't know. But there was an answering signal. All in code. But look here, Daniel..." He looked down at the toecaps of his brown brogues; they gleamed like polished brass. Old soldiers might fade away, but not their shoes. "Miss Kaplan... was sighted two weeks ago. She caught the ferry from Dover to Ostend. A woman matching her description – but not her passport – got on a train going east. To Antwerp."

I found I wasn't breathing. I inhaled and waited.

He went on. "Any idea where she was going, Daniel?"

I knew. I knew exactly where she was going. Her notebook left me in no doubt. There's a connecting train at Antwerp. One a day. Started running again in January. It was all in her notebook. I'd read the entries as journalist's notes for some article. Not as travel plans.

"I think she's gone to Berlin." I sat down again and took out a fag. I played with it while I waited for my brain to catch up. Cassells exchanged glances with Wilson.

"That's our guess too, Daniel. How did you know?"

"Just some things she said. And now this." I pointed at the transmitter.

"Any idea why?" Cassells probed.

"She was being followed. Maybe she panicked," I suggested.

"Maybe she went home, McRae. Back to her master." Wilson held my gaze for an age, watching me digest this.

I counted to ten. Then twenty. "So, what now?"

They looked at each other. "Are you still... interested in her?" Cassells asked.

Was a bird interested in flying? I kept my face smooth. "Depends."

Cassells took a deep breath. "We're curious about who she was in contact with. And why. Things are pretty fluid over there. What with the Russians and all that."

All that was a considerable understatement. Why couldn't the bloody English ever say what they really felt? From what I could gather, Berlin was a wild-west town with four competing sheriffs – Russians, Americans, British and French – lording it over a starving populace of ex-Nazis and current criminals. What the hell was Eve doing there? *If* it had been her on that ferry, and *if* she had been heading to Berlin.

"Why don't you ask your agents there?" My collar was beginning to feel tight.

"You know her. And she's more likely to be persuaded to return with you."

I looked at him.

"You're an old SOE hand. We'd like you to go to Berlin and bring back Ava Kaplan."

That night I lay on my bed thinking about Cassells' request. I'd promised to give him my answer the next day. I felt rushed, pressured. The disclosures about Eve were so totally unexpected that I couldn't marshal my thoughts. What I couldn't puzzle out was Cassells' interest. Why did the British Secret Service want her back if she was the "minor agent of a defeated enemy"? He said they didn't want to punish her; the war was over, she was doing her duty as a German citizen no matter how misplaced her loyalty. But they wanted to know why she was still transmitting to Berlin. And who was on the receiving end. Why did she flee to Berlin? To get away from her pursuers or to join up with her old network? If so, what were they up to? Was this some last-gasp Nazi group that wouldn't surrender? Cornered SS trying to flee the country?

Cassells had appealed to my sense of duty, without realising that I'd worn my allegiance down to the stub. I was sick of the lot of them. Tired of rationing and restrictions, fed up to the back teeth with secretive bureaucrats meddling in people's lives. Sickened by wars and their aftermath: refugees and orphans, innocents raped and killed. God help us, we were already talking of the new threat; our former allies had opportunistically stolen half of Europe while we were otherwise engaged. Uncle Joe was beginning to look as bad as Adolf when it came to grabbing land that wasn't his.

I hated my job: the petty crimes and jealousies, the rages and brutality, the infidelities and lies that made up my daily diet. They didn't pay me enough to absorb all their frailties and transgressions.

And it seemed I was pretty useless at picking women. Falling for a ghost six months ago, carrying a torch for a snooty accomplice to murder, and now fixating over a German spy. Eve had lied to me; had she been using me too? Had she been faking what I saw in her eyes and the way her body responded? Had I been on the receiving end of the artifices of a consummate Mata Hari? Why pick me? I had nothing to tell her, no secrets to be revealed on her pillow.

A few weeks ago I had found an old map of Scotland sticking out of a pile of rubbish left out for the dustbin men. I dusted it down and bought a cheap glass frame for it. It now hung on my office wall to remind me of my roots. I walked over to it and scoured the empty spaces of the Highlands and the Outer Hebrides. Maybe I should buy a one-way ticket to the Shetlands and take up poteen-making? Wrapped in a tartan plaid, striding the glens with my faithful collie bounding over the heather, rounding up my sheep. A hard pure life, living off mutton and tatties, washed down by my own hooch. Bliss.

Who was I kidding? I'd go mad within a fortnight. And what about Eve? Could I forget her that easily? How would I live without knowing what happened to her? Whether she was dead or alive. Whether she *was* a spy – and why. And of course, finally and selfishly, whether she loved me. That's all that really counted. I couldn't give a toss whose side she was on, as long as it was mine. And I had to find out.

Next day I phoned Cassells and told him I'd do it. He seemed less enthusiastic than I expected. But he agreed to put the wheels in motion to get me into that divided city, to pick among the ruins for my lover, the German spy.

FOURTEEN

Cassells offered me a choice. I could follow Eve by ferry and overnight military train into Charlottenburg station, the rail terminal in the British Sector. But it was faster by air, if they had a spare seat. They were running a shuttle service out of RAF Northolt to Berlin. A brace of Avro Yorks was plying the route. The York was a fairly new passenger plane using the trusty Lancaster's wings, engines, tail and wheel assembly wrapped round a wider fuselage. There were no nose or tail gun blisters on this craft, just a line of portholes running the length of the plane under each wing. The planes ferried forces mail and senior officers into Germany's heart.

I spoke to the pilot before we took off. His RAF tunic was plastered with medal ribbons from bombing trips that had stopped only eighteen months ago. He said he still tensed his buttocks as he flew over cities, waiting for flak to erupt through the thin skin of the Lancaster and mess up his bowels. He'd only recently stopped putting an upturned tin hat under his seat. But it was nicer doing the trip in daylight under your own steam, instead of trying to hold position in an armada of two hundred bombers. Nice, too, to land and get a cuppa at the other end instead of dropping your stick of incendiaries into the inferno below and going straight back.

The only problem was the Russians, he explained. "The Reds won't let us fly over their turf. The route we take is an air tunnel. Everything outside the city and for about seventy miles to the west of us is under Russian jurisdiction. Pain in the arse. You wouldn't think we'd fought on the same side. Thank God the Americans got the south west. At least we have Templehof."

Besides the pilot, navigator and radio man, there were eight Army brass and two big sacks of mail for our garrison. The racket from the four Merlin engines at take-off was deafening, but dropped to a steady comforting drone after we were airborne. The Army types had documents to read, or kip to catch up on, and left me to it. I had a front seat just behind and below the raised deck where the pilot sat.

As the plane rumbled through the air, I thought of the landfall ahead. My dream back in '42 – and that of most of the blokes I'd fought with – was to march into Berlin after giving the Germans a bloody good hiding. But weeks before D-Day my war had been rudely interrupted. As a reluctant guest of the Gestapo I had indeed ended up in Germany, far to the south, the soft south, among the rolling hills of Bavaria. Not that I saw much of the pretty countryside, or rosy-cheeked frauleins and thigh-slapping men in lederhosen. I was tucked away on the outskirts of a dozing village outside Munich, a village that had survived eight hundred years without anything more important happening than a failed cabbage harvest. Until the Nazi master bakers arrived with barbed wire and an unusually large set of ovens.

I was finally going to see Berlin, the pre-war capital of louche, but it left me curiously flat. I'd seen pictures of the city in *Pathé News* at the Odeon. The streets full of flag-waving loonies saluting a funny-looking bloke with a bad shave. The buildings built to last: heavy stone, four and five storeys high, with balconies sprouting haphazardly. Lots of trees down wide boulevards sprinkled with outdoor cafés, and an overhead railway. A solid respectable place that just happened to be home to the world's biggest megalomaniac.

Hitler knew his Berliners. He knew that underneath the stuffy demeanour lay suppressed passions. I'd read Isherwood, of course. He'd made Berlin sound racy and degenerate beneath the decorous surface. All those private bars and streets lined with smiling prostitutes, female and male. I wondered how much of it was left after the Russians arrived with vengeance in their hearts and lust in their loins.

I whiled away the three hours with a German dictionary and notepad and pencil, trying to fill the many gaps in my language. From time to time I broke off to do further translations of Eve's notebook – I still couldn't think of her as Ava – using a teach-yourself guide to Gabelsberger's shorthand. One phrase cropped up twice in her most recent stuff. She mentioned Berlin and something called a hellish door. Code words? The entrance to somewhere fearful? Or just my bad translation?

The captain announced we were beginning our descent. I peered out of the Perspex window just as we broke through the last of the summer clouds. The city sprawled out below and we could see the destruction on all sides. The RAF had done us proud. It made the Blitz look half-hearted. For a second I almost felt sorry for the poor bastards, then I remembered that it was the same poor bastards who'd set up a thousand concentration camps across Europe. This wasn't a handful of psychopaths in black uniforms keeping a peaceful citizenry in their thrall; this whole nation had got right behind their Fuehrer with unbounded enthusiasm for getting rid of the *untermensch*. And their *unter* women and kids. Still...

I couldn't see a complete block of buildings intact. There were odd patches of green where the city parks had been, but they were pockmarked and treeless. Only stumps and felled trunks remained to remind Berliners of their shady walks. The roads seemed clear, though. The rubble had been bulldozed into neat piles ready for rebuilding. It would keep a few brickies in work for the foreseeable.

We made a last bank over the city and straightened up. Ahead was Templehof airport, a great semi-circle of Doric columns and portals. Very Albert Speer. Just the thing for those torchlight parades. In front of it, embraced by the arms of the airport buildings, was the runway itself, with parked planes littering the central area.

Templehof was right in the heart of the city. It seemed too small to take our plane. As if we would run out of runway and plough into the streets all round it. I could see some tanks and ack-ack guns along the southern perimeter. What were we defending against – a German insurrection or a Russian take-over? We dropped lower and I felt the wheels shudder and drop. Our speed fell and we bounced once, twice, then bumped to a halt. We eased ourselves out of our seats and climbed down on to the tarmac. It was hot. The air shimmered and trembled.

A bus came scurrying out from a long flat building with more than a hint of the Parthenon about it. An American flag fluttered on top of the colonnades. The bus picked up the Army blokes, the crew and the mail. I stood like a lemon for a while. Then a Jeep headed my way from one of the caverns under the terminal. As it drew up I could see it was driven by a corporal wearing signaller's badges.

"Captain McRae, sir?" he called out.

Captain again. Is that how Cassells had set it up? I walked over to the Jeep and the soldier leapt out, saluted smartly and threw my battered case in the back. He was a good-looking lad – lad! I must have been all of five years older than him. Smartly turned out in battledress with his black beret at a rakish angle. I imagined he had no trouble pulling the frauleins. I got in beside him.

"You can drop the Captain stuff, Corp. And the saluting. Civvy street now. The name's Danny."

He looked at me to make sure I wasn't taking the piss. "Fine by me, Danny. I'm Vic." He tossed his beret under the dashboard, slammed the Jeep in gear and we shot off. Now I could see that the dozen or so planes stacked off the runway were American B-47s.

"Where are we going, Vic?"

"Don't you know, sir? Danny?"

"This was all arranged in a bit of a hurry."

"I'm to take you to Colonel Toby. Toby Anstruther. Mil Int."

Military Intelligence. Seemed a good place to start.

"It's not far. We're on Kurfurstenstrasse. In the Brit sector."

Despite the warmth of the day, I felt a curious chill. The German street names were bringing it all back to me. There is a harshness about the language that makes it peculiarly suited to giving orders. I found my hard-won vocabulary rushing through my head like water in a mill-wheel.

"You all right, Danny?"

I shook my head. "Fine. Just a bit queasy. Bumpy ride. How long have you been here, Vic?"

"Six months. I'm on a two-year stretch."

"What's it like?"

A smile lit his face. "Did you bring any fags?"

"A carton. Why?"

"That makes you a millionaire. You can buy anything with a pack of fags. Booze. Women. Anything. I've got my own gaff, here. A two-bed flat just round the corner from the office. In Kantstrasse. That's Kant, not...."

"I get the picture," I laughed.

"But it might as well be. The women drop their drawers for a cup of real coffee. If you want anything while you're here, just say the word." He rubbed his nose with his finger and gave me a wink.

Spivs in uniform. Human nature will out in any conditions. "Your own flat? Is there anywhere still standing?"

"Sure. Take a close look."

We drove through the barbed wire gate at the airport perimeter and out on to the Templehoffer Damm that seemed to run towards the city centre. If there was a centre any more. Rudimentary street signs had been set up at junctions: poles bearing bashed original plates retrieved from the shattered buildings, or wooden signs with white writing. They seemed more like markers for an archaeological dig.

But my view of the city from the air had been too fatalistic. Sure, whole buildings had been razed or turned into black stumps, and there were more piles of bricks than habitable structures; but there were functioning parts. Kids played at soldiers on the bomb sites, clambering on burnt-out tanks and trucks. Here and there little groups of women in headscarves tugged at the mounds of stones.

"What are they doing?"

Vic laughed. "That's the *Trummerfrauen*, the rubble-women. They're reclaiming the bricks. Paid by the number. It's either that or whoring."

Some of the women had hammers and were chipping away at the mortar. Others stacked the cleaned bricks in neat piles by the roadside. Riding in the livery of the victor, I felt embarrassed at witnessing their puny efforts. I shouldn't have; here was a spark of hope that hadn't been extinguished. One or two straightened their stiff backs and looked at us as we swept past. I turned my face away.

Maybe it was the heat of the day that made me conscious of the smell: a pong of drains and brick dust, especially when we rolled to a halt at intersections to let a convoy go by.

Vic laughed. "You'll get used to it." He must have seen my nose twitch.

"Hardly surprising. Do the sewers work?"

"Everything works. Sort of. We've got the street lamps on again, the underground, some trams and of course the bars. They all work. All rationed, mind. Unless you know where to get it." His nose got another rub.

"See over there." Vic pointed to his right. A big, bashed building stood adrift in a sea of flattened rubble. I could make out giant columns supporting the façade. I'd seen it on a hundred newsreels.

"The Reichstag. What's left of it. In the Russian sector now."

I stared at it, trying to visualise the little madman at work there, planning to rule the world but in fact wrecking his own country and redrawing Europe. One man. How was it possible?

It was a short drive. There was little traffic, mostly military. Old men pulled prams piled high with wood – broken floorboards for cooking-fires. Gaunt men in Wehrmacht greatcoats, faces dirty and eyes hollow, hovered at crossroads like the spirits of hanged men. I felt like a tourist gawping at the ruins of an ancient civilisation. Berlin was in worse shape than London, but there was a horrible symmetry of suffering. Maybe this was the war to end wars. Then I thought of the Red Army spread like a rash across East Europe. But surely the Soviets had had enough of war? Hadn't they lost enough men?

We dodged and dipped our way round and through potholes caused by our bombs and filled with shattered house bricks. We pulled up outside a three-storey stone building: 233 Kurfurstenstrasse. It looked like an office, insurance or the like. There were no guards or barbed wire to put the spotlight on its new occupants. Vic straightened his tie and pulled down his tunic. He dug out his beret, dusted it down and jammed it on his head.

"After you, *sir*." His eyes met mine. Time to put on our ranks.

We pushed through the main door and climbed two flights of stairs. Through open doors we could see secretaries and office staff. But it would be wrong to describe the scene as bustling. In fact, there was a distinct air of lethargy. A secretary filing her nails here, two others nattering there, and one bloke chatting up another girl. I realised I was hearing German spoken, and understanding most of it. Something stopped me from mentioning my shaky skills. We came to a closed door. Stencilled on the glass were the letters "OIC MIB". Vic knocked. A voice said, "Come!" and he pushed open the door. Vic stood to one side.

"Captain McRae, sir!"

"Thanks, Corporal," I said, and walked in trying to keep my right arm down by my side.

"Come in! Come in, McRae. I'm Toby Anstruther."

He was bald and bouncy, and his uniform belt hung loose to give his well-fed midriff some *lebensraum*. I guessed his age at late forties. The pips of a half-colonel sat proud on the uniform of the Lancashire Fusiliers. Probably saw active service in the Great War and was seconded by his regiment to Intelligence for this one. I thought I saw a Military Medal ribbon among a decent collection. I was beginning to feel underdressed.

We shook hands and he pulled up a couple of easy chairs over a coffee table. I'd barely sat down when the door swung open and a very pretty girl came in bearing a tea tray. Toby caught my eye as it travelled admiringly over her tight pencil skirt.

Her dark blue eyes smiled at me. "Do you have everything, sir? Can I get you something to eat? A sandwich?" She pushed back her pitch-dark hair and I only just bit my tongue from making a smart-arse reply. I smiled at her. Who wouldn't?

"Thank you. I have everything."

When she had sashayed out the door, Toby grinned at me. "A perk of the job. All the girls here are bilingual, of course. Some of the units have German lassies but it's a tad early for that in Mil Int, don't you agree?" He poured the tea and continued.

"You're one of Gerry Cassells' old team, then? Did good work. Hardest job of them all. Behind the lines, no one to talk to, and if caught…" He mimicked a noose tightening.

"Something like that. I have to say, I felt a lot safer being shelled by Rommel than interrogated by the Gestapo."

"Quite." Anstruther looked me up and down. Behind his piggy little eyes was a shrewdness; not your born leader but nothing much would get past him. "So, you're out here looking for a girl, I'm told. A German agent. Copeland or Kaplan, take your pick. Funny, I used to read her column. Hardly seems likely."

"No, it doesn't. That's why I'm here. It doesn't add up."

There was the same long look from him, as though he was drilling into my head. "Cassells seemed quite clear." He reached out to his tray and pulled the slim folder off the pile. He opened it and scanned the papers. He knew every line. And could read between them.

"Says they caught her *in flagrante*? Transmitter under bed, code book, the lot. Seems fairly conclusive…"

"Two men looking at a piece of metal sticking out of the ground. One sees the fin of a bomb, the other an old cooker."

"But a transmitter, Danny?"

"Ham wireless operator?"

He put on a wry smile. "Whoever she is, you both want the girl. I'm here to help."

"I appreciate that, Toby. But where to start? This isn't my patch."

"It would help to know why she was here."

"If we knew that…"

"Quite. But let's assume she is a German spy. She could be trying to make contact with her old team. The man or woman who was running her. Agreed?"

I nodded. He went on. "If that's the case, what I can say is she's probably not in our sector. We keep a pretty close eye on who's seeing who round here. So do the Yanks. The French? Well… the French do their own thing, but we're on pretty good terms with them." He tapped the file. "When I got wind of this I put some calls out. We asked them to keep an eye out for ripples. Anyone asking questions."

"And?"

"Nothing so far. But that was only a couple of days ago. My hunch is that she'd go where the climate is a little warmer for ex-Nazis. The Russians got here two months before us and had the run of the place. After raping every woman over ten and under ninety they installed their own tame Krauts in charge of each district, running them along the same lines as the old SS. We're beginning to push things back in our own sectors but the Germans seem more comfortable under... how shall we put it?... strong leaders. The Russians are happier to make use of the former Nazi top men than we are. If I were her, looking for my old playmates, that's where I'd look first."

"Can I travel into the Russian sector?"

"Ye-e-s. They have plenty of patrols, but that's mainly to keep their own soldiers out of trouble. It's not as if there's a fence or anything. Yet."

"Do I need a pass?"

"We'll fix that. But for God's sake be careful. The place is a thieves' kitchen. Roaming in gangs. They'd murder their grandmother for a packet of fags. All nationalities. Poles, Czechs, Russians... the flotsam of war, Danny."

"Can I get a map? Can you show me where to start?"

"I can do better than that. I'll lend you Corporal Vic for a few days. He speaks the lingo and knows his way around, particularly the shadier spots, I'm afraid. Don't let him corrupt you."

FIFTEEN

Vic was smirking as we left Toby's den. The mission obviously agreed with him. We hopped into his Jeep and he whizzed me round to the Tiergarten Mess, a block of flats requisitioned by the British Army, and left me to sort myself out. Luxury. I had two small rooms to myself. The sitting room had a wireless and a couple of sagging chairs, with a little fold-up table by the dirty window. The walls were in a heavy patterned wallpaper with vivid rectangles where the previous occupants had hung their framed photos of Kaiser Bill or Goebbels.

A tiny scullery ran off it, with a sink, a gas cooker and a wall cupboard. With a fine sense of British priorities the cupboard held a little caddy of tea and some sugar, along with a kettle, two cups and saucers and a couple of plates. In the bedroom I found a single bed and a wardrobe. The floor had worn but clean carpets over the lino. I took my shoes off, lay down on the bed and lit up. All hunky-dory.

Vic called again at six p.m. in civvies, hair glistening, and looking like he was born to wear silk ties and white socks. He was chewing a large wad of gum. I felt like a bank manager alongside him.

"Got cash?" he asked.

"I've got these." I showed him a handful of dollars, surprising gifts from Cassells. *You're sort of on the payroll, Daniel.* "And these." I pulled out a packet of cigarettes and patted my pockets to show the rest of my supply.

"What about one of these?" He slid his hand round the back of his trousers and pulled out a gun. It was a 9mm Belgian Browning High Power automatic. Used 9mm bullets. Thirteen to the cartridge and one up the spout. A nice weapon and a good crowd stopper.

"Do we need them?"

"Where do you think you are? Finchley? We're averaging two hundred robberies and five murders a day. And that's just the official numbers."

I walked over to the wardrobe where I'd hung my coat and few belongings. I lifted my socks and pants and retrieved the heavy Luger I'd purloined from my altercation with Gambatti's boys. God knows how the Navy version had turned up in the East End. The extra length gave it greater accuracy over Vic's Browning, but it needed to be kept spotless and oiled if it wasn't to foul up.

"This do?"

Vic whistled. I made sure the safety was on and tucked it into my waistband in the small of my back. I hoped there were no real cowboys out there. By the time I withdrew the long barrel from my trousers, flipped the safety and aimed the thing, I could have been outdrawn by a Girl Guide.

"Any idea where to look, Danny?"

I thought about the tangled words in Eve's notebook. I'd found some references to Berlin but nothing that made sense. Not without some context.

"What's the layout? I mean, how's this place set up?"

"Simple. Draw a line north to south, splitting the city in two. The Ruskies have everything east of the line. We share the west with the Yanks and the Froggies. We're in the middle, the French above us and the Americans in the south."

"Where would you go if you wanted to lie low?"

Vic laughed. "This whole sodding place is an escape hole."

"Toby said old Nazis hang out in the Russian sector. Make sense?"

"Maybe. Let's take a look."

I saw the expression on his face. He knew this was hopeless. But I had to try. We left the flat, pockets bulging with fags, cash and guns, and headed for the wild side of town. Vic left his British-marked Jeep in the safety of the courtyard behind the HQ. We strolled along the edge of Tiergarten. It had probably once been a great green landscape like Hyde Park, full of trees and pleasant walks. Now the trees had been scalped by shrapnel, and the open grassy areas were gouged and pitted by bombs. Expired tanks and smashed small aircraft littered the park. It would take a very long time to turn it into a lovers' haunt again.

My stomach flipped; ahead of us loomed the very symbol of the Third Reich: the great outline of the Brandenburg Gate, looking remarkably unscathed. Vic nudged me and pointed to our left, at a series of new arches standing apart from the rubble.

"What's that?" I asked, staring.

"It's the Russian Monument to their dead. Opened last week. Bags of big hats and red flags."

"Didn't take them long. Why here? Why in our sector?"

"They didn't expect to give up any of Berlin."

We walked on towards the Gate. Now I could see the damage: great lumps chewed out of the stonework and one side demolished. But it still dominated the central crossroads, and framed the Unter den Linden beyond. We walked through the central arch and found ourselves gaping at a massive picture of Joe Stalin guarded by some bored Russians sweating in greatcoats. They glanced at our cards and we walked on down the avenue. They would have to change the street name or find themselves some new Linden; all that remained was stumps amid the rubble. Vic pointed us down some side streets and we began to sink into old Berlin. The smell of bad drains increased.

We started in the few bars that were open. I had a couple of Eve's newspaper photos pasted on to card and wherever we went, I discreetly showed it to the barman and some of his regulars. Sometimes I bought their interest with a cigarette. We had to be careful; there were usually some Russian NCOs or officers having a drink. No squaddies – they were kept leashed in their barracks. There were also quiet men sitting alone, supping coffee and watching the room over the top of a paper.

We entered one bar down a set of steps and through a leather curtain. We left the daylight outside. Inside was all gloom and dank with only dim light from some paper lanterns illuminating the dark corners. It reeked of stale beer and fags, and a faint residue of vomit. The clientele fitted in well: shabby and grey, with lifeless eyes that tracked us to the bar. My neck hairs rose.

Vic ordered me a beer. It tasted of stale water. We surveyed the room and its handful of drinkers. They looked sorry that Hitler hadn't conquered the world. Maybe next time.

The murmured conversations were restarting at the tables around us. I was just about to walk Vic out of this rat hole when I felt a tap on my shoulder. I whirled. He was thin and intense, wearing a coat and hat despite the warm evening. "Papers, please," he asked in German.

The bar had quietened. The barman moved into the shadows.

"Who might you be?" I answered in English, knowing full well who he was.

His face tightened, but he stuck to German. "English? Show me your papers."

"I say again, pal. What do you want?"

I felt Vic squeeze my arm. "Don't, Danny. Just show him our papers."

The man slid his hand into his coat, and I waited for the gun. I could feel the weight of the Luger against my spine but not even Roy Rogers could draw in time. He pulled out a folded card. He opened it and I could see Cyrillic script and his ugly mug. It looked important. I assumed he was NKVD, the Russian security boys.

Vic interrupted. "Of course, sir. Danny, show him your papers." Vic handed his over and I followed suit.

"What are you doing here?" He wanted a fight and I was tempted. Jumped-up little bureaucrats have that effect on me. Vic must have seen my look. He interceded again in German.

"We're just having a quiet drink, sir. No trouble. This is my friend's first time in Berlin. I'm showing him how well the reconstruction is going, especially in the eastern sector." He smiled. The little prick didn't return the smile.

"Perhaps it is better to continue drinking in your own sector." It wasn't a question. We finished our beers and left. But we didn't head back, not immediately. We went from bar to bar, café to club down the darkening streets. None of them lived down to my expectations of Berlin as the fun capital of Europe. There were one or two lamps working but not enough to join up the pools of light. I became conscious that the number of Russian two-man patrols was increasing. Sometimes they stopped us and asked for papers. Vic's papers and his fractured German seemed to satisfy them. They reminded us of curfew at ten p.m. and left us with a shrug.

I tried to picture Eve in one of these dives but couldn't. I no longer felt I knew her, far less where I might find her. Some of the bars were little more than knocking shops that Mama Mary would have been embarrassed to be seen in. The atmosphere was a cloying mix of stale booze, fags and gallons of cheap perfume to drown out the smell of unwashed females. It wasn't through choice, I'm sure; shampoo and bath salts were as hard to find as a virgin over twelve anywhere in the Russian-occupied zone.

By nine-thirty my feet were killing me, and I'd drunk too much watered-down beer. Vic was ready for more but I needed some shuteye. I planned to strike out on my own tomorrow during daylight to see what I could see. The underground had stopped running for the night. Rather than face another walk past a line of good-time girls all hoping to pass as Marlene Dietrich in the moonlight, we found a taxi. I crawled to my room, slumped into bed and was out like a candle.

I woke with a bad head and a weak stomach. I dealt with both over a massive fry-up in the mess. We seemed to be looking after our boys out here. The locals might be starving in the street, but in here we could eat all the bacon and eggs we could manage. I noticed some of the blokes filling their pockets with hunks of bread and pats of butter, even wrapping the odd sausage in newspaper. I asked one of the other diners what was going on: saving something for a mid-morning snack? He laughed. They were feeding their girlfriends on the sly. Food and fags, and a roof over your head could buy the plainest British squaddie the most bewitching product of Hitler's selective breeding programme.

I'd been thinking about how to find her. It didn't seem likely that she frequented the dumps we visited last night, unless she hoped to find who she was looking for there. Maybe if I could imagine her target I could get on her wavelength? Let's assume she was a spy and let's assume she's looking for her spymaster – where would a senior spy locate after the spying stopped? There were several possible answers.

He – let's call him Fritz – could go straight, get a job in civvy street and forget his past dark arts. Unlikely; there were no jobs, and spies don't change their spots.

He could switch sides and work for one of the Allied security services. Much more likely. I replayed my conversation with Toby Anstruther. The Russians had been here longest and had already sewn up a number of senior positions. It was just the sort of rats' nest that would suit an out-of-work spy with flexible morals. But I doubted I would get very far with that line of questioning.

The other profession that Fritz could easily turn his hand to was the black market. He'd be used to shady deals and working on the margins of society. He'd know how to run a network and would already have good contacts. He was naturally ruthless and deceitful, and could work both sides of the law. That's where I'd start. All I had to do was find the black market.

The lovely lady who served me tea in Toby's office gave me

instructions and a short moral lecture before I fled her beautiful eyes and walked towards Potsdamer Platz. She told me that markets continually sprang up and died around the city depending on demand and the leniency of the authorities.

The nearest one tended to materialise in the wide open space on the line between the British and American zones. It could hardly be missed. With exquisite irony the black market operated in full view of the burnt-out shell of the world's largest department store. When I arrived, there was already a great crowd. A few armed MPs wandered around but didn't interfere. The authorities recognised that when currency becomes useless, bartering is the natural order.

As I merged with the crowd it became clear what was important here among the ruins. Cigarettes were the common currency, but anything could be swapped for anything else if there was a demand for it. Soap was a luxury and required a full pack of American cigarettes per bar. But there were stalls, wheelbarrows and squares of cloth on the ground, holding candles and cakes, second-hand clothes and shoes, weapons and kettles, pots and scratched 78s, dirty postcards and poetry books. Men with big pockets and hessian sacks showed off their finds: a few decaying potatoes; a lump of coal. It was the fag-end of a society, and in its way brought home to me how close we were. And how stupid it had all been.

This was Petticoat Strasse, with its spivs and shysters, fishwives and conmen, mugs and fraudsters. The smells were much the same: tobacco everywhere; a pungent tang from a stall selling coffee made from acorns; the great unwashed wearing the same clothes day in day out; nostril-twitching perfumes and hair-cream made from cooking oil. And as I watched and listened and tuned into the language, I began to feel strangely at home. If a camp with barbed wire and gun towers could fairly be called home.

I stopped at lunchtime for a beer and a black bread sandwich of some strong cheese. Refuelled, I pressed on through the afternoon. I repeated the process in two other spots, one to the south in the American sector and one to the north in the French. I followed the same pattern in each: threading my way through the crowds, stopping here and there to ask, in growing self-confidence, if they had seen the woman in the photo. I chose the ones who stood back a little, or who flitted between groups and who whispered in others' ears. I got shakes of the head and curt *neins*. From one I got a long cool glance. He reached inside his jacket and brought out his identity card. He was American, security services.

"Watch who you're talking to, buddy." I guess my accent wasn't fooling anybody.

I was doing something, but the heat was oppressive and my feet were killing me. I was beginning to lose heart, and thinking about calling it a day, when I heard a phrase that made my ears twitch like a pony's. A phrase I'd found twice in Eva's notes. *Hellish door*. Two middle-aged women in headscarves were gossiping while they rummaged through a pile of third-hand clothes.

"Excuse me, Fraulein. Hellish door? What is that?"

The fat one eyed me up like I'd just pinched her huge bum. "*Hallesches Tor*, you fool. Everyone knows that."

"It is a place, then?"

The slimmer one sighed. "Hildie, he's from Hamburg. Hear him. Yes, *Hallesches Tor* is a place. Old Berlin. In Kreuzberg. It's caught between the Reds and the Americans. Don't go there if you want to come back with both balls!"

The women roared at their humour. I laughed with them and pressed them into giving me a better picture of this segment of the city. The way they described it, my pronunciation wasn't far wrong. Even before the war it was a slum, they said. Rats as big as the children, and full of cutthroats, gypsies and Jews. I asked of black markets in the area. They told me of a very black market off Wassertorstrasse, where you could buy fresh meat, if you weren't fussy if it came from a rat or a Jew. They laughed some more, but I sensed they weren't entirely joking.

I limped off, my leg and feet aching but my head throbbing with excitement. I went back to my room and had a wash and a cup of tea. I had time to grab a bite at the canteen and then I set off again.

Dusk was already gripping the Leipziger Strasse as I passed the giant portrait of Stalin and slipped into the Russian zone. I began to notice the difference in the sectors. Here, there were fewer working gas lamps, and – maybe it was my imagination – something in the attitude of the people, something more closed and wary, that distinguished them from their cousins in the west.

I recognised Wassertorstrasse by the cobbled paving and the old stone gate that must have marked the city boundary centuries before. Here the streets were even narrower and darker. Hardly a lamp remained, and the rubble from ruined tenements lay where they'd toppled. Thin paths led through the mounds of stones, and the smell of raw sewage hung in the air like a curtain. Old posters of Brown Shirt rallies stained the walls. Swastikas were carved in the stones. Scrawled denunciations of Jews still held sway.

The tenements themselves were three and four storeys tall, with narrow closes and broken windows. Washing hung from poles stuck outside some of the open windows. Rubbish lay in the streets, wrapped round the piles of bricks and slates from bombed buildings. Though it was already too dark to see properly, thin and dirty kids still ran in and out of the entries screaming and laughing, oblivious to their bare feet and hollowed cheeks. I stopped and looked around me, and wondered if I'd taken a wrong turning in time and place, and wound up back in the Gorbals.

I was aware of eyes on me from windows and doorways, and for comfort I shifted the gun, tucked into my waistband at the back, round to the front. Shooting my own balls off suddenly seemed like a lesser risk.

I pressed on and emerged on to a small enclosed square with one entrance and one exit on the far side. It was like a ghoul's convention. The scene was lit by a central bonfire and the pale glow from the windows of a bar. Clumps of people stood round talking and haggling. Here and there people had thrown rugs down on the cobbles to present their shoddy wares in the best light. Crockery and food lay in dark piles. I'd found the black market.

Some of the groups shunned the firelight. They were in complete darkness except for the red glow of a cigarette or a struck match. I felt an intruder. I had no wish to approach anyone and show them Eve's photo. I stood back in the shadows, watching, thinking through my next steps.

I'd all but decided to beat a retreat when I saw her. A fleeting glimpse. A profile, a cast of the shoulder. But it was enough. My heart stopped. I drew back further into the shadows to watch her go from one group to another, always checking around her. She didn't see me. She wore a knee-length frock of some dark material. On her head was a familiar beret, less bulky than before. She carried a shopping bag, its straps over her shoulder. At last she broke free and walked off into the night, heading away from Wassertorstrasse and deeper into the Russian zone. Hardly breathing, I began to follow her.

SIXTEEN

She walked fast, in that purposeful way I knew so well, going somewhere, doing something. There were one or two others around and I kept to the opposite side of the street. She turned down an alley and we were again on cobbles. It made her heels click louder and I grew more conscious of my own footsteps. I daren't lose her, but I couldn't get too close. Once she glanced round but kept going. A patrol stopped her under a gas lamp. They joked with her until she showed her papers, then let her go and picked on me a hundred paces behind her. They seemed to take for ever reading my documents, warned me about the curfew and finally let me go.

I looked down the narrow street. It was deserted. Frantically I trotted after her. There was a crossroad ahead. She must have turned off. I had to get there before she disappeared completely. A much narrower alleyway ran at right angles to this one. I peered down the dark shaft to my left and listened for a foot-step. She could have gone into any of a dozen tenements along here; the entries were black and forbidding. I darted over to the other side and stared and listened. All I could hear was the blood in my ears. Then, faintly, I heard some steps, far down the alley. I plunged into the gloom. The walls crowded round me. I could almost touch both sides at once.

I was deep into the wynd. My eyes began to adjust and I made out dustbins and a great pile of rubble. I skirted it as best I could, stumbling and clutching the wall for support. I clambered down on to the cobbles and straightened up. That's when the world landed on my head. I fell forward, with a great weight crushing my skull and sending fireworks off inside my eyeballs. I thought part of the crumbling building had collapsed on me. I was dazed and on my hands and knees when the blow came again. This was no act of God, and this time it was final.

"Bring me some water."

It was her voice from a distance, so I knew I was dreaming. But I stirred my head anyway and felt pain blasting through me. I heard a gasp and realised it came from me. I lay panting, moving my hands and legs trying to feel the rest of my body. I seemed to be on a bed, lying on my side.

"Take it slow." She was speaking again. This time she was closer.

Another groan. I opened my eyes. Pain washed through my skull again. "Oh, shit." I managed.

"Danny, if I lift your head, can you take a drink?"

Impossible. It would hurt too much. "Yes."

I felt her hand go under my neck and ease my head up a fraction. The pain clutched at my eyes. "Sick," I got out. She eased me back down and rolled me further over so that my face was at the edge of the bed. She stood up fast, and came back with a bowl, just in time to catch my vomit. It brought great gasps from me and I felt myself sliding back into unconsciousness.

Time passed and I heard voices: hers and a man's, or two men. I couldn't make out what they were saying. They saw me stirring again, for she came over. I felt a cold damp cloth on my head and its soothing effect seeped into my brain. I thought I might live. It was like coming round from one of my worst migraines. I inched myself up on to my elbow and my head didn't drop off. I opened my eyes again and she was there, facing me, leaning forward on a wooden chair. Her eyes were full of worry. That made it a little better.

"Nice haircut," I said.

She grimaced and ran her hand through the stubble of her once glorious mane. The worried look left her, to be replaced with irritation. Which hardly seemed fair.

"It'll grow. What the hell are you doing here, Danny? How did you find me? Don't you know you can get killed around here just for your shoes?"

"It's nice to see you too, Eve. Or is it Ava?"

She sat back in her chair and eyed me closely. "Who sent you?"

I didn't answer. I wasn't sure how to. I sat up by swinging my legs on to the floor and letting the weight pull my body up. For a moment I thought I'd pass out. I held my head in my hands till it passed. Gingerly I touched my scalp, checking the plate first. It seemed intact and may even have absorbed some of the blow. Alongside it were two lumps as though goose eggs had been pushed under the skin. One was bloody. Both hurt like hell. I raised my eyes. A small room with a sloping ceiling: an attic? A table. A sink. A heavy wardrobe. Curtains drawn across the window. Two beds and two mattresses on the floor. I was on one of the beds. Three men sat smoking and watching me. One was a bearded giant, one looked about fifteen with big sad eyes, the third bald and with glasses held together with tape. All three were scruffy with mistrustful eyes.

"Was it you or these beauties who socked me?"

Eve nodded behind her.

"Did they know it was me?"

"How could they?"

"Just wondered. Some girls get huffy if a bloke can't take a hint."

"Danny! Will you cut it out? Why are you here? How did you find me?"

I dabbed at my head with the damp cloth. It was still coming away bloody.

"Give me that." She grabbed it and took it to the sink. She rinsed it and wrung it out. She handed it back to me, and raised an eyebrow.

"I was looking for you. Why else would I come to this hell hole? And I found you by chance. Sheer bloody chance. What were you doing at the black market?"

"Buying food. You don't see any Co-ops around here, do you?"

"Why are you so angry with me? I'm the one with the headache."

Her face softened. "Sorry. Look, we didn't know it was you. I knew someone was following me. I walked in a circle. The boys here keep a lookout. I gave them the signal." She shrugged.

"Where did you pick them up?" I turned to them. "Do - you - speak - English?" They just gave me baleful looks.

"Stop it, Danny. You still haven't explained how you got here. How did you know I was here, for one thing? And where did you get the papers? Who are you working for, Danny?"

"I need a fag." She went to the table and retrieved my own packet and lighter. Only half the packet had survived. I looked over at the three smokers. "Cheers, fellas!" I saw my papers and the gun on the table.

I lit up. Dizziness ran through me, and I thought I'd be sick again. I steadied, then I felt better.

"OK, Eve or Ava or whatever your name is. Here's my story…"

I told her about my run-in with Gambatti and watched her face to see if I could elicit – what? Sympathy? Doubt? Repentance? She gave nothing away. I told her of being waylaid by Wilson and the meeting in her flat next day with Cassells. Of seeing the transmitter and the revelation that she was a minor spy. That she'd fled England for Berlin to meet up with her old spymaster, else who had she been communicating with in Berlin in code? I explained how it was then the most natural thing in the world to agree to come looking for her, here at the end of the world. Maybe I shouldn't have said I came because I loved her and didn't care what she was; it was about what she and I could become. But I did. This time there was a reaction. Her lips pursed and she shook her head.

"You idiot. You damned fool." She said it softly. And idiot that I am, I read something into it that probably wasn't there and smiled at her.

"Maybe. But I'm on your side. Whose side are you on?"

"Does anyone know you're here? I mean, in the Soviet zone. Will anyone be looking out for you?"

"There's a guy called Vic. An army corporal. He's my guide-dog. He may be waiting up for me. But the main problem is Colonel Toby. I'm supposed to report in to him each day. If they don't hear from me by tomorrow morning they might get curious. I don't know if I'm important enough for a search party, but there might be some heat."

"Can you make it to the table?"

"Sink first."

I got up, holding on to the bed, and waited till the room had steadied before lurching over to the basin to be sick again. That made the head worse for a while. I ran cold water and splashed it over my head until the coolness numbed the aches. As I straightened up Eve threw a towel at me; I grabbed it, dabbed myself part dry and joined her at the table. She laid out mugs and plates and knives, and brought a pan over with steam rising from it.

"Coffee?" she asked.

"Acorns?"

She smiled and shook her head. "Last drops of Camp. All the way from London."

She poured the coffee and the three men joined us. I studied them. The giant looked to be older than the others; his black beard was flecked with grey. The other two were in their mid-twenties, dark-eyed and dark-skinned. From somewhere in middle or southern Europe. They still hadn't said a word.

Eve placed a paper bag in the middle of the table. She opened it and revealed a sweating half-sausage. She placed a heavy black loaf by its side and cut off chunks. The men attacked the meat and the bread as though they expected it to be taken away from them at any minute. I cut off a slice and chewed some bread and waited. She looked paler and younger. The short hair did that. Made her big features more pronounced. Made her boyish and vulnerable. I could see her mulling over what to say to me, what to do with me. She kept my gun at her side, handy for her right hand. And I'd seen her use one. If she was who they said, then she'd be familiar with this weapon. Both made in Germany.

Finally, she had eaten enough and sat supping her coffee. "OK, Danny. Here's my story. You can believe it or not. I can't prove any of it." So she began...

"They were right on one thing: my name is Ava Kaplan. I was born here and grew up here. My father was a doctor and a local official. My mother was a teacher. They could have lived in one of the smart areas of Berlin. But they chose to live here, in Hallesches Tor, because they were needed. They were good Germans, Danny. Germans. But they were also Jewish."

She let the word hang in the air and echo in my own memory. I wondered which camp they'd ended their days in, and whether they'd died together. Sometimes at the end, it's the only important thing.

Eve continued, "Father used to visit London before the war. He loved England and all it stood for. Especially the bookshops. He taught me to read English and to love its literature." She smiled at me. "He sent me to school in London for two years when I was sixteen to perfect my English. Despite the rise of the Nazis Father saw no reason to worry about his position; he was an important member of the community. A valued doctor. My mother taught in a German school, not a Jewish one. Even the Brown Shirts would not be so stupid. After Kristallnacht he began to fear for me and my mother. He sent me back to London in 1938 for my safety. My mother wouldn't leave him. She couldn't believe it would come to... this."

"So you weren't a spy," I said with relief.

She gave me a wry smile. "Oh, yes. Yes, I was. At the start. They tracked me down. I mean the SS. In London. Heinrich Mulder, one of their top agents. He told me that my parents' lives were at stake unless I helped them with some *research*, he called it. He offered to protect them if I did this small thing."

"Was it small?"

"To start with. I didn't know what to do. I had been getting letters every week or two from my parents, but when war broke out they stopped. I don't know if they were prevented from writing to me or whether MI5 intercepted them."

"Bastards."

"Yes. Bastards. By then my English teacher had helped me to get a job as a journalist. Mulder was back in Berlin now. We communicated by transmitter and the occasional dead letter drop. There were other agents in London. Mulder told me to use my job as a reporter to meet people and send back information. Mainly he wanted to know about morale. And defences in the city. Whether London could hold out much longer. Where the factories were."

"So you played along." I guess there was a hint of reproof in my voice, though God knows I would have done the same thing for my folks.

She placed her mug carefully down on the table and looked me in the eye. "Danny, I played along for all of five minutes. I contacted the British Secret Service and told them what was happening." Her voice was low and steady. A vein jumped in her forehead.

"You what? Cassells said you worked for the Nazis. You mean…"

"I worked for both sides. That is, I worked for MI5 while pretending to work for Mulder. We were called the Double Cross team. A unit codenamed B1A within MI5. Most of the others were spies sent over by the Nazis. MI5 caught them before they'd had their first sip of English beer. We had their codes. Have you heard of Enigma? Bletchley Park?"

I shook my head. She waved her hand as though it didn't

matter, or she couldn't say any more. She went on. "We knew every time they sent an agent over and were waiting for them. Lots were happy to turn and work for Britain." She paused. "The alternative was a firing squad. I was unusual. I came in under my own steam. We made up stories to send back to Germany. Disinformation. I was good at my job. The English gave me more money. The Germans promoted me to Major. Our biggest success was Normandy."

I sat back in my chair. My head pounded as I struggled to make sense of it. Who they hell was I to believe? Her, of course.

"Why would Cassells lie to me? Did he know all the details? Did he know you were working for us?"

She shrugged and took a cigarette from my packet. Her side-kicks helped themselves too.

"I don't know. We were an autonomous unit. My English handler kept things pretty close. But I would have thought when I went missing…"

I tried a different tack. "Why did you come back to Berlin? Who were you in contact with up to a couple of weeks ago?"

She flicked her ash on the floor. "I came back for my parents. I had one or two letters from them through my German drops in London. That was part of the deal. My father didn't say much; he wasn't allowed to. But it was clear they were under pressure all the time. Threatened with… well, it was pretty vague… loss of privileges, he said. But I knew he meant the camps. But the letters stopped completely in January '44. Maybe Mulder found out I was playing both sides. I came to find them."

"And…?"

She shook her head. "I knew it was a waste of time. When the war ended I wrote to them. Every week. Nothing. Then I got a response." Her eyes flicked to the men beside her. "My letters were being opened."

"The Nazis?"

"No. Let me introduce my friends." She pointed to the big bearded man. "This is Gideon. And these are Joseph and Ariel."

Gideon held out his huge paw to me and smiled. "Shalom, Danny." Joseph the kid and Ariel the bald followed suit. Ariel tugged at his wire glasses. He said, "Sorry about the head, Danny," in good English.

"It's OK. You're Jewish?" I said unnecessarily.

Gideon broke in. "Jewish Brigade. We got out of Berlin in '39. Got to Lisbon and then London. Joined up in 1940. We fought with the British Army in Italy. We came back after the war to see if we could find our friends and relatives who stayed behind. There was no one."

Young Joseph cut in, suddenly animated, as though he'd been released from a spell.

"Every one, gone! Wiped out! These murderers, these sadists destroyed us!"

Ariel reached out and touched Joseph's arm; he clearly kept the boy under his wing. He spoke tenderly to him. It sounded close to German. I recognised the throaty sounds of Yiddish from my camp days. The words formed in my mind. Joseph sat back and took a deep breath.

"So we decided to do what we could," went on Gideon. "Some Jews had survived. They'd lived secret lives here. Not all Germans were rotten. And others came back. This was the only home they knew. They were born here. We are helping them find each other. We have contacts who have lists… of the camps. We also help people to get to Israel."

"Past the British blockades," Joseph added contemptuously.

Eve cut in. "A second cousin of mine survived and knew Gideon. They went looking for others of the family. They found Germans living in my parents' flat. But one of the neighbours had *kindly* intercepted my letters. All of them. Gideon wrote to me."

"And your parents?" I asked quietly.

"They were taken away two years ago."

"But I thought you were getting letters…?"

Eve suddenly looked weary. Her shoulders slumped. "They tricked me. Mulder tricked me. He forced my parents to write several letters at once and didn't date them. It doesn't take much to add a date later."

"I'm sorry. Have you been to their flat?" Then I realised.

She looked at me funnily. "You're sitting in it. This floor and the one below. Though we've only taken this floor."

"What happened to the Germans who…?"

Joseph grinned at me and drew his finger across his throat. I looked round at them. They stared back at me defiantly.

Eve glared at him. "We threw them out, Danny. A few bruises."

"We should have…" Joseph again sliced his throat. "It's what they did to us! I am sick of Jews being slaughtered! Now we fight back, Danny."

"I understand all that you're saying, Eve. And I believe everything you tell me. But why did you disappear? Britain must have been grateful to you. The risks you took. They would have helped. Surely? Why all the pretence?" I ran my hand over my hair and winced. The bumps seemed bigger.

She got to her feet and began pacing. "It's complicated. It was about six months ago I found out that my parents had vanished. I've been in radio touch with Gideon and my cousin several times since. There's no doubt I'll never see my parents again. I had only one thought: I wanted Mulder's head. The British wouldn't let me have it."

"You went to them?"

"It seemed the natural thing. I wanted to know if Mulder was still alive and how to find him. At first my case officer in London was helpful. But then he closed down on me when he realised my intention. He indicated that Mulder might have survived, but wouldn't tell me if he was in prison or on trial or taken by the Russians."

"But *we* know!" cut in Ariel. His glasses flashed at me.

Eve stopped walking. "He's here. Alive and prospering. He is one of the district controllers set up by the Russians. I demanded that London let me come here and settle things with this swine. They told me to drop it. It had got political, they said. What the hell is political about murder?"

"Were they the watchers?"

She shrugged. "That was my guess."

"So you faked your disappearance. Made it look like you'd been kidnapped or murdered, and came here? You're here to get even?"

"An eye for an eye..." said Ariel, rubbing the tape between his lenses.

"Hasn't there been enough killing?" I asked.

She rounded on me, her eyes blazing. "Not nearly enough! Not nearly! Do you think this swine should get away with it? That he should get a nice job and everything is forgiven and forgotten? Is that your morality, Danny?"

Ariel leaned across the table to me, his eyes gleaming through his specs. "Ava – Eve – said you were in Dachau. How can you *not* want to kill these scum?"

"Because that's how scum think! That's what scum do. When does it stop, Ariel? When the last man's left standing?"

Eve sat down again. "Do you believe in evil, Danny?"

"As an entity? As some amorphous opposite force to good? No. Do I think some men are evil and are incapable of remorse or contrition? Yes. I've seen it. Experienced it." I bent my head and parted my hair. They could all see the livid scar that ran through my scalp.

"But you'd let them go on living? Hoping they'll change, see the light?" she asked.

This was what I still wrestled with. I'd seen humanity at its worst and its best in the camp. Afterwards I'd watched in sickening incomprehension the *Pathé News* showing the other camps being liberated. My gut reaction was to find every one of the guards and follow up every link in the chain of command and string them up, personally. But in more rational moments I found myself arguing that enough blood's been spilt, and revenge leaves an emptiness in the heart. The rational moments were still pretty rare.

I raised my hand to ward off her attack. "No, I don't think the SS will turn into choir boys. But would shooting *him* let *you* sleep easier? I've lost my God. My country has gone to the dogs. And the woman I fell for turns out to be a double agent." I tried a smile to soften the rhetoric. It came out a grimace. "The only thing I'm certain about is that there are no certainties. Look where it got Hitler. Eve, I don't know what's right and wrong any more. Did I tell you Gambatti offered me a job? I actually gave it serious thought. That's how far I've slid."

She examined my face for a long time, as though she'd never seen it before, or would never see it again. "You said you were on my side," she said.

I nodded.

"*This* is my side." She put her hands out and touched the nearest shoulders of Joseph and Ariel.

I walked over to the sink and rinsed the cloth. I pressed it on my head. It was beginning to feel easier. I still had questions. Why did Cassells lie to me about Eve? Who'd been following her in London? If it was MI5, were they concerned for Eve or Mulder? Who killed the man I went to meet in the bar? But my poor bashed brain had taken all the news it could absorb for one night. I returned to the table and sat down.

"You know where Mulder is?" I asked. She nodded. "OK, what's your plan?"

SEVENTEEN

It was too late to try to get back to the British zone. The curfew was in force. Eve tossed me a blanket and I lay down as best I could on the bare floorboards. My head hurt no matter how I lay, and I wasn't ready for sleep. Maybe it was the bad coffee. I listened to the sound of the others' breathing, easily distinguishing Eve's in the dark. I wondered what was going through her mind. Was she wishing we were lying together back at my place? Or had I simply become a nuisance, someone getting in the way of her plans to murder Heinrich Mulder? Frankly, I wasn't opposed to his removal. I just didn't think it would change things. But the repercussions for her could be immense. On the other hand, he hadn't arranged for the death of *my* parents.

It was a bad night, and a grim morning. I had the world's worst hangover without any of the pleasure. We made our plans over stale bread and bitter coffee. They gave me back my gun and papers, then Joseph escorted me to the British sector. The streets were quiet, but it wasn't the quiet of peace. Mist was clearing from the broken buildings and a wind was stirring the dust and debris. The reek of decay made me gag. There was a feeling that we were only in the lull of battle and that war could break out again at any time.

Vic was waiting for me outside the Tiergarten mess, pacing up and down, smoking like an expectant father. He saw me and came charging over.

"Where the fuck have you been, Danny?" Gone was any pretence at "sir".

I must have looked a sight. My suit was crumpled like a tramp's, my shirt had blood on it and my tie was in my pocket.

"I had a bit of a run-in with some thugs last night. I'm OK, but that'll teach me to go out looking for action."

Vic looked a little mollified. "Looking for a bint, were you? All you had to do was ask old Vic, you know. Any size, any shape. Where did you end up, then? The state of you."

I tried to look suitably chastened. "Two of them. I got away when a patrol came by. I begged a bed for the night somewhere in the Red zone. An old biddy let me in. Cost me five bucks. I need some breakfast and a wash."

"The Colonel is waiting for you. But you'd better get cleaned up and fed first. C'mon."

Colonel Toby was keen to know what progress I'd made. I expressed disappointment and frustration but vowed to go on trying at least for a few more days. Toby was encouragement personified and urged me to keep my pecker up. I vowed to do so, and left his office wondering how I was going to keep the pretence up and for how long.

"Vic, I need to do this my way. Thanks for your help. I can get around myself now."

"Sure, Danny. It's just that I was ordered to look after you. Look what happened when I wasn't around."

"My fault. I'll sign something to get you off the hook if you like. I just want some space. That's how I work."

"Tell you what, let's meet for a drink at the end of each day. That way I can check you're OK, and maybe I can help too."

We split up and I went straight back to my room and fell into a coma till early afternoon. I woke a little dazed, but human again. Even the bumps were going down. I dressed and walked out into the hot July sun, feeling amazingly cheerful for someone getting himself involved in an assassination. I was beginning to know my way about, and headed for the entrance to the U-Bahn on Kurfurstendamm. By the time I found it I was regretting not wearing a hat; my head was frying.

The station gave welcoming shade, but the respite was brief. Beyond expectation, Berlin's underground was operating again. But because it was one of the few cheap modes of transport left, other than bikes and the rare tram, the station was heaving with sweaty humanity. Strike that: this wasn't humanity, it was a mob. When the train got in they surged forward and besieged the doors, so that people wanting to get off couldn't. It was chaos, and every man for himself. I called on my training on the Northern Line and plunged in with elbows and feet. We shot off into the tunnels, heading east. By the time I fought my way out of the carriage six stops down the line, I was nearly asphyxiated with the stench and heat.

The warm afternoon air was a blessing; I gulped it in hungrily and lit up to get the taste of the journey out of my mouth. I gave uncle Joe a big smile as I left the U-Bahn station and headed towards my rendezvous with Eve in Holzmarktstrasse. I was close to the main station and the river Spree now. The area had taken a lot of hits, but as she promised I found the little cake-house open at the corner of Warschauerstrasse. She was sitting in the cracked window wearing her beret and looking just like the girl I'd left a hundred years ago in the Strand. She even raised a smile for me when I joined her at the table, and we kissed on both cheeks. Berlin suddenly seemed the most welcoming place on earth. All I had to do was talk her out of this mad idea.

"You really speak the language?" she asked in German.

I replied in kind. "Camp Deutsch. I don't know how it sounds compared to the real stuff."

She giggled. "You've got a northern accent."

"Two of my bunk mates were from Hamburg."

"Keep it up. It's fine. And better than English around here. How's your head?"

"Healing." I looked round. There were a few other customers supping from cups and nibbling at a flat grey slice of cake. "Just like old times."

She got serious. "No, Danny. It isn't."

Message received. "So what are we here for?"

"Don't look now. Across the road, to the left of the gutted building, there's an intact one. Do you see it?"

I waited a second, sipped the tea – it tasted of nettles – and casually turned and looked through the net curtains. "A four-storey building with a Russian flag. Looks like a hotel. Two Russian soldiers on guard duty. A big car outside, with a driver."

Eve smiled as though we were talking about the weather or the price of sauerkraut. "That's the District Controller's office."

"You mean...?"

She nodded. "Mulder. That's his office. That's his car. Those are his bodyguards."

"Same routine?"

"Clockwork. But we only found him four days ago. Around now – 14.30 – he comes out by himself. The guards salute and his chauffeur jumps out to greet him. He ignores them and walks off down the road and turns left."

"Then?"

"He goes into a house halfway down the street. It's a block of apartments. He comes back exactly one hour thirty minutes later. He goes to his office... he leaves at six."

"Where does he live?"

"We don't know. We've tried to follow him but all we had was a bike. We think it's in one of the suburbs. They still have trees there."

"Who's in the apartment? A girl?"

"There are ten names. We watched but couldn't see where he went inside. Yesterday after he'd gone in, we saw a curtain close on the second floor. We can't be sure."

"But you're not going to take him on the way in or out?"

"No. We need that hour and a half. You can get a long way in that time."

"But not out of Berlin, Ava."

"Don't *you* call me that," she hissed.

"Trying to stay in character. The point is, this bloody place is an island. It's surrounded by red sharks. You can't just drive off into the sunset."

"So what do we do, mister smarty pants?"

"Let it go, Eve. It won't bring them back. There's been enough."

Her eyes tightened with anger and her mouth thinned. "You don't know what it's like, Danny."

"I've been on the receiving end." I pointed at my head.

She shook hers. "You just got in their way. They tried to kill us *all*, Danny. Do you have any idea what that's like? To be hated so much? It wasn't just my mother and father. Not just my aunts and cousins. Though they're all gone. It was my *people*. My *race*." Her throat was flushed with anger.

"But this... won't end it. Come back with me to London. We can work it out. We can put this behind us."

She rubbed her eyes with her sleeve till they were red and sore. "You can. I can't. Go, Danny. Go back and leave me to this."

Customers were looking. I didn't care. "Eve, I had to ask. Had to be sure. I'll help."

She peered at me to see if she could trust me. "How?"

"I'm not new to this business."

She acknowledged it with a nod. "If you have any bright ideas about how to get into the flats while he's there, I'd welcome them."

"That's the easy bit. How are you going to get away? You need to plan an exit. Let's talk to your boyfriends."

"They are not my boyfriends."

"Four beds, one room? Very modern." I wished sometimes I could shut up.

"Do you really see it like that?" she said with a piranha smile.

"When I can't say what I feel I make a joke of it. You know that."

"Danny, this isn't the time or the place for feelings." She swivelled her eyes round the handful of customers in the café.

"Or the language. I have big holes in my vocabulary. We didn't get much practice chatting up girls in my language school."

She looked exasperated. "Let's go." She picked up her bag and got to her feet.

"Tell me one thing first?"

"What?"

"Before. When we first met." I didn't know how to say it. Either in English or German. "Was it a set-up? Was it all a sham?" Like I said, I wished sometimes I could let things go.

She hovered, and I thought she was going to walk away. Then she sat down, clutching her bag. I tried to read her eyes. They were dark and serious.

"Let's just say I hadn't intended to get involved. But I did. And then I began to worry about what I was getting you into. That's why I tried to get you to back off." She smiled and touched the stubble of hair peeping out under her beret. I felt an iceberg melt inside.

She went on more forcefully, "You're a bloody limpet, Danny McRae. But I'm glad you're here. You can help with the plans. But I'm not letting you get involved in the job itself. Now, can we get out of here before I have to drink another cup of this stuff?"

I took her arm as we picked our way past the potholes and abandoned wrecks. Inside I was feeling good. At another level I was more scared for her than ever. It took us half an hour to walk back to her flat. We were about to turn into the alley when we heard the shouting. Then the shots. We ran to the corner and peered round. A military truck blocked the way. Some Russian soldiers stood on guard less than ten feet away with weapons at the ready. Eve made to go into the alley. I grabbed her arm and steered her on. We heard an order, someone was shouting in our direction. We stopped and turned. An officer and two soldiers walked towards us.

In bad German he demanded, "Papers. Papers! Where do you live?"

"How are your papers?" I whispered.

"Finest German forgeries. Let me do the talking." She smiled and turned to the Russian.

"Of course, Colonel. What is the problem? We live down there, Staufenstrasse." She pointed back in the direction of the British zone, then dug in her bag and produced her documents. I did the same.

The officer was young and tough, a lieutenant who didn't mind being called colonel by a pretty girl, but clearly took his job too zealously.

"This says you are British." He peered at her suspiciously. I could see the dark stain of sweat round his serge green thick shirt collar. He wore one of their enormous hats as though he'd stolen it from someone much bigger. His two soldiers stood either side of him, weapons raised and pointing at us. They looked nervy.

"We are both British. I am a journalist accredited to the occupation forces. This is my research assistant." She pointed at me. I smiled and nodded.

"What are you snooping for here? This is the Russian-controlled sector."

"It is not illegal?"

He agreed it was not, but his tone suggested it was only a matter of time. There was more shooting and shouts. The young man got more flustered. He didn't know whether to run and see if he could join in the action or keep sightseers away.

"There is nothing to see here. Get on your way." He stuffed the papers in Eve's hand. I took her arm. She held her ground.

"But what is going on, Colonel? Is there a riot? Do you have a black market gang pinned down? There are so many criminals. It is so brave of you and your men." She gave him her most dazzling smile and I could see him almost bursting to tell her just how brave he was.

"It is nothing. Some Jewish agitators, we are told." He stepped closer and lowered his voice. "Between you and me, the Germans were on the right track, you know. These Jews are still up to their old tricks." He all but winked at her. She screwed her face up sympathetically. He stood back, and saluted.

"Good day, Fraulein." He nodded to me and turned and ran his men back to the side of the truck to see what was going on.

Eve's cheeks were red points. Her eyes were ablaze. "You see?"

"All I see is we need to get the hell out of here and come back later. Let's go." I took her arm, this time without encountering resistance, and marched her off down the street, bitter tears coursing down her face.

We holed up in my room. The guard at the door barely lifted his head from his paper. He was used to afternoon dalliances. For a while she sat on one of the chairs in the sitting room. I made tea and we drank it in silence, looking out the net curtains as the day faded. For that little while I was almost at ease. Just being able to turn my head and see her there. To make fresh tea and get her smile of thanks. I knew the world was revving up outside and was like enough to crash through the door at any time. But for an hour or two we were out of it.

As the light turned yellow she stood up and walked through to the bedroom. I sat still.

"Danny?" Her voice was soft. I stood up and walked to the door. It was dark and I waited till I could see. She'd drawn the curtains and was lying under the covers in the bed. Her clothes were piled neatly on the chair. It was a flashback.

I walked over to where her face lay on the pillow. "Is this what you want?"

"Silly man, get in."

I took my clothes off slowly, not wanting to rush anything, and padded over to her, feeling the rough carpet and then the cool linoleum. Her face was away from me when I pulled up the cover and slid in behind her. Her body was hot and naked, and I buried my face in her soft neck. I stroked her shorn hair and realised how little I'd known of her ears. I ran my hand down to her breast. She turned to me and we lay looking into each other's eyes. I wondered if she saw a stranger too?

Our lovemaking started slowly and finished in a flurry of limbs and tossed sheets, and we lay cradled in each other's arms till the skin cooled. I got up, went through to the sitting room and brought back two lit fags. We lay smoking and wondering who was going to talk first. I wished no one would.

She said, "When it's dark, we will go back and see, OK?"

"Why not stay here? I could sneak some food in and we could hole up for days."

She pinched my nipple. "You know we can't. They have been brothers to me. We must find out."

"It might not have been them they were after."

"Hah. We should have shot the Nazi swine we evicted from my parents' home. They sold us out. Ariel was right."

"What if they're dead?"

She lay quiet for a while. "I hope they are dead. If the Russians took them alive, they will wish for death."

"And then? Will you come back with me? To London. Or Glasgow. I could show you my home. It's different up there. Quieter. Except Saturday nights. We could be away from all this."

She rolled over and sat up. I watched her bare back, counted the knobs on her spine, reached out, touched her hip. She flinched.

"I can never go back. There are others here I need to contact. I promised."

"Promised what?"

She twisted round so she could see my face. She shook her head. I studied the hollows and curves of her body, the velvet skin of her breasts and sheen of fine hair over her limbs like a sleek seal. I got up, and walked round to her side of the bed and held out my arms. She stood up into them and I held her body close to me as though for the last time, and we kissed. As we dressed we talked and I won the argument. I would go to her parents' flat and find out what had happened. She would wait for me nearby.

It was a wonderful evening, soft and warm. We walked hand in hand, the picture of young love, she in her pretty frock and beret and me tie-less and jacket unbuttoned. I would have left it behind but I needed somewhere to carry my papers and to cover the handle of the Luger jutting from my waistband at the back. We separated at a bar just before the Russian sector. An enterprising barkeeper had rescued some tables and chairs from the rubble of a hotel and made a little pavement café among the ruins. I left her nursing a beer and holding a spare key to my room in case I wasn't back before curfew.

The alley was deserted when I peered down it. No trucks, no soldiers. I could almost have imagined it. And yet, and yet... as my feet crunched through the rubbish and the debris, I noticed small things: a pool of glistening oil, empty shell cases, fresh half-truck caterpillar tracks. I saw no one. All the curtains were drawn and the windows closed, except one: it was Eve's flat. A curtain flapped and the remnants of the window frame dangled from the remaining hinge.

The front door lay on its side, splintered and smashed. I peered into the dark stairwell and saw bullet holes on the wall. A long series of dark marks streaked the floor. I didn't remember them. I bent down and studied them. They were dark brown. I put a finger out and touched. Dry.

The tang of spent ammunition and explosives hung in the air. I pressed on up the stairs. I noted the odd bullet hole and more of the smudge marks, as though something had been dragged down.

Ahead was Eve's flat. The front door was still on its hinges but it was badly holed. I walked through. Straight ahead was the lower floor which had been used by local Germans. Up the stairs was the attic room where Eve and the men had taken me. I listened and thought I heard a sound ahead of me. Nothing. I took out my gun, undid the safety and cocked it. I began to climb the stairs. I got to the top and stepped over the threshold.

The room was torn to bits. The walls and ceiling were splattered with bullet and shrapnel holes. The window frame had been blown out. Shards of glass lay across the floor. The beds were wrecked and their covers shredded. The table and chairs were smashed against the wall. A bullet-riddled mattress lay across the debris. I could see the three of them making their last stand behind the upturned table and mattress. Against machine guns and grenades, it wouldn't have taken long.

A pair of crushed spectacles lay by the mattress. The dark smears here were thicker and led to two pools close to one another. This time so much had been spilled, it hadn't completely set. I bent and touched. My finger came away red, and I smeared it on a corner of a curtain.

I started back downstairs, then heard it again. From the room below. I crept along the short corridor. My gun led the way. I got to the opened door. I jumped forward holding my pistol in both hands.

"*Hande hoch!*" I shouted. A familiar enough term to me, but never before used *by* me. It was the favourite sport of one of the camp sergeants. He would line up outside the hut and make us stretch our arms in the air. It was a way of testing how fit we were and whether it was worth feeding us. He would pace up and down the line of faces twisted in pain and fear. He was a master of the game. He would wait till our shoulders were burning and our arms trembling like branches in a gale, then he'd start to count down from fifty. Slowly. Anyone who couldn't keep his arms above his head before the final *nul* was marched off, never to return. You could try to practise, but with too little food it might simply expend precious energy.

I heard the sob. It came from behind the couch. I called again and the sob became two, then three, then ran into a litany of weeping. A head appeared. An old face with a scarf holding grey hair in place.

"Don't kill me. Don't kill me." She edged out on her hands and knees and got to her feet. She wore a shabby dress and a pinny. Her face was streaked with dirt and tears. I lowered my gun.

"What happened here?"

"Don't kill me. Please don't kill me."

"Just tell me what happened. What happened to the men who lived upstairs?"

"The Russians came. Are you Russian?" The panic dissolved her face again. There were red-haired Cossacks, I'd heard.

"English." It was simpler than Scottish.

Some of the lines left her brow. "The Russians. They came for the Jews. No one likes the Jews. They were hiding up there."

"Are they dead?"

She shrugged her shoulders, and rubbed at her cheeks. "I suppose. Some of them. There was a lot of shooting. Then a big bang. Then it was quiet. They took two bodies. Such a mess. Blood on the stairs. And look at my ceiling." She pointed up. Large bits of plaster had fallen leaving the wooden laths on show.

"*Two* bodies. Only two? Are you sure?"

"I saw two. They asked me. After. If I'd seen the woman."

"How did they know?"

A furtive look slid over her face. "It wasn't me. I didn't tell them."

"Who did?"

"You're not Jewish? You don't look Jewish. People round here don't like them. They're the cause of all this. Anyone could have told the Ruskies."

"Haven't you done enough to them?"

Her face of misery clammed up and she wiped it dry with the edge of her apron. She patted her hair under her scarf; she wasn't as old as I'd first thought, maybe in her fifties.

"Do you have a cigarette?" she asked.

I gave her one and lit it. She inhaled as though it was pure oxygen. She sat down on the arm of her couch. She pulled her skirt up to her knee and crossed her bare legs. They were white and blotched with broken veins, but still slim.

"There was a girl," she said. "Probably their whore. But she wasn't here when they came." She dragged deep on her cigarette and blew the smoke in a long funnel.

"Were they looking for the girl?"

Again the shrug and then a lowering of her eyes so that she looked at me from under her eyelashes. "Do you want a girl?" She smoothed the skirt round her knees and pulled off her scarf. She shook her hair. The grey roots showed through the badly dyed dark hair. She ran her hands through it and sucked her lips to bring colour to them. I stared at her, disbelieving. But who was I to judge, in this place at this time? I turned and made for the door.

"Don't go, *liebchen*. We could have fun. I could get us some food. Give me two dollars and we will eat like royalty. Ten, and you could spend the night with me."

I turned and looked at her. She was standing hands on hips in what she must have thought was a provocative pose, but was more like a child playing than a middle-aged woman. Her attempt at a coquettish smile barely hid the terror of her daily fight for life. She might have been a respectable *hausfrau* once, nice clothes, greeted politely by shopkeepers and petty officials. There would have been a husband, now perhaps rotting in an unmarked mass grave outside Moscow. She must have seen the pity in my look. Anger flushed her face and brought the tears again.

"Get out! Get out, you smug English swine! You did this! Your bombs! Look at what you've done to us!"

I took out my half-empty packet of fags and placed them on the floor and left her sobbing. Her curses followed me into the street.

*

Was I surprised to find Eve gone when I got back to the café? No. The barman – after a dollar tip – told me she'd left with a man. A big man. With a great black beard. She'd left a message for me. She said – and here he screwed up his face to recall the words – *she knew what I'd find. She had business to do.* And it seemed Gideon had found her.

I set off back to my digs. I knew the business she had to do. I prayed to whatever gods still had patience with this city and this people that I would be able to stop her before it was too late.

EIGHTEEN

All I knew was that Eve was with Gideon They were both safe – for the moment. But Gideon's size and intensity made him conspicuous. If she was going to make a play for Mulder and it involved a giant with a nose like a battering ram and a beard that could shelter a murder of crows, the chances were high they'd be caught. What were they planning? To go in with grenades and guns blazing? A suicide mission? Had our lovemaking yesterday been a way of saying goodbye?

At five in the morning I was sitting on my bed with my head in my hands, waiting for the dawn. A full ashtray sat at my feet. A thin tendril of smoke from my last fag rose into the dead air. The thought of venturing outside made me want to curl up in bed again. Berlin was getting me down. I felt I'd been washed up on the blackened beach of a remote island at the end of time: me and the other flotsam of a corrupt society. Rotting hulks littered our shoreline. The survivors were fighting among themselves, for food and water, for their very lives.

I gave myself a mental kick and dragged myself to the communal bathroom. I shaved and washed and scoffed a life-giving breakfast in the mess. By nine o'clock I was standing outside, hope set on a low flame, waiting for Vic. I'd met him last night and asked for his help. It was a tall order.

By nine-thirty I was thinking of abandoning my vigil when I heard a great toot. Coming towards me was a massive German staff car, the three-pointed star on its radiator glowing with power. All it lacked was a brace of swastikas fluttering from the bumpers. Vic sat at the wheel, waving with one hand, steering and smoking with the other.

"Will this do?" he asked innocently as he drew up and wound down the window.

"I asked for a set of wheels, Vic, not the Kaiser's personal runabout. Where the hell did you get this?"

He rubbed his nose. "Contacts. It was liberated from the garage of a big cheese in the ritzy part of town. Some say it was Goebbels' personal transport, or his bit on the side."

"It's – how can I put this – a wee bit conspicuous. That's all."

He looked hurt. "Don't you want it then?"

I suddenly saw the humour in all this. "Course I want it. Vic, you're a bloody hero. Now show me how to drive this heap of tin. I don't want to demolish the Brandenburg Gate. Not after all it's been through."

God knows how he found the petrol, far less the car itself. But driving this luxurious tank made me feel much better. It certainly drew glances. I left him, mid-morning, with his admonition *not to bend the bleeding car, if you please, Danny-boy* ringing in my ears. I lied when I told him what I was up to – *impressing a bint, Vic, old pal* – or he might not have handed over the keys so easily.

As I sailed through Checkpoint Charlie – trust the Army to come up with a truly forgettable name – I got saluted by the two Red Army soldiers. I drove down the Holzmarktstrasse and parked along from the little café where Eve and I had watched the District Controller come and go. With plenty of Russian soldiers wandering about it should be safe from petty thieves, unless they wore officer tabs.

I settled down with a pot of tea and the four-page German newspaper that claimed to be the *Neu Berliner Zeitung*. I was conscious of curious eyes from the *grosse frau* in charge of the café and some of her customers, but when I challenged them by returning their glances they went back to their soft susurrations of local gossip.

Lunchtime dragged on, and I was beginning to think nothing would happen. Which was when it did. Across the street there was a flurry of movement. Soldiers slapped their rifles in salute, and out stepped Heinrich Mulder. He glanced up and down the street and walked quickly off in the direction of his apartment. I paid my bill and left, coughed the big car into life and eased its nose into the street just as Mulder disappeared round the corner. I double-declutched, found second, and felt the V12 engine pull the car up to walking speed. At the turning I stopped so that I could see down the street. Mulder had already vanished. I left the engine running but rolled the window down so I could hear any ructions.

At first there was nothing to disturb the hot, quiet day: just a pair of old women shambling down the road with string bags distended by some nameless bloody parcels – leg of dog? fillet of cat? There were two cars parked – neither of the stature of mine – one to the left near the flats, the other on the far side. Much of the street was intact, with only the odd toothless gap. Suddenly a shadow flitted from a gutted façade. A figure darted across the street towards the flats. Another, larger, broke from the same cover and moved more slowly, resolutely in her wake. Eve, then Gideon. I wondered how they would do this. They didn't know which flat Mulder used, neither could they easily get through the communal front door.

The pair of them skulked in the entrance porch. They peered up and down the road, but saw nothing suspicious in a big parked Merc at the end of the street with a driver conspicuously reading a paper. I shifted the paper, in time to see Gideon take a couple of steps into the street, turn round and run back into the porch. A crash told me he'd hit the door and the door, presumably, had lost. He didn't come out. Eve looked round again and disappeared through the porch. They were in. But they still had to find the right flat. I guessed their approach would be as subtle as their door entry technique.

The seconds dragged into minutes. How long did it take to knock on ten doors? I caught a movement in my mirror: a troop of soldiers – six, no, eight – was collecting outside the District Controller's office. An officer barked orders. They snapped to attention, then were dismissed. Four stayed behind and began to take up duty positions. The other four, their shift over, walked smartly off in my direction and broke ranks. They slung their weapons casually over their shoulders and pulled out fags. It was a scene echoed in every army on earth. The changing of the guard.

They were ten yards from the corner of the Controller's street when the sound of the first shots reached me.

It was though they'd been electrocuted. The fags went flying and the rifles came round into their hands. They sank to their knees, waiting to see who was firing at them. There was a further shot, then cries from round the corner. The four men dashed forward and peered round. Two took up positions, one kneeling, the other standing above him, weapons to their shoulders. The other two ran for the furthest side of the street and took up the same stance. When Eve and her wild man ran out with smoking guns in hand they'd be shot down like rabbits. The cries had turned to good old-fashioned screams now, and were clearly coming from the flats.

Sure enough, like a bad gangster movie, Eve ran on to the pavement with a pistol in her hand. She turned back to wait for Gideon just as one of the soldiers shouted in Russian at her. Whatever the words, it was clear he wanted her to stop, disarm and put her hands above her pretty head or they would blow it off. Before she could comply, the big man lumbered out. She screamed at him and they both dived for the cover of the parked car. That was enough for the squaddies who'd lost a number of their mates fighting their way into Berlin. They let rip with a first round which pinned down Eve and Gideon. In case the soldiers needed any more convincing, a big arm broke cover and sent a couple of bullets whizzing towards them. The firing squad opened up.

Another figure suddenly took centre stage. A young man ran out, waving his fists and screaming for help. If he wanted to die his timing was perfect. He was right in the crossfire and took at least two bullets before pitching into the gutter and lying there, twitching and groaning.

A smart guy with a lust for life and a borrowed car of some distinction would have eased said car into gear and headed for the quiet side of town. Maybe the country. Check out the lake. Do some fishing. A smart guy.

I dropped the clutch, put it into first, revved the engine and let the gears bite. The big nose shot up and we lurched away. I spun the wheel even as I crashed into second. By the time I was passing the first open-mouthed soldier I was doing over twenty. By the time I was level with the man rolling in his own blood I was at thirty. I hit the brakes next to the parked car and squealed to a halt. I shouted out the window.

"Get your stupid backsides over here!"

Two astonished faces peered over the bonnet of the parked car. They saw who it was and ducked down again. I looked in my mirror. The four soldiers were moving forward, firing from the shoulder as they came. The first bullets punched into the boot with a loud thunk. I ducked just as a bullet smashed the rear screen. Eve and Gideon appeared in front of me and darted to either side of the car. The rear doors opened backwards and gave cover. Eve got hers open and dived in. Gideon didn't. He took position on the running board, with one big hand holding on through the window. He began shooting at our pursuers. I slammed into gear, hit the accelerator and stalled the damn thing.

I glanced back. The soldiers were flat on the ground. One of them was curled up clutching his belly. The others were getting their shots in. I prayed I hadn't flooded the carb. I switched off, then on again, pressed the starter. It stuttered and rumbled in protest, so I tried again, foot well clear of the accelerator. The engine coughed, then roared and gave a great belch of smoke from its exhaust. I found first gear, worked the pedals and shot off, with bullets chasing us. The madman on my running board continued firing and cursing at them and their ancestors while clinging on for dear life.

I hurled us round the corner, stopped and screamed, "Get in, you big bastard!"

The big bastard duly obliged and I began to head north, round the Red sector back towards either the American or British.

"You've been hit! Oh, God, Gideon, you've been hit!"

Not a word of thanks, just concern for her partner in crime. I looked in the mirror. Gideon was holding his shoulder. Blood was oozing through his fingers. His face was slate grey.

"Where can we go? Is there a safe house? Did you have a plan?" I shouted.

"Don't shout at me!" she shouted.

"Why the hell fire shouldn't I?" I yelled as the adrenalin washed through me. "You're a bloody madwoman! That's what you are. And I'm even dafter!"

We glared at each other in the mirror for a long few seconds. She sat back. I heard a rip and saw she'd torn off a bit of blouse. She stuffed it on to the big man's wound. He groaned.

"We didn't plan this."

"You mean you didn't have an exit plan?"

She glowered at me. "Can you get us to the French sector?"

"I can if all the checkpoint guards are blind drunk. You look like a pair of assassins. And there might a be a wee problem explaining bullet holes, a smashed window, and a man bleeding to death in the back seat."

"He's not dying!"

We sped on, aware that the soldiers would have run back to the Controller's office. They would be able to radio or phone ahead. They might already be waiting for us.

"Did you get him?" I asked, and looked for her eyes. She wouldn't oblige.

"Yes."

"Feel better?"

"Shut up. Just shut up!"

"Who was the screamer?"

"He was with Mulder. His little friend. A cosy little love nest."

There was a groan from Gideon. "Filth," he managed before passing out.

We were on the Unter den Linden now, hammering towards the Gate. I looked ahead and could see a flurry of activity at the Russian checkpoint. They were moving a Jeep across the exit. Two groups of soldiers were setting themselves up either side to man the gaps. I gunned the pedal and felt the great engine roar. Its bonnet rose up like a ship meeting a big wave, then settled down as the springs rebalanced.

We were a hundred yards away and I could see the officer shouting out commands. The soldiers settled into firing positions, aiming straight at us.

"Get down!" I shouted to the back seat. I lowered my own head so I was peering though the rim of the wooden steering wheel.

The officer shouted again. Some men brought their guns up. Some began to get to their feet and move to the side. The officer screamed at them and suddenly bullets were cracking towards us. The screen smashed and metal pinged on metal. There was a big bang and an awful grinding noise. The fan had taken a hit.

I was twenty yards away. I swung the nose towards the smaller of the two groups, the one furthest from the shouting officer. They saw me and leapt away like salmon heading to their spawning pool. I clipped the rear end of the Jeep, sending the two soldiers on it flying. Our momentum lifted the Jeep like a cardboard box and flung it against the great slabs of the Brandenburg Gate. We tore through the arch, ripping off the remaining wing mirror as we went.

The Americans weren't lined up in force but had been attracted by the sounds of shooting. I wasn't about to run down the guys who saved me at Dachau so I swerved and made a screeching detour round the sentry box. The GIs raised their rifles but didn't open up. Then they realised bullets were coming their way from the Soviet lines. They dived for cover and let fly at their former allies.

"We've just started World War bloody Three! I hope you're happy now!" I shouted at Eve through the rushing wind that tore over the bonnet and through the smashed windscreen. I adjusted the mirror to see her. She was staring ahead, silent. Gideon was on his side in her arms. He looked very dead.

The Merc sounded like a tractor and looked like a target in a shooting gallery. I hauled the wheel round and tore down narrower streets but even here there were British and French troops on patrol or manoeuvres. We were as discreet as a stripper in a pulpit. It was only a matter of time before we were stopped – and I didn't have a story that even started to make sense. The word would also be getting around: top-level shouting matches between Red officials and their Western counterparts.

"Is he dead? Is Gideon dead?"

She barely raised her gaze. I slowed, turned down a blind alley and did a U-turn so we were facing back out, and stopped. I leaned over and felt Gideon's neck for a pulse. There was a faint beat. At my touch the big man groaned and stirred. His eyes flickered, then sprang open. They were clouded with pain.

"Where – are – we?" he managed.

"Oh, Gideon! Gideon, you're going to make it!" Eve fingered his face. I didn't disillusion her. This man was at the end of his days.

"Where…?"

I answered, "Through the Brandenburg. The British zone. Not far from the French sector. They're after us."

"Get me up," he said to me. "You, get out and help me into your seat."

I guessed what he planned. "Gideon, take it easy. We'll get you help."

"Now! Do it!" he demanded with all his remaining strength.

I got out and looked at the car. Vic would kill me. Shattered screens, bullet holes in the big fenders and mudguards, and the engine and boot shot to pieces. I hauled open Gideon's door and slid my arm under his shoulder; with Eve pushing we got him out and on to his feet. He was swaying, and I doubted I could hold him for long. Now I saw the blood pouring down his chest. We both looked at his feet; already there was a pool of red. His shoes were filled and his trousers soaked.

Gideon looked at me. He smiled. "Get me in."

By this time Eve had worked her way round to our side. "What are you doing? Gideon, don't do this. We can get help."

I manoeuvred him next to the driving seat and he sank down with a great sigh and moan.

"Help me."

I kneeled and pushed his legs and feet into the footwell.

Eve was weeping. Gideon said something to her and she jerked up. The language. Yiddish. All I got was *The story. Tell the story…* I couldn't make out Eve's response, but it sounded like a denial. She didn't want to do whatever he said. Then he silenced her with another few words, guttural and hacking like a bad cough. She stopped and nodded. Again I heard the words "Tell the story…" She said yes. She reached inside his jacket and fumbled around. She pulled out something and held it up to me: a set of keys.

He turned to me. "Give – me – the – gun."

I looked in the back seat. I saw his big Mauser pistol and

drew it out. It had three shots left. I pulled out my own Luger. It had a full chamber of six. I gave him the Mauser in his right hand and laid the Luger across his lap. When the first was empty he could reach easily for the second. Eve was sobbing again and softly saying *no, no, no*. Gideon murmured to her. She nodded and leaned over and kissed his brow.

"Start me up," he said.

"Use third. Don't change." He nodded.

I reached across and pressed the magneto. I waited a second or two and then pressed the starter. The big engine roared and the broken fan screamed. I shut the doors and Gideon crashed the car into third gear. The nose tensed and he released the handbrake. The Merc juddered off towards the main road, kangarooing and near to stalling. He didn't wait to see if any cars were coming, just shot out, hauled the nose round and pointed back the way we'd come.

We ran to the corner just as he got going. The car looked a mess and sounded worse. Gideon waved his gun at us. I caught the words "Next year in Israel!" and he shot off down the street just as a Jeep and half-truck hurtled towards him filled with troops.

Gideon fired at them and the Jeep swerved and nearly flipped. He sped past them with his horn blasting. The Jeep and the truck turned and began the chase back towards the Russian lines. We heard more firing, much more than from one hand gun. Klaxons went off all round the city centre. It was like an air raid.

We lost sight of Gideon's car as he made the turn towards the Gate and launched himself along the cobbles. From a long way off we heard the sound of gunfire, then a great metallic bang. A little later we saw smoke appearing over the buildings.

"Eve, let's go. We have one chance."

She jolted as if I'd struck her. "It doesn't matter. Go without me. I don't care."

I took her by the arm.

"Let me go."

"You may not care if you live or die, but I bloody do! I need you to show me the safe house. Come on!"

At last she seemed to be seeing me.

"He's dead. He gave you this chance, Eve. *Tell the story*."

She swayed. I steadied her. There was blood down her side. "Are you..?"

She shook her head. I grabbed her under one arm. We tottered down the main street like a pair of Glasgow drunks and began heading away from the Gate. I heard sirens behind us. The chase would be on soon enough.

NINETEEN

I held her close as we walked, partly because she needed the support, partly because I did, and mainly to cover the crimson smears down her frock. By now I reckoned we were well into the French sector, north of the British zone. Occasionally a Jeep or a truck klaxoned past, racing towards the Gate. This was a four-nation rumpus.

We came to a halt outside a block of damaged flats down a side street. Eve was still clutching the keys. For a few fruitless turns she couldn't open the hall door. At last we tumbled through. A man was standing in the corridor, waiting to see who was trying to break in. From some hidden reserves, Eve flashed him a smile and turned to me with a *liebchen* and a patting of my cheek. I tried to look suitably entranced. She waved her keys at the old man. He shrugged; another whore, a city of whores. He closed his door and we slid into the flat.

It was in darkness. The curtains were drawn and the room smelled of old clothes and old food. There was a sink in one corner, a toilet in the hall, a tiny bedroom through a door. Eve didn't collapse. She tore off her dress and stood by the sink in her brassiere and knickers. Her slim body was streaked with dust and blood, and bruises were appearing down her arm and leg. The old scar on her thigh was livid. She was shaking from head to toe. It wasn't cold in here.

She waited for the rust-brown water to run clear, then thrust her arm under it and cleaned it best she could. Then she lifted her leg and washed it too. She plunged her dress under the tap and soaked and massaged it until the water ran red.

I looked in the bedroom and came back with a sheet to drape over her. She flinched but I gripped her shoulders till the shaking subsided a little. I began to rub her body dry. She let me do it. I found a blanket and wrapped it round her. The shakes seemed to be getting worse and I moved her over to the couch and made her lie down. She lay trembling as though she had the flu, and stared at nothing.

I tried to be useful. I dug into the one cupboard and found a tin pan, some coffee essence and a can of milk. I boiled water on the one hot plate and made her coffee. She didn't drink it.

A long while later as the evening drew in, she fell asleep. I lay beside her on the thin rug and tried to join her. I couldn't. My brain was racing, trying to figure out how to get us out of this mess. Nothing came to mind.

It was dark when she stirred. This time she accepted a hot drink. I found sugar too and she supped it like nectar. We kept the light off for no other reason, I suspect, than we didn't want to see each other's faces. I checked her dress. Though the room was warm it was still damp. By morning it would be creased but wearable – Berlin wasn't currently the capital of high fashion. I gave her a cigarette. It was time to talk.

"Did you have any plans after…?" I meant after the killing. She understood and shook her head.

"A suicide mission?"

She shrugged under her blanket. I was getting fed up with this.

"OK, Eve, do you feel happier now you've killed a man?"

Even in the gloom I could see her eyes glistening with tears. "If you must know, I didn't. I was the feint. I just knocked on every door until we found him. Gideon wouldn't let me do it."

Relief – of sorts – washed through me. "So it was Gideon?"

"What does it matter? I went there to do it. I set him up. I might as well have pulled the trigger."

"Did anyone see you? The boyfriend, did he see you? Did he see who did it to Mulder?"

"I suppose so. He answered the door. I told him I was looking for Herr Mulder. I had a message from him from the office. When we heard Mulder call out from inside, Gideon appeared. He shoved the boy out of the way. Mulder was in bed. He tried to hide under the sheets when he saw Gideon with the gun. Then he saw me. He knew me, I think. I hope so. I aimed the gun at him but I couldn't fire. He smiled when he saw that. But he stopped when Gideon blasted him. Then the boy was screaming and throwing fits, so we ran. The rest you know."

I didn't know how this would play out. But Eve could still be hanged as an accessory – if anyone missed Mulder enough to care.

"What was the story Gideon wanted you to tell?"

"Don't tell me you learned Yiddish too? You're beginning to make Dachau sound like a Jewish finishing school."

"It nearly finished me." It almost made her smile, so I went on.

"I only picked up a smattering of words, but I knew what language he was speaking. All I got was 'Tell the story'. What did he mean? Can I help?"

Her eyes were soft in the gloaming. She did smile this time. She shook her head. "You've helped beyond words, Daniel McRae. Beyond words. I don't know why. I don't deserve it. I haven't been very kind to you. But thank you for what you did today."

"It was… interesting," I managed.

"This isn't your fight. It's time you left it to us."

"Us?"

"The people who want a bit of land to call their own. Where we won't get marched off to die in camps. Is that so much to ask?"

"No. It's not." I shook my head. "What was the story?"

She pulled her knees up against her chest and pulled at her cigarette. It glowed red in the dusk. I settled down on the carpet. She began.

"Everything I told you was true. Mulder and my parents, and working for the British."

"But…?" I asked.

"No buts. All true. But there was more to the Jewish contacts. When they found out who I was and what I did – the reporting side – they wanted me to join their group. *Irgun*. The *Irgun Svai Leumi*. Part of the Jewish Resistance Movement."

"How could you join that gang?! They murder our boys! A month ago they blew up all the bridges in Palestine!"

"And what did the British do?! Arrested three thousand Jews and put them in a concentration camp! Where did you learn that trick?"

"They were terrorists!"

"As much as the SOE in France!"

"Oh, come on. We were fighting for our lives against the Nazis." Even as I said it I realised how stupid that sounded from her perspective.

She gave me a look and went on. "We are reclaiming our land, Danny. *Eretz Israel*. The land of Israel. My father used to finish the Shabbath by saying *Next year in Israel*. For a thousand years Jews all over the world have been reminding themselves of the land they left. *Next year in Israel. This* is the year."

I had nothing to put on the scales on the other side. The Scots too have had their Diaspora. The Clearances. And I know from letters to my mother from her sister in Canada that the further away they travel, the more Scottish they get. They talk wistfully of returning to a mystical land they've never seen. They do everything in their power to make themselves stand out from their neighbours. Tartan in Calcutta and Burns Nights in Sydney. Bagpipes in Argentina and highland games on the prairie. Wailing "Auld Lang Syne" at new year. But despite these provocations, no one tries to massacre us. Not even the English. How could I argue with this woman?

"They wanted me to become their information officer. Propaganda if you like. God knows, the Jews need some good press. They wanted me to spread the word. To use my contacts and my position to give their side of events. All we hear is the British version."

"We're only just over the war. What do you expect?"

"Justice? Isn't that what you fought for? I thought that was why I was on your side. You seem to have a short memory."

"We have a job to do in Palestine."

"The British Protectorate," she sneered. "But it's only the Arabs you protect."

"Not always. Balfour promised you your own place. The war changed everything."

"Not the war. *Oil*. You need oil. The Arabs have it."

She had a point. I changed my angle.

"What exactly were you expected to do?"

"Tell the story. Whenever something happened that involved the Jews, I was to give their side. Hell, even if I just told the truth – like a reporter should – it would make a change. You have no idea how biased it all is."

"Have you done anything yet?"

"No. But Gideon said… never mind."

"There's something coming up?"

"Maybe."

I sensed it was useless to press her. Instead I asked, "Why would Cassells lie to me about you?"

"About working for the British? Maybe he wasn't told. Secrets within secrets. Maybe he felt silly, losing an agent."

"Then why did he send me after you?"

She thought for a while. "Berlin is a mess. The chances of a complete stranger finding me are nil. You knew me, knew how I'd think."

"I thought I did."

She had the grace to look sheepish.

We were silent for a while. I had one more question that I dreaded asking.

"Why pick me, Eve? Why did you get me involved? It wasn't chance, was it?"

"Leave it, Danny. Just leave it."

"After all this? I can't. You owe me this."

We stared at each other. Something passed over her face. She took a deep breath.

"I told you, MI5 ordered me to drop my Mulder inquiry. I should have pretended to let go. I didn't." She smiled ruefully.

"So they began tailing you?"

"Someone was. They wanted to stop me. And if I disappeared they would know where I'd gone. They might even have warned Mulder. God knows why. I needed to get them off my trail. Make them think I'd been kidnapped. Maybe killed."

"You set it up to look like Gambatti. You'd targeted him long before you met me. You just needed a sucker to get you closer." I couldn't help the accusation in my voice.

"I needed your help."

"Why my help? Why me, Eve?"

She ran her hands over her face. "You were on the front pages. You were in the right business. You could get me access to the underworld. And..."

"And?"

"You'd probably spot the watchers."

I thought for a long minute. "So that when you vanished I'd be able to back up the kidnap story?"

She nodded. "More or less."

"I don't get it. The moment I began to tell you about the watchers you clammed up. You denied it. You ditched me, Eve, because of them!"

By the moonlight seeping through the curtains I could see the glitter trickling down her cheeks. She rubbed the blanket at her eyes.

"You'd just saved me from two of Gambatti's hard men. Gunmen. You didn't think. Just acted. A big daft hero."

"So?"

"If that's how you were going to react... If I was in worse trouble... you were going to put your life at risk."

I shrugged. "And?"

"I hadn't expected... it wasn't supposed to happen."

"What?" I asked softly.

Her voice was at a whisper. "That I'd fall in love. I didn't want you dead."

I got up and sat beside her on the couch. I put my arms round her and held her while she shook and wept. A while later I guided her through to the bed and we lay on it, spooned together like babes in the wood. Sleep quickly carried her away from me. I lay for what seemed hours, waiting for the running feet in the night and the shouts of *Raus, Raus!*

TWENTY

Next morning I ventured out. We were starving and I had a couple of dollars left for food. I also wanted information. I assumed the manhunt for us was well under way. Four Russian soldiers had seen the three of us hightail it from the scene of the crime. Mulder's lover boy – if he survived – would corroborate. And a dozen terrified sharpshooters at the sector checkpoint had seen three ashen faces bearing down at them in a two-ton Merc. The Brandenburg Gate was a congregating point right smack in the middle of the city. We could hardly have got more publicity out of the front page of the *Daily Trumpet*. The question was, who would be coming after us? The Brits? Russians? The military? Police? Or the lot of them?

Much depended on how Gideon's death-and-glory mission had climaxed. Had he got far enough away to divert them from us? Had he died in a fireball so violent that they couldn't tell if there were three bodies in the car or one? Or had he ground to a halt, still alive, and been tortured till he'd disclosed who we were and where we were hiding? My guess was Gideon had died fighting or in the explosion we heard. If they had taken him alive and made him confess in his dying minutes, we would have had a reveille from Russian storm-troopers.

It was a glorious day and the sunshine gave me unwarranted hope. I no longer had a gun to hide so I went without my jacket. I was in grubby rolled-up shirtsleeves and open neck. But I'd borrowed Eve's beret to hide my red hair. It was tight but not much different from my old army version. I decided to wander back up the road to see what I could see at the Gate. A cliché of my own making: the criminal returning to the scene of the crime. Stupid if there was anyone around who could recognise me.

I tried to walk nonchalantly, hands in pocket, as I came to the corner of the last building before the roads opened up and led to the Gate. I stood with my back against the wall and lit up, as though I hadn't a care. The Gate was about four hundred yards away in open ground. The sun was behind me so I got a good view. There was a cordon round one part of the Gate and if I screwed my eyes up I could make out the burnt wreckage of the car. Gideon hadn't fooled around. He'd gone straight for it like Jimmy Cagney charging the Feds, both guns blazing and roaring like a stag in heat. There were plenty of guards round the wreck, some in Russian uniform and some from our own side. There were also plenty of gawpers, so I didn't feel too conspicuous wandering over.

I feared seeing the charred body of Gideon in the heap of twisted metal, but the car was mercifully clear of burnt remains. The front was stoved in and fire had swept through the rest, but it was recognisably my Merc. *Vic's* Merc. Where Gideon had hit the wall was blackened in smoke. Guards were shoving people away. I asked one of my fellow ghouls what had happened.

"A madman killed himself in protest at the rationing."

"No, no," another guy interrupted. "It was one of Hitler's generals. He had been hiding but became insane and made a last assault on the Russians. A brave man," he whispered.

I would get no sense here and turned and walked away. A voice behind me called out, "McRae? That you, McRae?"

I walked faster, trying to put people between me and him. I broke clear of the crowds around the gate and began to trot. It was never a good idea to run in a place so brimful of guilt. But the guy behind me wasn't to be shaken off.

"McRae! Stop, Danny! Stop or I'll shoot, so help me God!"

I stopped and turned round and waited for him to catch me up. He was breathless but he was also in uniform and holding his service pistol.

"Hello, Vic."

"You stupid sod! I nearly shot you."

"In the back? Vic, how could you?"

"Because of what you did to my car, you bastard!" He was right in my face and angry, but at least he'd lowered his gun.

We locked gazes till he laughed. "What the fuck is going on, Danny? Have you any idea the shit I'm in? This car isn't – *wasn't!* – exactly inconspicuous. I got hauled out of bed at five this morning by a bunch of pissed-off Redcaps wanting to know why I'd tried to demolish the fucking Brandenburg Gate, and mow down half the fucking Russian army in the process? Not to mention – not to *fucking* mention! – shooting District Controller Heinrich fucking Mulder himself!"

"Vic, I can understand you're a wee bit upset…"

"A wee bit fucking upset!"

"Vic, don't shout. You'll draw attention to us. Let me buy you a beer and explain." I took his arm and led him like a recalcitrant child back to the shelter of the shattered buildings. We found a bar, and though it was barely nine o'clock they found us a beer each. I made him pay.

"I'm sorry about the car," I started.

"*You're* sorry!"

"You're shouting again."

He sat back and folded his arms. "I'm waiting."

I checked the room. The barman was listening to the radio, a mix of news and music from Voice of America. The only other customer was three tables away and staring into his cup – reading his tea leaves maybe. I leaned forward to Vic and told him everything that happened, more or less. In fact, rather less than more.

I didn't tell him the Jewish resistance stuff, and I was at pains to make him believe that Eve hadn't pulled the trigger on Mulder. But a British court might not see the difference between doing the murder and helping at it. Come to that, I might have some serious explaining to do in the dock as well.

Vic interrupted me at the start but as I got to the last twenty-four hours he listened to me in silence with his arms folded. When I stopped, he lit another fag and shook his head.

"I have to hand it to you, Danny. You've been in this town less than a week and you've managed to cause an international incident. That takes talent. I saw old Toby this morning. Scraped him off the bleeding ceiling I did. He was mental. Would have wrung your neck with his bare hands if you'd walked in the door."

"That's comforting."

"But he's calmed down. A bit. Now his current mission in life is to get you off his patch as fast as your little legs can pedal."

"What about Eve?"

"Her too, I imagine. They want her back in Blighty, so I guess they'll take the pair of you back. Then you can sort it out from there. And we can get on with turning Berlin back into the cabaret capital of Europe. If that's all right by you…"

I didn't tell him where we were hiding. I agreed to meet him, same place, same time tomorrow to hear how Toby wanted to handle it. The bar could be approached from a number of angles and though it had more board than glass in its windows, I would be able to check if there was a platoon of Redcaps waiting to pounce. On my way back I did some hard bartering in one of the open markets and carried my treasure to the flat. It didn't look so tasty set out on the table.

"You should have sent me," she said, prodding the blackening spuds and cabbage and the dark red sliver of fatty meat.

"If you're going to complain about it…"

"Joking, joking. You did well, Danny. I can make a meal out of this. But we won't bark too loudly in case the meat twitches, eh?"

She'd evidently got over the shock of yesterday. Her face had some colour in it again, and she'd managed to wash her hair in the sink. It was damp and combed flat against her head like a Twenties flapper. While she rinsed and cut up the food I told her about my run-in with Vic.

"Are you sure you weren't followed?" she asked.

"I'm trained in this stuff."

"Can you trust him?" She put a pan on to boil. She threw the meat into the little frying pan and it sizzled and filled the room with saliva-inducing smells. I chose not to sniff too deeply in case I could identify its provenance. Meat was meat.

"I don't know. He might set me up tomorrow. Haul me off in a paddy wagon. But it's a risk we need to take."

"Is it? We could lie low. Stay here till it went quiet. Try to make contact with some of my other friends."

"Irgun? Haven't they got you in enough bother?"

She turned to me, her face red – maybe it was the heat of the stove.

"It was my decision, Danny. Nobody forced me. This time."

I held my hands up. "Sorry. I still find it hard to see you as a double-agent."

"Me too, Danny. Me too."

"What about this big scoop? This propaganda event Gideon was talking about? You know what it is, don't you? When is it?"

She was suddenly back at the cooker, meddling with the food. I let the silence grow. Finally she turned to look at me. There were beads of sweat on her brow.

"I don't know exactly. It's in Jerusalem."

"A raid? A bomb? A street riot? What?"

"I can't tell you! No one will get hurt."

"When?

"Soon. Very soon."

"Where are we? This is July…" I realised I had lost track of the days.

Eve clearly had her finger on the pulse. She took a deep breath. "Today's the twentieth. It could happen any time, he said."

"Today? Tomorrow? Next month?"

She shrugged.

I pressed her. She was finally coming clean. "What were you to do?"

"I drafted a few words."

"Like a press release?"

She nodded. "I suppose."

"Then what?"

"Gideon was to send it out on the wires. Telegraph a man in Reuters in New York. He was going to spread the text. I was to phone in my report to my news desk. A scoop, as you call it.

Then I was to get exclusive interviews with the heads of the Jewish Defence Agency."

"Would the *Trumpet* print it? It's not your normal headline."

"This is big enough to be different. We would have the edge on everybody else. Old Hutcheson would make it happen. This would be news."

I looked at her, wondering again if I knew anything about her. I whispered, "Christ, Eve. What is it? What's so big that it would make such news?"

She shook her head. "Enough. I've said enough. Just leave it."

"One last question. How will you know about it, now? How will you hear? You've lost your contacts."

She turned and walked over to the sideboard. She reached out to the wireless and switched it on. The screen glowed faint then a steady yellow. The set began to hum. She turned the knob and began to switch through the stations. Ghost accents and languages whistled past until we heard the distinctive voice of the BBC Overseas broadcast. I'd heard those clear, comforting tones many times sitting in a tent in the desert in North Africa or at dead of night in France crouched over an illicit radio, listening for coded messages.

"Good old Auntie," I said. "Leave it on a bit, there's a girl."

And for a while, we listened to the everyday rhythms of *Music While you Work*, then *Educating Archie*, wondering at the barminess of a ventriloquist act on the wireless. We ate our food and felt like we were living on an island of domestic bliss. Bing Crosby crooned at us and I nearly asked her to dance. But I was scared she'd think me daft, and the moment would sour. So we had another fag. The fried cat wasn't bad either.

TWENTY-ONE

I met Vic as arranged at nine o'clock the next morning. It was drizzling but warm. Before going inside I checked out the café as best I could through the steamed-up windows, and saw no one I didn't want to meet. I entered and added my own cigarette smoke to the cosy fug. I took a seat with my back to the wall and easy access to the kitchen and the back exit, and waited. The radio warbled away in the background. Four other customers sipped at their coffees and pulled at their fags.

Vic arrived and shook off the rain from his mac. He looked a wee bit happier this morning.

"OK, the deal's on," he started.

"You mean we're forgiven?" I asked.

He sat back and lit up. "Even the Pope wouldn't forgive you for what you did to my car. But seems the Army's prepared to draw a line under this. Toby wants you out of his hair ASAP."

"And Eve?"

"Bit more awkward there. She might have to travel separately. Under guard. Our MPs will escort her back. She is a Nazi spy, you know. Not to mention knocking off a senior Russian administrator in Berlin."

"She's not a Nazi anything! She's a Jew. She was forced into working for these bastards to keep her parents safe. Fat lot of good that did. And she was a double. She worked for MI5."

"Quiet, man," Vic hissed. "Keep it down. So – I might have got it a bit wrong. Nobody tells me anything, you know. I'm only a bleedin' corporal at the end of the day. I'm telling you what Toby told me."

"Well, you can tell Toby to stuff his offer! I'm going back *with* Eve and without a bloody escort of Redcaps, or not at all. Maybe we'll talk to the Americans, or find our own way home."

"All right, all right. I get the picture. But I wouldn't count the Yanks as pals, if I were you."

"Oh, why not?"

"Let's just say they're as pissed off about the uproar as we are. You don't understand how big this guy Mulder was… Danny? Are you listening?"

"Shut up." I'd caught something on the radio. More details were coming over. A bomb. A big one. In Jerusalem.

"Thought you couldn't speak the lingo, Danny?" Vic nodded at the radio where a newscaster was excitedly reporting the event in German. "Danny? Where the fuck are you going?"

I was already out of my seat and heading for the door. "I'll be in touch, Vic." I shouted.

It was tipping down. The rain drummed across the pavements and settled the dust on the bomb sites. The streets were filthy rivers. I splashed my way through and arrived at the building, panting and soaked to the skin. The door to the flat was open. Eve was sitting in the gloom listening to the BBC's half-hourly newsflashes. Her face was strained and she'd been crying. She looked up at me and away.

"Was this *the story*, Eve? Was this what Gideon meant?"

She didn't reply. She just looked at me like I was on the other side of the river Hades. The living side.

"Eve! Answer me! Are we in even more shit?"

Slowly she focused on my face. Her voice was light, mocking. "We? You and me? I think not. This isn't your fight. Whereas *we* – me and the other Shylocks – are in trouble again."

By coincidence, the announcer was tolling the news. "Jerusalem is in shock – scenes of devastation – massive bomb attack – the King David Hotel has partly collapsed – dead and missing now over fifty and expected to rise – among the dead are many British, Arab and Jewish workers – no warning…"

"No warning?!" I asked.

She snapped at me. "Of course there was a warning! That was the plan. We wanted them out of there and then the bomb was to go off. It was to show them what we could do. The French embassy got their warning. They listened. No one got hurt."

"Are you saying the British were warned but didn't buy it? They ignored it? Is that what you're saying?!"

"Stop shouting! I don't know!"

At least she was engaged. Her face was blotched with anger. There was a growing pool of water round my feet. I went to dry myself, and came back wearing a towel. I sat at the table and drew on a fag. We were well into my last pack. Eve was standing looking out the rain-streaked window. The radio was off. She turned to me.

"Danny, it wasn't supposed to happen like this. Assuming it did." She nodded at the radio.

"So now you think the BBC is lying?"

"I'm a reporter. Everybody lies. Even your saintly BBC."

"Why that hotel?"

"It's the headquarters of the British Protectorate. It was to send a message. Irgun wanted to let them know they weren't impregnable. That it would cost them."

"Seems it has."

"We didn't want them killed! There *was* a warning!"

I raised my hands in acquiescence. "How can you check?"

She took a deep breath. "There is a man with a transmitter. American sector. Out in Grunewald."

I turned on an electric fire and hung my shirt and trousers in front of it over the back of a chair. We waited an hour till the rain cleared. My clothes were still steaming when I put them on. I looked like I'd just climbed out of a washing machine and hadn't got as far as the mangle, far less the iron. We stepped into the street. Water lay in huge pools unable to clear from the blocked drains. Vapour swirled across the concrete and rose from the ruins like smoke as the sun poured down. The air smelled like a jungle, wet and fœtid, mixed with the pervasive stench of drains and soaked plaster.

We kept to the back alleys as best we could, heading west. We didn't speak much. What was there to say? We eased into the crowd on the Potsdammer Strasse and picked up a crowded bus heading south. If you squinted, it could be Oxford Street: people walking and shopping and chatting in the sun. But the occasional gap or gutted shell jarred. We trundled down Rhein Strasse and into Berliner Strasse. After twenty minutes the buildings began to thin out, and not just because of our bombing. We were coming into a residential area, the suburbs, with individual homes set back from the road among clumps of pine trees.

"This is where the rich live. Used to," she corrected herself. The damage was less, but an occasional swathe of large houses and pines had been obliterated as though by a giant scythe. We got off the bus in what seemed to be a forest glade, and proceeded on foot down one of the pine-dark avenues. It was much cooler here. The trees were dripping and dank after the rain. The area should have felt luxurious, exclusive; individual villas set in a cool forest, their owners living some Aryan dream. Instead, the homes were crammed side by side in the shade of the heavy trees.

"Why are they all jammed together?"

"Cost of land. Everyone wanted to be here even if they had no elbow room. As long as the next elbow belonged to someone rich."

"No wonder they liked Hitler's plans for *Lebensraum*."

Studded among the pines the villas were a jumble of styles. Tall rambling wood-clad chateaux next to cubist steel and glass. It was a mess. Many of the houses had boards over the windows and doors. Some had obviously been looted, their entrails hanging out of wrecked windows. We saw no one, though I fancy the odd curtain twitched.

We stopped outside a tall wooden house with a tiny front garden and wood fence. It must have been a fine home in its heyday. Four storeys, wood-clad with big shutters and a wide porch. I imagined a rocking chair and a glass of beer on a summer evening. We pushed through the gate and walked up the path, and we'd barely begun to climb the steps to the porch when the door crashed open. A skinny, wild-eyed man came out. He wore glasses and a shirt buttoned up to the neck but no tie.

"Ava! Is it you? This is a black day. Who is this? Come in. Quick, now!" His quick-fire German hit us like bullets. He kept casting his eyes about, as if worried what the neighbours might think.

We walked into the hall and he slammed the door behind us. We stood in a slab of light from the glass panel above the door. The house smelled of cabbages and death.

"So, it's true, Willi?" she asked.

"Who is this, Ava?" He pointed at me.

"A friend. A good friend. He saved us. Gideon and me. Though…"

"I know, I know. Gideon is dead."

"Are you sure? He was hit. But he might have…"

Willi was shaking his head. "Ach, you mustn't hope, Ava. They say he hit the Gate and ended up on the bonnet still shouting at them and firing at them. They shot him to pieces." Her face melted. "It was quick."

Willi suddenly slid past us like a ferret and headed up the stairs. "We have other things now. Come. Begin's been waiting for you."

We followed him up to the top floor and into a room where the ceiling angled down and the window was boarded up. There was a desk and two chairs. On the desk glowed a radio transmitter and receiver with headphones and a microphone. Willi made straight for it and began to tune it. He turned the volume up and the set hummed and warbled. At last there was a steady pitch.

"Come in, Menachem, come in. Menachem, this is Willi calling." He spoke now in a heavily accented English.

There was a static burst, then, from the loudspeaker, a distant voice. "Willi, this is Menachem. Is she there?" The voice was strong, speaking in English with a guttural mid-European accent: Polish? Russian?

"Hold on, Menachem."

Willi handed over the headphones and seat to Eve. She hooked on the phones and picked up the mike with professional ease.

"Shalom, Menachem, it's Ava. What happened? Is it true?"

"I made the calls myself. One to the British in the King David. One to the French embassy next door. And one to the press. The British had twenty-five minutes to clear the hotel. They did nothing."

"Did the French listen?"

"They closed all their shutters."

"I don't understand. The British are not stupid."

" But they are arrogant. A British officer said *We don't take orders from Jews*! The whole corner of the hotel, above the kitchens, it's gone. Those idiots!" His voice rose higher and higher with every utterance. Then he broke off.

"Any of our people?" she asked.

"No one in the squad was hurt. It went like clockwork. Such a waste…" He suddenly sounded bone weary.

"Listen, Menachem. We have to act. More than ever we need to get the truth out. We must tell the world what happened."

There was silence for a while except for the background hum down the line. "Ava, do you think there is anything we can say that will be believed? Already they are talking of a Jewish massacre. Already they are saying there will be vengeance."

"It's all the more important! We must get our story out, Menachem. Tell them we issued a warning."

His angry voice dripped down the line. "Do you think it matters? So many dead. Young girls, our own people in the kitchens… Is this the way we build our promised land? There has been so much blood. All we wanted was a scrap of desert. A place we could be safe."

Eve's jaw was clenched. She shook her head.

"Menachem, Menachem, we have to try. I'm going to contact our Reuters man. We'll get the message out. I'll contact the

British press. They'll listen to me. We have to try." Her fists were clenched on the table.

"Try, my dear. Try. What is there to lose? Listen, are you safe? Can you get out of there?"

She turned and looked at me. "Don't worry about me. Shalom, Menachem."

"Shalom, Ava."

Eve sat back and took her phones off. She wiped her face and turned to me.

"Willi, do we have a phone? Does it work?"

"Yes, yes. They repaired the lines last week. But I haven't dared…"

"We must dare, now!" She turned to me. "I'm going to make some calls, Danny. Can you amuse yourself for an hour?"

Eve placed calls with the operator and after a long wait, wonder of wonders, got patched through to New York. She spoke to her man in Reuters, but he seemed to be having a convenient bout of amnesia. He denied all knowledge, denied he knew her, denied the truth as she saw it.

She turned to her radio transmitter. From the world's radio stations it was clear that the real message wasn't being picked up. The constant refrain was that the casualty number had risen to eighty and was expected to climb. There was widespread condemnation for this *act of evil* by these *unspeakable terrorists*. Eve scrubbed at her hair, her face getting pinker by the minute. At last she flung off her earphones and sat back. We shared our last cigarette.

"I've got to get back. I need to see Jim Hutcheson. He'll listen to me. He'll print the story."

I didn't say anything. Even if she could get through to Hutcheson he wouldn't believe it. Wouldn't want to.

TWENTY-TWO

We left Willi wringing his hands and asking what would become of him. The authorities would tap the phone calls and come looking for him. We had no advice. We walked back in silence through the steaming pine woods, back to the city stewing in the sulphurous heat of late afternoon. The buses seemed to have stopped. Tainted petrol or a hold-up by one of the marauding gangs. It took us four hours to reach the safe house, sweaty and footsore, and out of cigarettes. Maybe it was time to give them up anyway. I made some tea and we sat glumly at the table and stared into our cups. I should have paid more attention to the sounds outside. I was vaguely aware of truck noises and a motorbike. But nothing prepares you for the sound of your own name being bellowed from the street via a megaphone.

"Daniel McRae! You are surrounded. You and Ava Kaplan cannot escape. Surrender now!"

We shot to our feet, teacups thrown across the table, staring at each other in the hope that we'd both misheard. My breath clenched in my chest. The cry came again. Even with the distortion of amplification I recognised Colonel Toby Anstruther's voice.

"Shit. We must have been followed." I realised I was talking in whispers, which was silly given the ruckus outside. I heard shouted orders and the pounding of army boots on the cobbles.

"Is there any way out? Is there a skylight? Where would it lead?" I had hold of her arms and was shaking her.

"Danny, Danny! There's no place to go. Even if we got on to the roof, we can't get off the building. We're trapped." Her eyes were pleading, telling me the game was up, that it was time to let go. I dropped my hands from her shoulders and let my arms slump by my side. It was over.

The shouts came again, this time with a warning of an attack if we weren't out in ten seconds. I went to the window and stood by the side, not wanting to make myself a target for any trigger-happy squaddie. I eased the window catch and flung it open. A gust of warm air came in and flapped the curtain round my face.

I cupped my hands and shouted, "All right. We're coming out. But on one condition." I waited, wondering if he'd heard me.

"What is it, McRae?"

"We're out of fags."

There was silence. No sense of humour. Then, "Come and get them. Slowly. With your hands in the air."

I walked over to her and without asking took her in my arms and gave her a squeeze. We clung like shipwrecked sailors for a moment then let go.

"Say nothing about Jerusalem. Got me? They know nothing about any connection to the bomb."

"But I have to get back to London, Danny. I have to tell the story!"

"The best way is to say nothing. Not yet. They're bound to throw us on the first train out of here."

She nodded, reluctantly. We grabbed our meagre possessions and left the flat. In the hall I pulled open the door and led the way, hands in the air. We were ringed by troopers pointing their rifles at our hearts. The Colonel stood directly in front of me. Alongside him was Vic, looking sheepish. A small crowd congealed at one end of the street, in which our downstairs neighbour was prominent. He folded his arms and made some sneering remark to one of the others. This city had got into the habit of snitching on its neighbours.

We were marched to the truck and shoved up over the tailgate. Half a dozen red-faced soldiers climbed in after us and squeezed on to the parallel benches. The familiar smell of wool uniforms and sweaty males filled the tarpaulin-covered truck. They kept their guns on us. As we settled down a packet of fags sailed through the air from outside and landed at my feet.

I looked at the boys in uniform. "All right, lads. I think these are for me. Steady with those guns." I slowly reached down and picked up the packet. Woodbine. Cheapskates. They'd do. I passed round the packet as we set off and we filled the back with smoke before we got to the British sector.

"You're a bloody fool."

"I know, Colonel. Sometimes there's no choice."

He harrumphed. We were sitting – Eve and me – in his office. There were two guards outside but none in the room. It was the first time we'd been together in two days. She looked puffy and ragged, much as I felt. We'd been grilled separately by Military Special Branch. I imagine Eve got the same round of questions as me. *Did you kill Mulder? Why him?* On the second day there was a sudden shift in direction and tone: *what do you know about the bomb in Jerusalem?*

We glanced at each other as we were brought into Toby's office, trying to read the other's mind. I hoped she'd kept as shtum as me.

Toby had been on the blower to London twice since we'd been sitting there. We were in big trouble. As well as the Mulder assassination and the diplomatic furore that had caused, London – or Berlin, maybe – had intercepted Eve's fevered phone calls to her Reuters man.

They'd also spotted signals from a radio transmitter in the same area. Whether they'd decoded them or not hardly mattered. They knew someone had been in contact with Palestine from the same area as the phone calls. No one mentioned Willi. I assumed he'd done the sensible thing and legged it. Whatever was known or guessed, London, and now Toby, wanted to know what we knew about the bombing of the King David Hotel.

"It's on the wireless," I was saying. "That's all I know."

"We believe that you – or at least the woman here – were in touch with known terrorists in Palestine. You, Miss, were sending them instructions. We want to know what these were, and how you are involved in this… this outrage!" Toby thumped his desk for emphasis. It didn't work; he was too round to do a convincing hard man. His act made me think that they didn't have the evidence to tie us to either Mulder or the bomb. All we needed to do was say nothing. Clearly not easy for Eve.

"The outrage is the British blockading a ship of refugees from finding a safe haven in the land of their birth!"

Eve's accusations were growing ever more melodramatic. Toby looked weary. We'd been going round this topic for an hour, getting nowhere. Suddenly Toby stood up. "I've had enough. It's time I handed you to the professionals. Corporal!"

The door burst open. Vic leapt in and stood quivering at attention. A faithful dog. I wondered if he'd mentioned my sudden language skills when the explosion was announced on the radio café.

"Sir!"

"Get on to London. Tell them we're sending this pair back. Fix a flight for the morning. Should be room on the post run. Take them away and lock them up overnight. Separate cells."

He turned to me. "Goodbye, McRae. I won't pretend it's been a pleasure."

He stood with his hands behind his back. No last handshake for me. We left under heavy escort and were deposited in the cells used for military prisoners. Vic had the decency to stop at the Tiergarten mess and pick up my suitcase and spare clothes. A WAAF was sent out to get some army-issue underwear and a skirt and blouse for Eve. At the cells – the largely unscathed civilian nick in the centre – we were given a chance to wash, and I had a shave. Funny how hot water and a smooth chin can perk up your day. I suppose it was reaction to the last few days, but I crashed on to the bare board of my cell, drew the rough blanket round me, and was asleep before lights out.

I jolted awake to the sound of a rifle butt banging on my cell door. I cowered under my blanket, waiting for the dogs to be let loose. The SS trained their giant Alsatians and Rottweilers well. The guards would pick a prisoner – usually wearing the pink triangle of a queer – and string him up naked by his hands three feet off the ground. When the hounds learnt to rip off the poor bastard's balls they were showered with praise. The dogs learnt fast.

"C'mon, McRae. Wakey, wakey."

I blinked and woke properly. Daylight was filtering through the dirty window into my cell. It was five o'clock and already warm. By six I'd cleaned up, dressed, and stowed away some eggs, bacon and sweet tea.

I met up with Eve in the back of the waiting truck. She looked as though she hadn't slept much. We exchanged tired smiles. Vic saw us off. His parting act was to slip a pair of handcuffs on my left wrist and Eve's right. Not quite how I hoped to be hitched to her.

"Is this necessary?" I asked.

"Boss's orders. My balls or yours."

"Fair enough. And, Vic – thanks for everything. Sorry about the car."

He avoided my eyes. "Yeah. Right. See you, Danny."

By eight we were sitting in the front seats of the Avro York at Templehof airfield. Apart from the crew and our honour guard of Redcaps sitting behind us, the plane was empty. Two of the huge propellers started up, then the other two, and we taxied out on to the runway. I wouldn't be sad to see the back of Berlin. It had been a madcap few days in a city of nightmares. The dark alleys of Hallesches Tor with its Nazi slogans still on the walls left me chilled to the marrow. We might have destroyed the Fascist infestation but I wondered if we'd really pulled out the roots.

On the other hand, I didn't relish our return to Blighty. I couldn't imagine this was what Cassells had in mind when he sent me over. And Wilson would be waiting. He'd like nothing more than a second round with me in one of his cells. Eve seemed more upbeat. Her face had some colour without the hectic hue of the past few days. She was on a mission.

"I'll get word to Jim Hutcheson when we land. He'll come to visit. I can still get the message out."

It was no good talking her down. Her enthusiasm and the conviction that she could reverse the negative news pouring out across the world was keeping her aloft. But I wasn't so sanguine about the reception she'd get. It's hard to change an image, and the poor bloody Jew has had a bad press since Shakespeare.

I grew aware that we were taking our time getting airborne. Air traffic on a go-slow. But there were agitated noises in the cockpit. I leaned out into the passage and tried to see what was happening. There was a lot of squawking between the pilot and the control tower. Suddenly the pilot unbuckled his straps, stood up and came back to us. The Redcap police behind us got up to hear him above the sound of the engines.

"We have a problem," said the RAF bloke. "Someone doesn't want us to leave." He stood aside to let the Redcap see through the windscreen in the cockpit.

"Christ! Ruskies?"

The pilot nodded. I hauled myself up alongside them, straining on the cuffs that bound me to Eve. I now had a view of the runway. Facing us, with gun barrels aimed straight at our nose, were two Russian tanks with a squadron of infantry on their wings. We weren't going anywhere any time soon. And neither was Eve's message to the world.

TWENTY-THREE

The Russian tanks were soon encircled by a contingent of American and British armour and troops. They could have held their own mini-war out there on the patched-up runway. We got reports second-hand from the control tower. Seems the Reds got wind of our departure and threw away the protocol handbook on how to stay pals with your allies. Those boys were mad. Mulder was an important guy. They wanted our skins, and had been prepared to invade our sector to get their hands on us.

On more than one occasion we heard an exchange between the tower and our friendly RAF guys that made it clear that handing us over was being seriously considered. I couldn't blame them; I would have chucked us over the side in a flash. I just hoped our team had more scruples. Besides, the enormity of the Russian invasion of the airfield would get through to the top brass. How could they let the Reds win this one? Regardless of how expendable we were, they couldn't lose face. Give the Red Army an inch and they'd take Poland.

The pilot shut the engines down and we waited. Eve fell into a despairing silence. Her chances of rebalancing the press reports were at rock bottom. The stand-off continued all morning. Almost on the stroke of noon we felt the nudge of the wooden stairs being placed against the hull. We'd long since opened the door to let some air in and smoke out. We heard steps on the ladder, then a head appeared. It was round and red and sported an American cap with three stars on it. The rest of the general's body eased its way through the door and filled the tight space between us and the cabin. The Redcaps struggled to get to their feet and get a salute in, and the pilot and navigator came down to the deck.

"Easy, boys," the general drawled. "No time for that." He looked straight at me with fierce blue eyes that could strip paint off a door.

"You McRae?"

"Sir."

"And I guess we know who you are, miss."

"And who might you be, *Major*?" asked Eve with all the tact of a turd in a punch bowl. I waited for the explosion. Instead he smiled. It wasn't a pretty smile. It wasn't a gentle smile.

"Why, excuse my lack of politesse, ma'am. I'm General Willard J. Stonecroft. And I'm minded to hand you and your boyfriend over to the Ruskies out there. Is that your preference?"

Eve eased back in her chair and didn't reply. Partly because I had a grip on her index finger that signalled I would break it if she said another word. I coughed.

"Sir, we'd rather you didn't do that, if it's all the same to you. We'd rather face the music in England," I said.

General Stonecroft stuck his thumbs in his belt that ran round his massive girth like the hoop of a barrel.

"Thought that might be your choice. But you know what? I don't give a squirrel's nuts what you think. We got a bigger thing going on here. Lieutenant?" He turned to the RAF blokes and spoke to the pilot. "We can't have these guys thinking they can bust into our aerodrome any time they feel like it, now can we?"

The pilot looked as though he didn't care one way or the other.

"So, you're going to taxi all the way back to the end of this here runway. Far as you can go. Then you're going to put the foot on the gas and get this tin can in the air. Preferably before you hit the tanks."

The RAF men looked at each other. They knew they were dealing with a madman.

"General, there isn't enough run-up."

"Sure there is. You don't think I got these from flying a desk?" He pointed at the set of wings on his chest. "I reckon there's plenty of room. If you get the revs up."

He waited while the pilot stuck his head out the door, conferred with his colleague and sized up the problem.

"General, is this an order?"

"If you like."

"What if the tanks shoot?"

"That's my job. I'm gonna tell those Red guys if they shoot you down, they get it too. We'll blast them to pieces."

"Well, that's all right then, sir," said the pilot. "Fair's fair is what I say."

The general looked at him suspiciously but grunted and slid back down the ladder. The flyers shrugged at us and slid back into their seats. We heard the general's Jeep racing away from us. A little later air traffic control told us to start up and taxi to the end of the runway.

We rolled away from the mêlée on the runway, and when we

ran out of tarmac we swivelled on the spot and aimed back down the long strip. The RAF team had switched into professional mode, their voices calm and unforced through the check routine. The noise grew from the big Merlin engines and the vibrations rose through the fuselage until the plane felt as if it would implode. We heard a last good luck from the tower and the brakes were released. Then we catapulted forward and the engines strained up through the revs.

Call me a masochist, but I wanted to see. I jammed my face to the porthole and peered forward as best I could. Ahead was the growing blob of machines and men. It looked very much like we'd plough straight through them. We used to play chicken on the swings up at the park. We'd make them swing faster and higher, and see how high we could go before we jumped off. Sometimes we'd work them up above the horizontal before making the great leap. One of my boyhood pals – Archie, who died over Dresden – broke his leg that way. This was one monstrous game of chicken. With more than a broken leg at stake.

As we hurtled towards the mass of armour, I saw some of the troops throwing themselves to ground. A few others scampered to the side. The two Russian tanks kept guns trained straight at us, while on their flanks the American and British took point blank aim at them. This was going to be some fireworks display. I couldn't look any more and sank back in the seat alongside Eve. There was no sound from the Redcaps behind us. Too busy with their rosaries, I suppose. I smiled at Eve and gripped her hand. And waited for either the tank shell or the tank itself to shatter our flimsy frame.

Suddenly the engines screamed louder and higher and the nose tipped up. We braced ourselves for the impact. Then the thunder beneath our wings dropped away. We were airborne, but were we high enough? I peered through the screen again and wished I hadn't. The tanks were rushing towards us. They were still holding fire, but we weren't going to make it. We couldn't make it. Up in the cockpit the pilot was heaving at his sticks for all he was worth. Slowly, slowly, we eased up and I saw faces flash beneath us, distorted in horror.

There was a big bump like you get when you land, and a double "Fuck!" from the MPs. Then we were up and away. We kept climbing, and the undercarriage came up with a thump and a groan of steel. The noise of the machine straining to stow the wheels continued then stopped. It started again then whined to a halt. It didn't feel good. But at least we were airborne. Eve had a line of perspiration on her top lip and her face was deathly. Mine must have looked as drained. The navigator came back to us. He had his professional smile on.

"All right back here?"

"Couldn't be better, Flight," I answered. "Bloody well done."

He nodded. "Well, we got up. But not so sure about getting down. We hit something and the undercarriage is jammed. Bit of a nuisance, really. Cuts our speed and could be a bit bumpy at the other end."

Flyboy's understatement meant we were probably going to crash-land. Frankly I was past caring. My nerves would only stretch so far. I was past hysteria and into stupor. I felt slugged. And I wasn't getting much support from my pal next to me.

You would think that sharing a pair of handcuffs would draw folk together, but we were miles apart. It didn't help to have two goons breathing down our necks, though they seemed more interested in the bars they planned to hit on their one night in England before the return trip in the morning. They were over-ambitious by half, but I envied them their youth and bravado.

The endless flight gave me plenty of time to think. To try to get some perspective on the last few days, few years. I realised I wasn't where I'd thought I'd be. Not that I'd had a crystal-clear picture of my future ten years ago. None of us ever gave it much thought, or spoke about it. It was too personal, some-thing only girls talked about. But there was an assumption and unspoken expectation that we'd get married and have kids. Like our folks. It's what you did. It's what everybody did. It was the path of least resistance. But now it seemed as likely as a squadron of pink pigs doing a fly-past for the King.

I realised that at some stage – before she disappeared – I'd been harbouring thoughts of a future with Eve. Like what she'd think of Kilpatrick. Or more interestingly, what Kilpatrick would think of her. She'd meet my mother, and I'd watch as these two women circled each other, wondering what each expected of the man standing between them. I'd take her walking through the town parks. Or we'd hop on a bus and go to Largs for the day and eat ice creams at Nardini's, and paddle in the freezing sea. I'd show her Arran and the bump of granite called Ailsa Craig, and the low-slung hulk of the Mull of Kintyre. But it wouldn't happen now. We'd come too far, seen too much. And instead of pulling us closer, our sojourn in Berlin had ripped us apart.

I still loved her. But it was a love for someone in my past. Someone who went away. Maybe – given her revelations – someone who was never there in the first place, except in my imagination. I glanced across at her, but she was staring inward like a yogi.

The plane droned on across the scarred earth of northern

France. Through breaks in the clouds I could see the land far below. I imagined it a year ago, after great armies had chewed up the ground with their heavy treads and high explosives. But it wouldn't have taken long for nature to cover our sins. New grain would wave in the summer heat and apples ripen in drowsy orchards. The rows of white crosses would glint in the sun in the great cemeteries from the first war. New mounds would be settling alongside them, filled with young men who'd never see the wheat fields of Iowa or Essex again. I fingered my scar and tried to tell myself I was lucky.

"OK, chaps," called the pilot. "We're over the Channel and heading for London. We're going into RAF Hendon. We've radioed ahead. It won't be the first time they've had a wonky Lanc drop in for tea."

Soon afterwards we began the descent, and I saw London spread out underneath us. We were tracing the Thames westwards. From the ground it was hard to get a perspective on the damage. From up here its scars were fully visible. Docklands and the area around the Tower of London displayed their wounds. St Paul's stood secure and insolent above the acres of devastation, as though its great dome was cannibalised from the flattened buildings all around it. We turned north and slid over Regent's Park, levelling out at about a thousand feet over Hampstead Heath.

Again we dipped, and the runway of RAF Hendon sliced the green sward ahead. We circled, waiting for the tower's instructions. At their bidding we tried twice, then a third time to lower the landing gear. But whatever had stopped the wheels coming up was stopping them going down. The last words from the pilot before he turned in for the landing were, "Brace yourselves." We needed no telling.

I didn't try to look forward this time. I took Eve's hand. It was cold and limp. "Just in time for the late editions," I said. She tried a weak smile but it didn't come off. The pilot called out the height. One thousand feet, eight hundred, six… a hundred feet…

The plane was flying level and true. I leaned out and saw a line of trees and beyond them some houses at the far end of the airfield. The runway was to our right. We were heading for the grass alongside. I prayed they'd had a lot of rain the last few days. I felt the tug on our wings as they extended the flaps and feathered the engines. The grass rushed towards us and a fire truck charged out to meet us along the runway. Bizarrely I saw one of the firemen hanging on with one hand, yanking on his bell rope. I don't know who he was warning, but we didn't need it.

We hit once and bounced, then a second time. When we came down for the third time we stayed down, skidding along the grass in a series of thumps and bangs. The flyboys had kept the nose up as long as they could but now it tipped and caught; our starboard wing went down and we pitched over. There was a great metallic screaming and a smashing and splintering as the starboard propellers buried themselves in the ground. The plane swung round like someone had grabbed its trailing wing. It tipped, and we were up in the air, balancing on one wingtip like a mad ballet dancer. Then we were falling back to earth and the whole shebang seemed to be fragmenting around us – then… nothing.

TWENTY-FOUR

I t was the second time in six months that I'd woken in a hospital bed with Gerald Cassells' face looming over me. I tried to focus and realised my left eye was blocked. I raised my hand to brush away the obstruction and hit my face with a plastered forearm. Pain shot up my wrist and I let the weighty cast drop back on the bed.

"Steady, old chap. You've got a bandage on your head. And broken wrist. Nothing fatal. Soon be up and about."

"Eye?" I mumbled, pointing at it with my free hand.

"Bruises and cuts, but still functioning," he said.

"Where is she?" I asked.

Cassells looked puzzled.

I unstuck my tongue from the roof of my mouth and tried again. His face relaxed.

"She's all right old chap. Better than you. Bit bruised and so on, but nothing broken. They're keeping her in the next ward."

I settled back. The relief washed over me. I began probing my body, flexing my limbs as best I could. Apart from the wrist, which had ceased throbbing, I felt stiff and bruised all over. Hardly surprising. They found us at the crash site, still strapped into our seats, but with bits of the fuselage in our laps. There was a big hole in the hull and firemen were already clambering around. I heard their shouts and the hissing of water on flames, and the fireman I'd seen hammering on his bell – I swear it was him – eased his head through the jagged hole.

They cut us loose – from each other and from the wreckage – and tenderly eased our bodies out on to the wet grass. They gave us both shots despite Eve's protestations. She wanted to get going, she had a story to tell, she kept saying. They didn't listen, just lifted her on a stretcher into the back of an ambulance. She was quieter by then; the painkiller must have got to her. As it was beginning to get to me. I felt myself slipping away and letting go, letting it all go.

I fought my way to the surface again. "Gerry, is everybody else all right? Did they all get out?"

He screwed up his face. "The Redcaps are fine." He shook his head. "But the RAF chaps in the front seats didn't make it. The nose took the brunt."

Shit. Shit, shit. They'd flown through the war, through ack-ack and clouds of shrapnel, against all the odds. Then they bought it, flying a pair of dumb civilians into London. Another bad joke, God.

"What happens now, Gerry?"

"You're clear to go, old chap. I'd stay in bed for a day or two then hop it. You did your bit. Got the girl, and all that." He suddenly looked sheepish.

"What about Eve? What happens to her?"

"Fact is, we need a bit of a chat with her." He was avoiding my eyes. "Bert Wilson has a warrant."

"Wilson! You can't let that animal near her! Remember what he did to me!"

"I know, I know. But, look, things have changed. He can't throw his weight around now. I'll see to that."

I shook my head. "Can I see her before she goes?"

He shook his head. "She's under guard. No one allowed. Look, it's only for a couple of days while they find out what she knows about the Jerusalem attack."

"A couple of days? Then what?"

"Then she's out. We might want a chat with her. Make sure she doesn't have any other ideas."

"Ideas? About what, for Christ's sake?"

"Look at it from our point of view. She came here as a German spy. All right, all right, she turned. But she went maverick. Killed a senior official in Berlin. She's somehow linked to the bombing of the King David. We think she's a threat, possibly a cell leader of a Jewish terrorist group. Wilson, for one, is wondering what she'll do next."

I sank back in my pillows and prayed they would never leave her alone with Wilson. Not even for two minutes, much less two days.

His Majesty's Prison Holloway is a Victorian folly. Its crenulations and turrets would look more comfortable perched on a hilltop in Scotland, a staunch defence against the marauding English. Instead, Holloway Prison for Women dominates the quiet Parkhurst Road in north Camden. It has its own little walkway up to it and its great doors look as though they've been welded shut. Two policemen superfluously guard an impregnable fortress.

For late August the day was cold and windy, as though autumn was coming in early. I was told ten o'clock, and it was already a quarter past. The two days had become four weeks.

And instead of a friendly chat at the local nick in Charing Cross, they'd quickly moved Eve to the safety and security of Holloway. Cassells didn't make it clear whose safety and security were at risk; it felt like Eve's.

I stood waiting with a taxi across the road. The coppers wouldn't let me closer. I tried to scratch the itch that gnawed away under the tight bandage on my left wrist. Suddenly the little door in the blank expanse eased open. A warder stepped out, looked around briefly and signalled. Eve emerged. She looked straight ahead. Her eyes flicked over me without recognition. She walked slowly down the path to the public pavement, looked left then right, and began to walk away. She was wearing different clothes from the Army duds borrowed in Berlin, and she carried a brown paper parcel.

I ran after her, signalling the cab to follow me. "Eve! Eve, wait!"

She kept walking. I knew she'd seen me, heard me. I got within reach and put my hand on her shoulder.

"Eve, it's me. Please stop. I've got a cab."

She stopped and turned to me. Her face was grey and wet. The flesh had fallen away and the big features stood more prominently. It was a truly stupid thought; she looked more Jewish.

"Go away, Danny. I don't want any more. I just want to get away from here."

"Be sensible. It's miles to a bus. I have a cab." On cue the taxi rolled up and sat next to us. She looked back down the long empty street, shivered and nodded. I helped her in and we set off back to town.

"Where do you want to go?" I asked.

She dug into her coat pocket and pulled out a folded piece of paper. "They said my flat's gone. I guess my landlady didn't want me back."

"I guess so."

"I have to stay here. Part of the bail conditions." She handed me the paper.

"Cabbie? Can you take us to Battersea?" I gave him the address.

It was a long ride. We were in silence for most of it. She sat with her head against the window gazing out at nothing. I noticed her hands; they looked thinner and longer. We pulled up outside a Victorian mansion block opposite the park. I paid the driver, wincing as the meter reached ten bob. I gave him a tanner tip and got out beside Eve. She was standing in the street gazing up at the redbrick façade.

"They said they'd left my stuff here. My clothes. Shoes. I have to report to the police station every day. It's round the corner."

"Who's paying?"

"They are. For a month, they said. Till I can find some-where."

This was unwarranted charity. Not like the Yard to care what happened to former guests of His Majesty. Wilson had set this up. He hadn't done with her yet. But why?

"Come on. Let's get you settled," I said cheerily. "Let's see if they left you a kettle."

She looked like she was going to protest, but then she clamped her mouth shut and fished out two keys. One was for the big main door. We went in and stood for a moment in the gloom of the hall till our eyes recovered. Her flat was on the third floor. We took the lift and emerged in a corridor lit by the sunlight from big windows.

The flat was stale and dark. I found a switch. A light came on in a tiny toilet and sink on our left. I could see a chink of daylight ahead, and I strode across the sitting room and flung the curtains open.

"Room with a view! Look, you can see the park."

She didn't respond. She sat down on the couch, still in her outdoor coat, and closed her eyes.

"Sleepy?"

She shook her head. "Danny, it's OK now. Thank you for all you've done. I just need some quiet." She closed her eyes.

I felt my resolve slipping away. Stupid, stupid me. I thought I was over her. Instead I'd been holding on to the tatters of a dream. That she'd come out of jail and we'd be able to pick up again. That with everything out in the open, we could at last be ourselves. But it seemed that *her* self wanted nothing to do with my self. I was a jilted teenager. And it stung.

"Sure, Eve. Just wanted to make sure you were all right. Check that Wilson had left you in one piece."

She opened her eyes and stared at me. I shrugged.

"I'll leave you to it. Call me when... Call me if you need anything. Otherwise..." I turned and made for the door.

"Danny? Wait. I'm sorry. I'm being a bitch. How's your head?"

I rubbed the new marks on my brow. "Hasn't spoiled my good looks."

"The arm?"

I waved my bandaged wrist at her. "You wouldn't have a knitting needle would you? I have a terrible itch."

It got a faint smile from her. "I heard we were lucky."

"And the flyboys weren't. Shame it wasn't the Redcaps. We could have made a run for it."

We went quiet again. I was at a loss. "Right, I'm off," I said.

"Do you want a cup of tea?" she asked.

We muddled about until we found the kitchen and the kettle. Someone had been thoughtful enough to provide a teapot, two cups, a strainer and a packet of tea. There was even a bottle of fresh milk in the pantry. Jam and a loaf and some butter in a dish. We made tea, and strawberry jam sandwiches.

"Was it bad?" I asked.

She sipped at her second cup and took a pull on her cigarette. "Was it bad?" She let the silence gather. Her big eyes filled. She kept brushing them with her cuff until they were red and puffy. She wasn't going to give in to tears.

"They put me in solitary. A little cell. Away from the others. Said it was for my own sake. They wouldn't let me sleep. Called me names. Nazi shit. Jewish whore. Better if I'd died in Belsen."

I reached out but she moved her arm. She kept going.

"I didn't mind what they called me. But then he started on my people. He made up lies about Gideon, said he was a deserter. A murderer. A child molester. Gideon? The man who won the Military Cross with the Jewish Brigade? He told me they knew what had happened to my parents. Knew where they were buried. Said he would tell me if I told them the truth."

"Eve. Who's *he*?" fearing the answer.

"Wilson. The one you said was at my flat. He hates *you*. He kept telling me you were scum."

"From him that's a compliment," I snarled.

"He wouldn't listen to the truth. *My* truth. Didn't want to hear about the warnings. Didn't want to listen when I said they had Arab spies in the British Mandatory Government. That they'd been the ones who'd deflected the warning. The ones who'd said it was a rumour."

"Is that true? Arab spies in Palestine, working for us?" I could believe it. We Brits have always had a thing about the desert. Rudolf Valentino in white robes, making the girls swoon.

"We know who they are. We know them by their terrorist names. I can give you details. But not Wilson. He wouldn't believe it. Didn't want to." She took some more tea. With her coat off I could see the bones of her shoulders. I wanted to hold her.

"What happened to MI5 and your pals there? The ones who ran, what was it, the Double Cross unit?"

"B1A? Yes. I asked for them. Asked for Tar himself. Tommy Argyll Robertson. The colonel in charge. They just laughed. Said I was making it up. They'd never heard of such an outfit." She shrugged. "Washed their hands of me, I guess. A Nazi spy is one thing, but a Jewish agent…"

Her voice was quieter now. "I kept trying to get some sleep. And every time I dropped off, they woke me. He told them to wake me. That was bad. I begged them for sleep…" She broke off, searching for the words.

"And the woman. One of the warders…" She couldn't get it out. "She kept doing a search. A body search." Her eyes blazed. "The others held me. She made me stand naked. And she touched me. She put her fingers in me. She enjoyed it!"

Her chest was heaving. "And all the time… all the time… *he* was there. Behind the grill. Watching me. I can see his eyes…"

She gathered herself after a while and started again in a whisper. "I couldn't take it, Danny. I couldn't help it. They made me. I was out of my mind…"

I whispered, "What? What did they make you do, Eve?"

"I told them I knew about the bomb. I told them about Menachem Begin. Told them he was the leader of Irgun. Told

them he didn't give a warning. I betrayed him. *How could I?*"
She broke apart again. I pulled her to me and held her for a
long time till the sobs stopped. She pushed back and went to
the bathroom and washed her face.

I was pacing the room when she got back. "We're going to
file a complaint, Eve. They can't do this to you. I won't let him
get away with it. That bastard!"

She took my hand. "But he *can*, Danny. You know he can.
Who'd believe me?"

I calmed down. I decided to go. Take the pressure off. Let her
sleep. The sun was dropping behind the trees.

"What will you do now?" I asked.

"See Jim. See if he'll print the truth. See if I still have a job."

"Then?"

She shook her head. "We'll see."

I couldn't help myself. "Do you want me to come round? I
mean…"

"Let's leave it, Danny. For a bit. I'll call you if I… You know."

I left her, left the building and walked into the park. I sat on
the wall watching the river, going over and over what she'd told
me. Why had Wilson let her go? Why hadn't he charged her? He
could have pinned a murder on her. He could have charged her
with accessory to commit terrorist acts. Had he got all he
wanted? It wasn't much of a confession. They probably already
had Begin's name against this action anyway. At least she was
out. Why look a gift horse?

When the parkie ushered me out I went home. Then I went
to the pub. Maybe the lads needed a beer. I did.

TWENTY-FIVE

I didn't expect to hear from her any time soon. Perhaps ever. So her voice on the end of my phone, two days later, was a shock, like a call from the spirit world.

"Danny, can you talk?"

"Yes. Where are you? Are you all right?"

"Can you come round? I mean, here to my flat in Battersea? I mean, some time, when you can…"

"Put the kettle on."

It took me the best part of an hour and three buses. I was still economising after that taxi ride from the prison. I buzzed her flat number and she let me in. When the lift reached her floor I found her waiting by the door. She still looked fragile but her face had a hectic flush. I soon found why.

"They won't print it! Hutcheson won't touch it, Danny. Wilson got to him. He showed Jim my confession! The bastard, bastard! Jim said he didn't believe it but it was too late anyway. No one would believe it. He didn't want to rake it all up again."

I opened my arms and she fell into them. She stood sobbing against me for a while. Her thin back and arms made me curse Wilson and all his kin. Finally I pushed her back gently from me, but held her by her shoulders.

"Eve, are you surprised? Forget the confession. You're a reporter. You know when a story goes cold. It's been nearly six weeks."

She freed herself from my hands and went and stood by the window. "I'm not a reporter. He won't give me my job back. He asked me how it would look if the paper had an ex-Nazi on the payroll."

"Wilson put in a good word for you, then?"

"What do you think?"

I walked over and joined her at the window. I looked out into the street. Two men were talking. Both wore coats and trilbies though it was mild and dry. One of them walked away. I pulled back, dragging Eve with me.

"Did you see him? I recognised one of them. The one I accosted in the street. Ages ago. The Yank. I'm sure it was him. Have you noticed anything lately?"

Her shoulders slumped and she reeled away from me and collapsed on the couch.

"Yesterday. It started again, yesterday. Why won't they leave me alone?" She began sobbing.

"You tell me, Eve. Is there anything you're keeping from me? Anything you're not saying?"

Her answer was to sob harder. I left her then, and as I emerged from the building, I tipped my hat at the bloke loitering across the road. He stared at me till I began walking away. I headed back to my office. I had a phone call to make.

While I was in the hospital Cassells had given me a number to call. It took less than twenty minutes before he phoned me back.

"Why are you still following her?"

"We're not, old chap."

"Then who is?"

There was a long silence from his end. "Look, let's do this over a drink…" He gave me directions to the Feathers, a pub in the side streets between St James's Park and Victoria, just behind the tube station. He was lurking in a booth in the empty lounge bar. A scotch was already standing on my side of the table, and an empty pint glass and a whisky sat in front of him. He had a fag going. I didn't know Gerry Cassells smoked, or drank for that matter. I sat down opposite and he pointed at my glass. I lifted it, nodded and took a sip.

"Your local?" I asked.

"I don't have a local."

"We could have met in the park."

"Twice round the pond and you'd meet the whole of MI5. This is quiet."

I could see why. There were a couple of blokes in the public bar, not talking, just reading their papers. The pub had an air of indifference. The landlord didn't care if you drank here or not.

"What's happening, Gerry?"

"What's happening? Hah! You might well ask." His usual clipped tones had slowed and elongated.

"I am. Tell me."

"You know there's a new war on, of course?"

I raised my eyebrows and waited. I wondered how long he'd been here. The pub had been open for an hour. There were other damp rings on the wood table.

He leaned over. "Us and them. West and east. Capitalism and commies. We're not shooting yet. But it's only a matter of time."

"What's this got to do with Eve? Or me, for that matter?"

He took a long drink of his beer, got up and walked to the bar. He walked faster than he should and stood gripping the counter until the barmaid deigned to serve him. Then he returned with foaming pints, and went back for two large whiskies. He made a dent in both of his glasses before continuing. He wiped the foam off his moustache.

"She got in the way. That's why. Meddling Eve. And her pals. The whole bloody ragbag of them. Stirring up the Middle East, just when we didn't need it."

"Gerry, what the hell are you talking about? She was on our side, remember? Your side."

He nodded. "Trouble with doubles is they get confused." He flapped his hand in the air. "Change sides once, they'll do it again. She did. Bloody Jewish underground."

"But it doesn't matter now, does it? It's all over."

"Hah!"

"Gerry, for fuck's sake stop going hah! Just tell me what's going on."

"S'not over. It's just starting. A new dance, but same old, knackered players. Change partners and dance with me." He stopped and looked around furtively. "Listen. The Reds are the bad guys now, so anyone who isn't a commie is a good guy. My enemy's enemy is my friend. Right?"

I gave him a long incredulous look. "You can sit there and tell me we're working with the SS now? The same rotten bastards who started all this?"

His face twisted. "You think I like it? You think we're all happy campers now?" He subsided. "It's not our show any more."

I guessed the answer but needed to hear it. "Whose show is it, Gerry?"

"The Yanks, o' course. New outfit. Central Intelligence. Truman set it up in January. Replaces all the old departments like the OSS. And they don't just gather intelligence. They *act*."

"Like SOE?"

"With more money. Buckets of cash. They're everywhere. We're tripping over them in Europe, Far East, Palestine…"

"Berlin?"

He nodded. "Buying intelligence. Using the old networks set up by the SS and SD. They argue that we're all on the same side against the commies."

Light dawned. "Mulder? Eve's old boss was on the payroll?"

Cassells nodded and gulped at his beer.

"That's why they're still following her?" I asked.

"Her and her new pals."

"Irgun?"

"Yanks don't want to lose any more of *their* agents."

"Why are you telling me this, Gerry?"

He lit another smoke and gathered himself up again. "Because it stinks! It bloody stinks. Can't change my spots. Lost good men and women to bloody Nazis. Now we're supposed to protect 'em. Well, I won't. Wilson can if he wants. But not me. Time I retired. Thinking of buying a pub. Down in Devon. Got my eye on a place. Noss Mayo. Little village by the sea…"

"Gerry! What about Wilson? What's he up to? Is it about Eve?"

"She shouldn't have gone after Mulder." He shook his head.

"Gerry!"

"Wilson is MI5's link man with the Yanks. He does it with relish. Loves the power. Likes how they operate. *Action, that's what it takes!* he keeps telling me. Not for me. Not my cup of tea."

"What's he up to?" I pleaded.

"He put your girlfriend in a little flat, yes? Battersea, isn't it? So he can keep an eye. And on you. And if necessary..."

He paused, then like some old ham actor, he drew his finger across his throat.

"He wouldn't dare! She was a British agent. Not even Wilson..." I forced myself to be calm. "What can I do?"

Cassells shrugged. "There's nowhere safe, old chap. But I'd get her away, get her out of that flat. No need to make it easy for him."

I left him there, still nursing his drink and looking like the saddest man in the world. I paced round St James's Park, my mind in turmoil. By the lake in the evening sunshine, Cassells' tale sounded like the ravings of a lunatic. I couldn't, didn't want to believe what he told me. But it all had the ring of truth. *In vino veritas*. And behind all this fear and craziness stood my bête noire, Wilson. Cassells described him as a sort of go-between for the American Central Intelligence Agency and British Secret Intelligence. But I knew Wilson. He'd be enjoying this. Sadists need victims. Like what he did to Eve in prison. Now he'd be waiting his chance to twist the knife. Personally. Away from official eyes.

I thought of the stray moggy I fed. I found it with a mouse one day. It didn't kill it. Not right away. Just caught it, roughed it up, let it go, and caught it again. Time after time. Until the mouse was so terrified and torn it couldn't move. It just sat there trembling until its heart gave out. The sun dropped behind the trees and a cool wind whipped across the pond. A sudden dread filled me. I walked smartly out of the park.

It was dark by the time I got to her building. I walked slowly, using the odd parked car for cover. There was no one around.

No sign of watchers. I looked up to see if I could see her window. It was hard to pick out one from the identical frames and curtains. The one I decided was hers was in darkness. I took a risk and walked over to her front door. I buzzed several times but got no reply.

"Forgotten your key, dear?"

I turned round and found myself gazing down on a bent old woman struggling with her string bag and a stick to climb the four stairs. I stepped down and helped her up.

"We've just moved in," I lied. "My wife said the buzzer wasn't working this morning."

"Happens all the time. I was telling the caretaker only the other morning. The milk is always late. And the dirt! Dear me, the dirt. Gets into the hall and everywhere. Never swept."

She dug around in her bag and finally pulled her purse out. She found her key and let me in. We shared a lift up to her floor and I carried her bag to her front door. I left her once she'd put her light on, and walked to the fire exit and down the two floors to level three. I eased the fire door and peered into the hall. It was dark apart from a single bare bulb glowing in the ceiling. I paced my way quietly to her door and put my ear against the wood. I could hear nothing. But under the ill-fitting door was a faint bar of light.

I tapped gently on the door, then louder. "Eve? Eve, it's me, Danny." Nothing. I kept up the tapping for a bit then drew out the two slender wires I keep in my top pocket. I slid one into the lock and felt for movement. It didn't take long. My SOE instructor would have been proud of me – though he was probably back in the nick again.

I pushed the door open and stepped inside. "Eve? Are you there? Don't worry."

I stopped dead. It didn't look as though she would hear me. The source of the light was the bedroom. It illuminated the chaos. Chairs tipped over, couch on its side and cup and teapot smashed on the floor. I walked into the bedroom expecting the worst. But there was no body, no blood. Thank God. Her few clothes were scattered on the floor and across the tumbled bed sheets. Eve hadn't gone willingly. But where? And was she still alive?

I left her flat in a cold fury. Where would Wilson take her? Back to prison? But the scene in her flat wasn't caused by an official visit. The boys in blue wouldn't have needed to turn the place over to get her to come with them. Waving a warrant would have done the trick. In her frail state she would have gone with them like a lamb to... I didn't finish the thought.

I stormed out the building, practically running. Bastards, bloody bastards! Why couldn't they leave her alone? My panting lungs turned to near-sobs until I pulled up short in the middle of Battersea Bridge and forced myself to take deep breaths. The lights were coming on along the Embankment and making the trees glow in silhouette. Slowly I let the river seep into my mind. Some calmness returned. I had to think. Had to plan.

An idea came to me and I shoved it away. Crazy ideas come too readily to me. But it wouldn't leave me alone. So I hopped on a bus heading back to Lambeth and changed to one for Camberwell Green. It was just nine o'clock. The George would be open for another hour. With luck, one or two of the lads might be around.

TWENTY-SIX

OK, it was a stupid idea. But it seems the lads were as far round the twist as me. They knew all about Wilson. I'd ranted about him over many a beer. How he'd used his position to get free access to Soho girls and how he'd beaten and abused them. How he'd nearly killed me. And what he'd done to Eve, the plucky girl who'd saved their skins in the warehouse robbery. If there was a way of paying her back, they were ready for it. They even offered to do it for free.

As luck would have it, Fast Larry was skulking in the bar. I grabbed him and put a message through to Pauli Gambatti. Larry lived up to his nickname. Quicker than the phone. Next morning one of Pauli's minions dropped by my office. This time he held a key in his hand, not a gun. It seemed Mr Gambatti was delighted to help. Wilson's reputation had preceded him. Furthermore Mr Gambatti graciously acceded to my request on the condition that I consider working for him. I said I'd give it serious thought. Why not?

I then put a call into Cassells. He gave me short shrift when I finally got through. Told me there was nothing he could do. And certainly nothing I could do. He couldn't tell me anything, and, no, he didn't know whether she was alive or dead.

My last call was to Scotland Yard. I asked for Detective Superintendent Wilson. I gave my name. I went through three pairs of hands before Wilson's sneering voice came on the line.

"What do you want, McRae?"

"I want to meet. It won't take long. I have something to tell you."

"Let me guess. You want to give yourself up. You want to confess to being an accomplice to the murder of a certain German official? Or how about the murder of a certain man in the Angel pub in Rotherhithe. Or how about the spate of murders of prostitutes in..."

"Shut up, Wilson. Do you want to meet or not?"

"Maybe. When? Where?"

"You're based at the Yard, right? Meet me outside at noon today."

"Today? That might not..."

"Noon. Today." I hung up.

I took Midge with me to Victorian Embankment and stationed him across the road, leaning nonchalantly against the river wall. The towers and turrets of New Scotland Yard shouted power and authority, just as the architect last century had planned.

By twelve-twenty Wilson hadn't shown and I was beginning to think I'd blown it. Maybe I should have been more conciliatory. Just when I'd given up on him, his tall dark form strode casually through the great front door. I was still surprised how much weight he'd lost, but it didn't make him less imposing. His thin hair was slicked back and parted carefully in the middle. He wore a new double-breasted suit that made my demob outfit feel shabby. They must pay well. He got within punching distance and stopped with a big supercilious grin on his face.

"You've got five minutes, McRae. Talk fast."

"Where's Eve Copeland?"

His grin got wider. "You mean Fraulein Ava Kaplan?"

"Where is she?"

He raised his big shoulders. "Now how should I know? Tried Berlin, have we? Probably gone off to join her Nazi pals again."

My fists were clenched and I'd almost forgotten why I was there, when we were suddenly interrupted.

"Scuse me, guv. You happen to know how to get to Trafalgar Square from 'ere?" asked Midge. He was talking to Wilson.

Wilson's lined face screwed up with annoyance. "That way." He nodded north and turned his back on Midge. I waited till Midge was well away.

"You abused her in prison, you sod. Forced a confession out of her."

"Did I?" he asked, all innocence. "Just doing my job. But listen, McRae..." He bent his head forward so that I could smell some cheap cologne. It failed to mask his breath. "I can see why you fancied her. Very nice." He cupped his hands beneath his chest and leered.

He must have seen my arm move. He stepped back smartly, out of reach. I unclenched my fist.

"Steady, McRae. Assaulting a senior officer on the very doorstep of Scotland Yard? Ten years for that. Minimum."

I got my breathing nearly under control. "Where is she? You set her up in the flat in Battersea. You had her followed. Where have you taken her, Wilson?" I heard my voice rising. Ten years would be worth it, if I could get one good punch in.

Wilson stepped further back and smirked. "No idea what you're talking about, McRae. That head of yours giving you problems again? Seeing things again, are we?" He made a show of looking at his watch. "Time's up. Disappointing, McRae. Disappointing." He turned and walked back to the Yard, leaving me seething. I curbed my instinct to run after him and punch him to the ground. I'd have my chance. Later.

It was simple. Midge had clocked him. By the end of day the lads had followed him and found out where he lived: in the rundown area between Bayswater and Notting Hill. He rented a basement flat in Moscow Road. Midge pretended he was a delivery man, and asked a couple of neighbours about Mr Wilson. He seemed to live alone, surprise, surprise. And got home early evening.

The boys were waiting next morning to check that Wilson emerged from the same place. They did it once more for luck in the evening. During the wait I visited Eve's building three times, pressing the bell until my thumb hurt. Nothing, and no sign of the watchers. I also inspected the area around Moscow Road. It was quiet and lined with trees. When I met Midge, Stan and Big Cyril in the George that night, I gave them the word. Tomorrow, on his way home.

We prayed he followed a regular pattern, and hoped he wasn't working late. We knew he took the tube to Notting Hill Gate and walked along Bayswater, left into Palace Court and then into his street. We decided to take him in Palace Court where the pavements were shaded by trees.

Midge sat in the driver's seat of the borrowed van. I sat in the back. Stan and Cyril patrolled the street; when Stan signalled from the Bayswater Road, Midge could see it in his mirror. Last evening Wilson had come back around six o'clock. It was half past already and no sign. I was getting cramp in my legs and dearly wanted to get out and stretch.

"Got him!" said Midge. I looked through the crack in the van door and saw Stan walking towards us from the road end. He would walk past us, then do an about turn to block off Wilson's escape. Cyril would be tailing our man. Midge and I pulled on the dark balaclavas and tugged them down over our faces.

"Remember, say nothing. Not a word," I ordered. Midge raised his thumb.

I peered out the crack. Stan was nearly level but no sign of Wilson. Then suddenly a bulky figure appeared round the corner. Stan passed our van and kept walking. At the far end of the street another big figure appeared. Cyril. It was all in the timing. The two men paced down the leafy street, Cyril a careful twenty yards behind Wilson.

Now I could hear them, almost as if they were trying to keep in step. Wilson was within five yards of our van when Midge shoved his door open so that it suddenly blocked half the pavement.

"Oi! You nearly hit me, you idiot," shouted Wilson. His flushed face peered in to the cabin to remonstrate with Midge just as I heard running feet from both ends of the street. There was shuffling, and the footsteps stopped.

"Don't move, copper. This is a gun and I'll use it. Now stand up slowly," said a panting Cyril. Wilson's face vanished backwards. I hoped Stan and Cyril had remembered to pull their balaclavas over their faces. The rear door was tugged open and Wilson stood there, his face a mask of shock and anger. He had the sense to put his hands in the air.

"In!" commanded Cyril. I eased back in the van to let Wilson kneel and crawl forward. He pulled his legs in and sat with his back against the wall. I noticed him adjust his jacket; didn't want his nice new suit crushed. I sensed Stan get in the front alongside Midge.

"Do you know who I am?" Wilson managed with some of his old bluster. "Do you have any idea what you've done?"

"Shut it," ordered Cyril, who by this stage had hauled himself opposite Wilson. Cyril pulled the door shut but kept the gun trained on Wilson. I said nothing from my corner, just handed Wilson a thick strip of blackout material. Cyril cracked his knee with his gun.

"Put it on. Nice and tight, now."

Wilson needed a further nudge with the gun barrel till he wrapped the blindfold round his eyes and tied it. Cyril checked for daylight then nodded at me. The doors at the front banged. Stan and Midge were in place. The engine started and we were off. I touched Stan on the shoulder and pointed at his mask. He and Midge got the message and took them off. Didn't want to draw attention to a van driven by two masked men.

Wilson made another plea. "Look, this is madness. You've got the wrong man. I'm a senior policeman. This will go badly for you. Just stop and let me out and we'll say no more about it. I'll forget this ever happened." It sounded very reasonable. But I knew none of the lads was seduced.

"Shut it!" said Cyril, pressing the barrel against his knee. Wilson slumped and was silent the rest of the journey across London.

The yard gate was chained. I got out and used the big key on the padlock. Gambatti had kept his word. I pulled the gates wide and the van drew in. Midge and Stan pulled their black woollen masks down again. While I closed the gates and relocked them, Cyril and Midge hauled Wilson into the building.

By the time I got inside they had him stripped to his vest

and pants. He was strapped to a chair with a rope round his body and his legs. He still wore the blindfold and I could see by the rapid rise and fall of his chest that his sense of outrage had been properly replaced by fear. I walked round him. Tufts of thick dark hair grew across his shoulders and back as well as his chest. He looked suddenly smaller, but I felt no mercy. Not after what he'd put Eve and me through. Cyril stepped forward at my nod, and ripped off the blindfold. Wilson looked like a startled deer. He could see the four of us standing, fully dressed, wearing our masks.

"Who are you?" came his strangled words. "What do you want? Just ask me. Anything. I'll tell you. I promise."

This was too easy, if it was true. I nodded to Cyril.

"You took a friend of ours two days ago. Where is she?"

"Who? Who is it?"

"Ava Kaplan," said Cyril.

Wilson's body tensed. "Who? Who are you?"

Cyril reached over and gave him a smack. Wilson's face flared.

"You bastard! You don't know who I am! You'll be sorry!"

"Where is she?"

"Never heard of her. You've got the wrong man."

Stan stepped away and I wondered what he was up to. He was back in a trice with a painter's blowlamp. Wilson's face was a picture. I almost stopped Stan but thought I'd see what came of it. Stan pumped at the handle to get the paraffin up the spout. He took out his match and lit the wick. He pumped it again and adjusted the flame. A jet of blue heat shot out and roared nicely in the quiet warehouse. I could feel the heat from four feet away. Stan stepped forward and Wilson's head jerked back.

Cyril asked him again. "Where is she?"

"I don't know!" he gasped, his head as far back as he could get it. Stan did a quick pass with the flame. A mound of black hair on Wilson's shoulder frizzled and burnt. Wilson shrieked. The smell of singed hair hung on the air. Stan moved the blowlamp down towards his groin. Wilson yelped and flung himself back. His chair tipped and he crashed to the ground. Midge and Cyril got him back on an even keel. Wilson was weeping and snivelling now. His vest had tucked up. A livid scar scrawled across his stomach and up to his chest; a reminder of his self-impalement on a chair leg the night he attacked me.

"So you remember who she is, then?" asked Cyril.

"Yes, yes. But I don't know where she is. We didn't take her."

"Who did?"

"I don't know."

Stan did a neat sweep with the torch across his bare hairy legs. Wilson shrieked and the smell of burnt hair filled my nostrils again. It was time to put a stop to this, if only to stop the foul stink. Besides, Stan was enjoying it too much.

"It was the Americans! They wanted her out of the way." He looked over at me. "McRae? Is it you?"

Stan pumped his torch again. I raised my hand and shook my head.

"McRae? It's you, isn't it? I didn't touch her. I swear. Let me go and I'll say nothing about this. I promise."

I had had enough of this masked ball. I ripped my hood off. "Keep yours on, lads." I walked round his trembling body.

"You didn't touch her, eh? What did you do to her in prison? I remember how gentle you were with me in a cell. Still up to your old tricks?"

"I swear, McRae. I didn't touch her."

"But you watched while they did! There are other ways of hurting a person. And by Christ, you hurt her!"

"McRae, I really don't know where she is. As God's my judge. It wasn't my doing."

"Is she alive?"

"I don't know. I don't know." He was whimpering now. I could see blisters forming on his shoulder and leg. I tried a change of tack.

"Why are the Yanks so pissed off at her?"

"She was screwing up their network. She killed their top man in Berlin."

"Why did you let her go, then? Why did you let her out?"

"Can you imagine the trial?"

"And besides, you knew the Yanks would take care of her once she was out."

He was silent.

"Didn't you?" I nodded to Stan, who leaned forward with his flame.

"Can you blame them? This was the second agent she killed."

"What? What are you talking about?"

"The Angel pub in Rotherhithe. The man you met."

I froze. "He was American? Central Intelligence?" I remembered his one word to me – *McRae?* – and how it sounded Irish. It was. Boston Irish.

"That's why they were after her."

"She wasn't there. She wasn't *there*, I tell you."

"But her Jewish pals were. She set them on him."

"Why did he agree to meet me?"

"They'd lost track of her. Didn't know what she was up to. They thought you could help track her down."

"Why the hell would I do that?"

"Because you wanted her back. You'd had a fight. She dropped you."

Why should I believe this man? He'd lied so often to me.

"And knowing all that, Wilson, you set her up in that flat. A sacrificial offering for your Yankee pals. Is that it?"

His silence was deafening. I'd had enough. I was past caring, one way or the other. The likelihood was that Eve was dead. And this man had put her in front of the firing squad. If I'd had a gun in my hand I would have shot him like a dog and left him to die. I was barely aware of the rattle of locks and the door opening behind me. The lads jumped and were quick to get into defence mode. Had the police tailed us after all? Then I smelled the cigar.

"Hello, Danny." Pauli Gambatti stepped over the threshold followed by three of his men. They were all carrying guns.

"Hello, Pauli. Fancy meeting you here. We were just tidying up."

"I can see."

He walked over and stood alongside me, gazing at Wilson's shaking body.

"Got what you wanted, Danny?"

"As much as I think I'll get."

"Then we'll take over. You can leave him with us." Stan handed over his blowlamp to one of the musclemen. The man grinned in anticipation.

"That wasn't the deal, Pauli."

"I gave you the premises. I didn't say nothing about your guest. I owe this one."

"What for?"

"We used to have some deals going. Him and me. Must have paid him a couple of grand in backhanders. For turning a blind eye. Ain't that right, Bertie boy?"

Wilson's wide eyes said it all. Gambatti continued. "Set you up too, Danny."

"What?"

"He heard you was looking for me. And after our little rendezvous here, he called me. I told him we'd had words. He asked me to arrange the meeting at the Angel for you. Depending what you knew, they were going to kill you."

I thought of the man's knife dropping from his dead hand. "You bastard!" I said to Pauli, but it covered both of them.

Pauli shrugged. "Business. Shit-head here was holding my cousin and good friend Alberto. He said he'd fix things with the judge."

"Let me guess…"

"Oh, he fixed it all right. Alberto is rotting in Dartmoor now. Twenty years, wasn't it, Bertie boy?"

"I tried, Pauli! I tried. For God's sake, man, I can't buy all the judges," pleaded Wilson.

"We had a deal. You broke it. It's payback time. You can go, Danny. And let me know your answer 'bout the other thing, won't you?"

I looked at Wilson. I looked at Pauli. I knew my answer. I'd sooner rot in Dartmoor with his cousin than join forces with this hoodlum. Instead, I smiled.

"I'll be in touch, Pauli. Go easy on him."

Wilson thrashed in his ropes. "Don't leave me, McRae! Don't go. They'll kill me! I'll help you find her. They'll listen to me. Don't go…!"

I led my lads from the warehouse, and never looked back. Even when I heard the screams. There was nothing I could do for Wilson. Not against three guns. Even if I wanted to.

TWENTY-SEVEN

Two months passed. Eve had vanished without even a mention on the inside pages. No one noticed, no one cared. Though I took comfort from the fact that they hadn't reported finding a body. I clung – stupidly – to the idea that the Yanks would let her go eventually. In the meantime, the only evidence of her existence was her notebook. I'd worked through every coded phrase and deciphered every word to see if I could pin down this butterfly that had flitted through my life. Given the notebook's importance to her I wondered why she'd left it behind. I would have loved to bounce the matter around with Prof Haggarty, but he'd signed me off a month ago. Still, it was worth a phone call to the lovely, tight-hipped Vivienne.

"Hi, Viv, it's Danny McRae. Are you doing anything on Saturday? Fancy the Palais? I bet you're a great dancer."

"Certainly not!"

"In that case, I'd like a word with your lord and master."

I could almost see her cheeks sucking in as she fought for her dignity. "That's quite impossible. The Professor is in consultation all morning. Besides, you are no longer one of his patients."

"Viv, it's not impossible. Not for a girl like you. Leave a message for the Prof and ask him to call me, there's a good girl. And if you change your mind about Saturday…?"

"Hmphh." She cut me off.

Haggarty called me within the hour. "You've been upsetting my lovely receptionist again, Danny. She's going to be a bag of thorns all day."

"Sorry about that, Professor. It's hard to resist. She needs to loosen up a bit."

"I do the analysis around here, thank you. I thought I'd cast you adrift? You're not having a relapse? Need a dream deciphered? Your bumps read?"

"Do you ever get off duty? Can I buy you a beer? I mean drop the patient-doctor thing? Now I'm not on your list?"

"Why not? A quick one, mind. After work tonight. There's a pub round the corner here. Marylebone High Street. The Cambrai."

His first Guinness hardly touched the side. He was a big man and I could see that he planned to get bigger. We batted the breeze for a while and then I got down to it, at his urging.

"This girl I was seeing."

"The reporter lassie?" He started on his second pint.

"That's the one. Turns out she was a spy."

"All women are."

I laughed. "A real spy. A German spy, as it turns out."

"Sounds like a good story. A four-pint story. I'll line them up."

Over the barrier of brimming black glasses I told him about her. Told him of Berlin and how I tracked her down with her notebook.

"That was the strange thing, Prof…"

"You don't drink with me and call me Professor. It's Mairtin."

"Mairtin, then. It was precious to her. She never went anywhere without it. Why did she leave it for me to find?"

"Maybe you've just answered that."

"She could have done it to make it look good. The kidnapping."

Haggarty was shaking his grizzled head. "No need, if I understand your story. No, I think she left it for you to find. She wanted you to come after her. Whether she knew it or not."

"What do you mean?"

"We're just puppets, Danny, and it's our subconscious that pulls the strings. Partly we're in thrall to the habits we picked up as kids. But mainly we just follow the groove of our nature. Free will is a grand notion." He went quiet. "But I think it's a bit of a con, so it is."

I must have looked sceptical.

"Take a look at yourself. How did you react when you found she'd gone to Berlin?"

"I went after her. I loved her, Mairtin."

"One man in ten, or a hundred, might have done what you did. Most would have stayed at home and pined. Not you. She probably knew that's how you'd react. She was counting on it."

"Why?"

"She didn't want to go, I guess. Her heart wasn't in it. Or maybe she was just plain scared and needed to know you were going to ride in on your white horse, Sir Galahad. It's like suicides. Some, anyway. They make sure they take an overdose just before their loved one comes home. Or they jump off a bridge into the river and find their arms making swimming motions involuntarily."

I took these thoughts home with me and nursed them to me as evidence that this affair hadn't been so one-sided after all. Whether she realised it or not. Of course, in some ways it made things worse. I missed her funny face. I could only picture her in the early days, when she was full of challenge and fun. And love.

While Eve's vanishing act had failed to cause a public ripple, Wilson's disappearance had generated plenty of column inches, often on the front page. It began slowly but then grew to a crescendo of speculation about a brave policeman missing in gangland. There was one cautionary call from Cassells just before I was raided and interrogated for eight hours at Charing Cross nick. But they had nothing to pin on me, not a shred other than a chance meeting the day before he disappeared. Why had I met him? What did we talk about? Did I still have a grudge over the Caldwell business? What was the link between me and the spy Ava Kaplan? And so on. But once I started to ask them about her, the whole apparatus closed down. I was ejected into the street and left alone after that.

Then things went quiet. The press were off chasing the latest accusations of corruption at the Board of Trade. Then Cassells called me and asked to meet.

I sat on the bench in St James's Park watching the ripples on the grey water. Summer had long gone and the trees were melting back into the earth. Their gold and yellow finery lay mouldering round their bases, and a cold wind probed my over-coat. I checked my watch. It was time to go. I left my park bench and walked round to the ale house. It was the same tawdry atmosphere. The same lack of customers. Cassells was nursing what looked like a shandy.

"What happened to the pub idea?" I asked.

"What?"

"You were going to buy a pub. Fill it with big-breasted serving wenches. Drink yourself to a happy retirement."

I swear he blushed. "A chap has dreams."

"So why are you still here?"

"I get a good pension. Just another ten years. Then I'm out."

"Despite the Americans?"

He shrugged. He drew patterns on his glass. "I also believe in it. There's wickedness out there. We may not eradicate it. We may not even make a dent in it. But would you have me stop trying?"

"There's too many people with beliefs. That's where the fighting starts."

"Like your girlfriend? Finding her cause at last? Fighting for it. Like we were."

"What *was* that again? I forget sometimes. Freedom, was it? Is this what freedom looks like? Is this what we do with it?"

"What a world-weary chap you are."

"Don't bloody patronise me, Gerald, *old boy*!" I felt a flush on my cheeks. I was angry with everything these days. "Sorry. It's all such a mess."

"Conscience?" he asked gently.

"For what?"

"Wilson. It was you, wasn't it?"

I held his gaze. "I didn't kill him. I don't know what happened to him."

He studied me. "Well, that's all right then. I needed to know."

I guessed. "They've found him?"

He nodded.

"Alive?"

He shook his head. "In the river. Very low tide. Body weighed down by chains. Covered in burns. Looked like a gangland killing. There was talk, a while back, that he was on their payroll."

I searched for some compassion in my heart and found none. Had I fallen so far? Seen too much inhumanity? Like a camp guard?

"Was this why you called me, Gerry?"

"Thought you might want to know. Also…"

"Yes?"

"Your girl. For what it's worth, the Americans deny it."

I nodded. He got up then. He pushed on his hat and gave it a firm tap. He smiled and walked out the door. He didn't shake my hand.

TWENTY-EIGHT

Winter laid siege to the capital and turned us all into hoarders. We hoarded coal and tins of Spam. We hoarded blankets and we hoarded our emotions. We each became an island of shivering humanity, too cold to talk, to meet, to reach out to each other. I filled another foot of shelf with bright orange Penguins, wondering, with each acquisition, if she would have liked it. I could afford more, now I'd given up the fags.

Surprisingly, business ticked over. I had a nice line in advising companies on security in their warehouses. Tommy Chandler had spread the word. It was enough to keep me in scotch and food. I'd cut down on beer too. I'd stopped going in to the George every night. It had got harder to keep up the banter with the lads after leaving Wilson to the hyenas. Even Stan looked like his conscience troubled him, or maybe he regretted giving up the blowlamp to someone else.

New Year came and went and there was no softening of winter's grip. They began to cut rations again. Disillusion set in with Attlee and co. Fine promises but none of them kept. It was as though we were tipping back into the gloom of the war years. But this time – apart from winter itself – we had no common enemy. Just each other.

I was sitting in my bedroom, a quilt pulled round my shoulders and the heat from two sullen briquettes cooking my shins. One hand peeked out to hold the latest book. The other nursed a scotch. It was early evening and sleet was falling past my window. The wet flakes sparkled briefly in the light from the street lamp and were gone.

The door was closed to my office but I heard footsteps on the stairs and then the landing. My outer office door was tried and opened. Someone entered. The steps were hesitant and soon came to a halt. I put down my book and shrugged off my quilt. I got up and opened the dividing door.

She was standing there, hands deep in her pockets, the scarf round her head dripping with melting snow.

"Can I come in?"

I inspected my glass.

"One too many."

"Not like you, Danny." Eve smiled and walked towards me.

"I've done with ghosts."

"Oh, I'm real all right." On cue the cat slid round the door and mewed. It ran forward waving its stumpy tail and wrapped itself round her legs. Eve bent and picked it up. She walked up close to me and dropped it on my chest. The cat hissed, sank its claws in me and leapt off.

"You're real all right." I rubbed at my wounds. "Are you staying? Dump your coat and come in. There's a bit of a fire in here."

She hesitated.

"Oh, come on, Eve. You're back from the dead. We can celebrate. A wee bit."

She pulled off her coat and hung it on the hat-stand by the office door. She took off the scarf and shook it and hung it on top. She walked back to me. She looked good, but different somehow. It wasn't till she came into the light that I realised her russet mop had grown back. It was also now a dark brown.

"Suits you. The hair."

She fluffed it in embarrassment. I poured her a whisky and topped up mine. We sat, me on the edge of my bed, she on my chair.

"Cheers," I said. We sipped.

"I'm not staying, you know."

I nodded and waited.

"Danny, I'm sorry. So sorry."

"For which bit exactly?"

"My vanishing act. Again."

"Houdini's got nothing on you. You could have told me."

"It wasn't planned. Not by me. Menachem arranged it. He sent two men."

I remembered a voice from a radio transmitter in a big house in Berlin.

"How is Mr Begin? Bombed any good hotels lately?"

"Danny! That's not fair!"

"Neither's this, Eve! I loved you, you stupid woman. I would have died for you. And what did you do?"

Her face twisted and tears started. A woman's trick.

"Don't you see? I loved you too, Danny."

"I note we're using past tense."

"It was the wrong time."

"And the wrong place. They should write a song about us. Why did you run away from me?"

"You fool! I didn't want you hurt. I had to do this."

"Didn't want to hurt! Not a letter. Not a word. You could have been *dead*!"

"You would have known!" She drew herself up. "A long time ago I told you that there was a boy in my life. Before all this. He was big and blond, the perfect German. But he was a Jew. He was going to follow me here. He never made it. He vanished in the round-ups of 1942. I pleaded with Mulder to find him, to let him go. But I knew he was gone. I knew."

She shook her head. We were quiet for a long minute.

"Why are you here? They'll be looking for you. The Americans. The CIA. They want your hide. You had one of their men killed in a pub. You killed their top turncoat."

"They can't touch me. I have immunity. I'm here for discussions. Confidential. When Menachem's men came for me they took me back to Palestine. Now I'm part of their negotiation team. We're giving evidence to the UN Special Committee on Palestine."

"Eretz Israel? You think they'll let you have your own place?"

"The UN might. And the British are fed up being policemen."

"Remind me. Why did we want to stop you?"

She smiled. "I told you before; the Arabs have the oil."

"What about the Arabs who live there already? Won't they mind?"

She shrugged. "They weren't born there. It's not their home. We made the desert green, and they started pouring in from all the other Arab states."

"So you'll boot them out. They become the refugees. A new Diaspora?"

She shook her head. "No. They'll have their own state. All we ask is that they let us live in peace. The world owes us this. It's time."

We made small talk then. So small that I don't remember a word of it. I kept looking at her and wondering what she'd do if I got up and kissed her. She was probably reading my mind for she never gave me that chance.

"I have to go. I shouldn't be here. I slipped away. One of the men is looking out for me. He'll be frozen."

She got up and I followed her out into my office. I helped her on with her coat and she tucked her hair under her scarf. We stood looking at each other like it was the end of the world. It might as well have been.

"Eve? It doesn't have to be like this. We could forget the past. I used to be good at that. A hard tap here –" I touched my skull "– and it's gone. We could start again. I could… Hell, I could come to Israel."

Her smile softened her face. "Oh, my darling, you'd hate it. All that sand. And the flies and the heat. Your Scottish…"

"Heat sounds good right now." But I nodded and smiled back at her. She stepped towards me and we embraced. I smelt her hair and skin again and was lost for ever.

"Goodbye, Danny."

The winter of the new year of 1947 turned out the worst in memory. The whole country seized up under a blanket of bone-breaking cold. The windows in my attic seemed permanently frosted over, like living in an igloo.

I read in the papers that the UN Resolution is likely to pass, even though the Arab countries are opposed. Sabre rattling; they wouldn't attack Israel, would they? What have they got to fear?

I think of her often and hope that she finds peace. She took the hard road. She could have merged into the shadows here and continued as a journalist. She could have had me. But that wasn't enough. She had to be creating the news, not reporting it.

She once told me that the battle between good and evil was never-ending and no one could be a bystander. You had to take a stance, one side of the line or the other. She got more lyrical, the journalist coming out: a lone voice gets swallowed up in the roar of history, but a chorus can be heard. I understand that. I'd even like to be part of something like that. Trouble is – and she knew this all along – I've forgotten where the line is.

Don't miss the new Douglas Brodie investigation

PILGRIM SOUL

As Glasgow is buried under seven feet of snow, a killer is on the loose and a deadly secret threatens to take Brodie to the edge of sanity.

Brodie is approached by the Jewish community in Glasgow to solve a series of thefts. But it isn't Brodie who catches him: the thief is found dead, knifed by the owner of the house he was robbing. When the householder is also found murdered, the whole community is in uproar - and Brodie's easy case has become a terrifying, violent mess.

The householder has only been in Glasgow for a year, a refugee from the Holocaust. But when Brodie investigates further, he discovers that the dead man wasn't a brutalised Jew, but a sadistic camp guard. Is there a group of Nazi guards hiding among the genuine Jewish refugees?

What starts as a small case soon escalates into a relentless personal quest for the truth. Meanwhile, Brodie is plunged back into the horrors he witnessed during the liberation of Poland - memories that haunt him still. And when it begins to seem that the guards are protecting someone high up in the old Nazi organisation, Brodie faces the biggest moral dilemma of his career...

Coming from Corvus
April 2013

ONE

There's no good time to die. There's no good place. Not even in a lover's arms at the peak of passion. It's still the end. Your story goes no further. But if I had the choice it wouldn't be in a snow drift, in a public park, ten minutes from my own warm fireside, with a two foot icicle rammed in my ear. This man wasn't given the option. His body lay splayed out in cold crucifixion on Glasgow Green, his eyes gazing blindly into the face of his jealous god.

I looked around me at the bare trees made skeletal with whitened limbs. High above, the black lid of the sky had been lifted off, and all the warmth in the world was escaping. In this bleak new year it felt like Glasgow had been gathered up, spirited aloft, and dropped back down in Siberia. So cold. So cold.

I tugged my scarf tight round my throat to block the bitter wind from knifing my chest and stopping my heart. I looked down on his body, and saw in the terrorised face my great failure. The snow was trampled round about him, as though his killers had done a war dance afterwards. Around his head a dark stain seeped into the pristine white.

A man stood a few feet away, clasping a shivering woman to his thick coat. Under his hat-brim his eyes held mine in a mix of horror and accusation. I needed no prompting. Not for this man's death. I was being paid to stop this happening. I hadn't. This was the fourth murder since I took on the job three months ago. But in fairness, back then, back in October, I was only hired to catch a thief. . .

'I'd be a gun for hire.'

'No guns, Brodie. Not this time.'

'A mercenary then.'

'What's the difference between a policeman's wages and a private income? You'd be doing the same thing.'

'No badge. No warrant card. No authority.' I ticked off the list on my fingers.

'No hierarchy. No boss to fight.'

I studied Samantha Campbell. She knew me too well. It was a disturbing talent of hers. Of women. She was nursing a cup of tea in her downstairs' kitchen, her first since getting home from the courts. Her cap of blonde hair was still flattened by a day sporting the scratchy wig. The bridge of her nose carried the dents of her specs. I'd barely got in before her and was nursing my own temperance brew, both of us putting off as long as appeared seemly the first proper drink of the evening. Neither of us wanting to be the first to break.

'How much?' I asked as idly as it's possible for a man who's overdrawn at his bank.

'They're offering twenty pounds a week until you solve the crimes. Bonus of twenty if you clean it up by Christmas.'

'I've got a day job.'

'Paying peanuts. Besides, I thought you were fed up with it?'

She was right. It was no secret between us. I'd barely put in four months as a reporter on the Glasgow Gazette but already it was palling. It was the compromises I found hardest. I didn't mind having my elegant prose flattened and eviscerated. Much. But I struggled to pander to the whims of the newspaper bosses who in turn were pandering to their scandal-fixated readership. With hindsight my naivety shocked me. I'd confused writing with reporting. I wanted to be Hemingway not Fleet Street Frankie.

'They gave me a rise of two quid a week.'

'The least they could do. You're doing two men's jobs.'

She meant I was currently the sole reporter on the crime desk at the Gazette. My erstwhile boss, Wullie McAllister was still nursing a split skull in the Erskine convalescent home.

'Which means I don't have time for a third.'

'This would be spare time. Twenty quid a week for a few hours detective work? A man of your experience and talent?'

'Ne'er was flattery lost on poet's ear. Why are you so keen for me to do this? Am I behind with the rent? Not paying my whisky bills?'

She coloured. My comparative poverty was one of the unspoken barriers between us, preventing real progress in our relationship. How could a reporter keep this high-flying advocate in the manner she'd got accustomed to? My wages barely kept me; they wouldn't stretch to two. Far less - in some inconceivable medley of events - three.

'The Gazette's just not you, is it? An observer, taking notes? Serving up gore on toast to the circus crowds. You're a doer not a watcher. You're the sort that joins the Foreign Legion just for the thrill of it.'

'Not a broken heart?'

'Don't bring *me* into this. What shall I tell Isaac Feldmann?'

Ah. Playing the ace. 'Why didn't he just call me?'

'He wanted to. But Isaac's from the South Portland Street gang. This initiative's being led by Garnethill.'

In ranking terms, Garnethill was the first and senior synagogue in Glasgow. It served the biggest community of Jews, concentrated on the West End and centre. I'd only ever seen it from the outside. Apart from the Hebrew script round the portal, more a pretty church façade than how I imagined a temple. Isaac's place of worship was built about twenty years after Garnethill, at the turn of the century. It looked after the burgeoning Gorbals' enclave. Jewish one-upmanship dictated that they called the Johnny-come-lately, the Great Synagogue.

Sam was continuing, 'I've worked for them before.'

'They?'

'A group of prominent Jewish businessmen. I defended them against charges of operating a cartel.'

'Successfully, I assume?'

'I proved they were just being business savvy. The local boys were claiming the Jews were taking the bread from their mouths, driving their kids to the poor house and generally living up to their reputation as Shylocks. But all the locals managed to prove was their own over-charging.'

'I suppose I should talk to them.'

'Oh good. I'd hate to put them off.'

They came in a pack later that evening, four of them, shedding their coats and scarves in the hall in a shuffle of handshakes and *shaloms*. They brought with them an aroma of tobacco and the exotic. Depending on their generational distance from refugee status, they carried the range of accents from Gorbals to Georgia, Bearsden to Bavaria, sometimes both in the same sentence. As a Homburg was doffed, a yarmulke was slipped on. I recognised two of the four: a bearded shopkeeper from Candleriggs; and my good friend Isaac Feldmann, debonair in one of his own three-piece tweed suits.

'Good evening, Douglas.' He grinned and shook my hand like a long lost brother.

'Good to see you, Isaac, how's business?'

'Better. Everyone wants a warm coat. Come visit. I can do you a good price.'

'I don't have the coupons, Isaac. Maybe next year.'

I grew conscious that the other three men were inspecting me. I turned to them.

'Gentlemen, if Miss Campbell will permit, shall we discuss your business in the dining room?'

Sam led us through the hall and into the room at the back. We played silent musical chairs until all were seated round the polished slab, Sam at one end, me at the other, then two facing two. I placed my notebook and a pencil down in front of me. I looked round at their serious faces. With the hints of the Slav and the Middle East, the beards and the lustrous dark eyes, it felt like a Bolshevik plot. None of your peely-wally Scottish colouring for these smoky characters. Sam nodded to her right, to the big man stroking his great brown beard.

'Mr Belsinger, the floor is yours.' She looked up at me. 'Mr Belsinger is the leader of the business community.'

'I know him. Good evening, Shimon. It's been a while.'

'Too long, Douglas. I've been reading about your adventures in the Gazette.' His voice rumbled round the room in the soft cadences of Glasgow. Shimon was born here from parents who'd pushed a cart two thousand miles from Estonia to Scotland seeking shelter from the Tsar's murderous hordes.

'Never believe the papers, Shimon. How have you been?'

I'd last seen him just before the war in the wreckage of his small furniture store in Bell Street. Some cretins had paid their own small act of homage to Kristallnacht. All his windows were in smithereens and his stock smashed. But the perpetrators hadn't been paying real attention; the legs of the daubed Swastikas faced left, the wrong way for a Nazi tribute. Unless of course they really meant to hansel the building with the gracious Sanskrit symbol. We caught the culprits, a wayward unit of the Brigton Billy Boys, personally led by Billy Fullerton who wanted to show solidarity with his Black Shirt brethren in the East End of London.

'Getting by, Douglas, getting by. But we need your services.'

'You want me to write an article?'

He looked at me through his beard. A rueful smile showed.

'We could do with some good publicity.'

'You need more than a Gazette column.'

No-one had to mention the headlines in these first two weeks of November: *Stern Gang terrorist arrested in Glasgow - 800 Polish Jews held in South of Scotland - MI5 searching for Jewish terrorists - Irgun Zvai Leumi agents at large…*

'Not even Steinbeck could improve our standing. But that's not why we're here. We are being robbed.'

'Dial 999.'

He shook his head. 'They don't come, Douglas. Your former colleagues are too busy to bother with a bunch of old Jews.'

Isaac interjected from the other side of the table. 'They came the first few times, but lost interest.'

Tomas Meras leaned forward, his bottle glasses glinting from the light above the table. Tomas had been introduced as *Doctor Tomas*, a lecturer in physics at Glasgow University.

'Mister Brodie, we pay our taxes. We work in the community.

We are *Glaswegians*. We expect an equal share of the services of the community.' His vowels were long and carefully shaped, as though he polished them every night.

I knew what they were saying. It wasn't that the police were anti-Semite. Or not, *just*. They were even-handed with their bigotry: anyone who wasn't a mason or card-carrying Protestant got third rate attention. Jews were at the bottom of the pecking order when it came to diligent community law enforcement, alongside Irish Catholics. On the other hand crime was rare in the Jewish community. Self-enforcing morality. Glasgow's finest were used to leaving them to their own devices until whatever small dust storm had been kicked up, had settled.

'First few times, Isaac? How many are we talking about and what sort of thefts? I mean are these street robberies or burglaries? Shops or houses?'

Shimon was nodding. 'Our homes are being broken into. Eight so far.'

'Nine, Shimon. Another last night,' said the fourth man, Jacob Mendelsohn, waving a wonderfully scented Sobranie for emphasis. As a tobacconist, he could afford them. It went well with his waved centre parting and his neat moustache. A Cowcaddens dandy out of central casting.

'Nine? That's an epidemic,' I said.

They were all nodding now. I looked round at these men and marvelled at the capacity of humans to uproot themselves and travel to a far-off land with weird customs and languages and make a home for themselves and their families. How did these innocents or their forebears fare when they encountered their first Orange Parade or Hogmanay? What use was their careful cultivation of a second language like English when faced by a wee Glesga bachle in full flow? Urdu speakers stood a better chance.

I thought about what they were asking from me. It didn't seem much, yet I wondered if my heart would be in it. I used to be a thief taker but I'd moved on. The world had moved on. Did I care? Was I still up to it?

'Gentlemen. . .' I flipped open my reporter's notebook. 'Tell me more.' I began scribbling in my improving shorthand.